Praise for Thomas McGuane's

CROW FAIR

"Bathed in insight, irony and a dark, knowing humor. . . . Ranks among [McGuane's] best work." —*Miami Herald*

"Dazzling. . . . McGuane rustles up some of his best stories yet . . . [and] continues to burnish his reputation with some of his most accomplished fiction to date."

—*O, The Oprah Magazine*

"A rich and fascinating portrait of Montana. . . . McGuane has both honed the edge of his already sharp tone and, paradoxically, become more sympathetic to the human condition." —*NPR*

"Brilliant, bittersweet. . . . *Crow Fair* is funny, of course: It couldn't be written by McGuane if it weren't. But undergirding his signature visceral, unpredictable humor is a new sense of wistfulness, nostalgia, and loss. . . . McGuane narrates his cautionary tales with fierce, energetic concern that at times feels almost like tenderness." —*Elle*

"Brilliant." —*Booklist* (starred review)

Thomas McGuane

CROW FAIR

Thomas McGuane lives in McLeod, Montana. He is a member of the American Academy of Arts and Letters and the author of ten novels, three works of nonfiction, and two other collections of stories.

CROW FAIR

CROW FAIR

STORIES

Thomas McGuane

VINTAGE CONTEMPORARIES

Vintage Books

A Division of Penguin Random House LLC

New York

FIRST VINTAGE CONTEMPORARIES EDITION, MARCH 2016

Selected stories previously appeared in the following: "Crow Fair"
and "Grandma and Me" in *Granta*; "River Camp" in *McSweeney's*;
"A Long View to the West," "The Casserole," "The Good Samaritan,"
"The House on Sand Creek," "Hubcaps," "Motherlode," "Prairie
Girl," "Stars," and "Weight Watchers" in *The New Yorker*.

The Library of Congress has cataloged the Knopf edition as follows:
McGuane, Thomas.
[Short stories. Selections]
Crow fair : stories / Thomas McGuane.—First edition.
pages ; cm
I. Title.
PS3563.A3114A6 2015   813'.54—dc23   2014018360

Vintage Books Trade Paperback ISBN: 978-0-345-80591-1
eBook ISBN: 978-0-385-35020-4

Book design by Betty Lew

www.vintagebooks.com

146028962

In memory of Barry Hannah,
1942–2010

The rest of you can eat me up.
I just record your behavior.

—*Marina Tsvetayeva*

Contents

CROW FAIR

Weight Watchers

I picked up my father on a sultry morning with heavy, rumbling clouds on the horizon. My mother had thrown him out again, this time for his weight. She'd said that he was insufficiently committed to his weight-loss journey and that if he hit two-fifty she wouldn't live with him anymore. She seemed to know he'd be heading my way: I had been getting obesity-cure solicitations over the phone, my number doubtless supplied by her. I was tired of explaining to strangers that I wasn't fat and of being told that a lot of fat people don't realize how fat they are or wrongly assume that they can do something about it on their own, without paying.

By the time my father got to me, he was well over Mom's limit, and he wanted to go somewhere to eat as soon as he got off the plane. He was wearing a suit, rumpled from his travels, but his tie was in place: a protest against the rural surroundings. I took him on a little tour of the town—the rodeo grounds, the soccer field by the river, the old-car museum. He was happiest at the railroad shops, the smell of grease rising from a huge disabled locomotive, mechanics around it like Pygmies around an elephant. "When's she go back to work?" he asked, his eyes gleaming. The mechanics didn't look at him; they looked at one another. My father was undismayed: they assumed he was management, he said.

At the diner, he asked if the chicken sandwich on the menu was actually made of chicken or was "some conglomerate." A blank stare from the waitress. He ordered the sandwich. "I'll just have to find out myself." He insisted on buying our lunch, but when the cashier counted the change too rapidly for his taste he pushed it all back toward her and said, "Start over."

A man in a suit was an uncommon sight around here, and the responses to him indicated bafflement. In the afternoon, I rowed him down the river, still in the suit. He brought along some pie from the restaurant and asked me not to hit it with the oars; he held both hands over the pie as though to protect it.

I made dinner at my house, a place he plainly considered a dump. He sat at the card table in a kind of prissy upright way that indicated a fear that the dump was about to rub off on him.

"What's this stuff?"

"Tofu."

"Part of the alternate lifestyle?"

"No, protein."

I hated to tee him up like this, but he couldn't go home unless I got some weight off him.

Dad owned a booking agency for corporate and private aircraft and had to act as if he could afford what he booked, but just watching him handle my thrift-shop silverware you could tell that he was and always would be a poor boy. He felt that he had clambered up a few rungs, and his big fear was that I was clambering back down. As a tradesman—I run a construction crew—I had clearly fallen below the social class to which my father thought I should belong. He believed that the fine education he'd paid for should have led me to greater abstraction, but while it's true that the farther you get from an actual product the better your chances for economic success, I and many of my classmates wanted more physical evidence of our efforts. I had friends who'd trained as historians, literary scholars, and philosophers who were now shoeing horses, wiring houses, and installing toilets. There'd been no suicides so far.

My father believed that anything done for pleasure was escapism, except, of course, when it came to seducing his secretaries and most of my mother's friends. He and my mother had been a glamorous couple early in their marriage; good looks, combined with assertive tastemaking, had put them on top in our shabby little city. Then I came along, and Mother thought I'd hung the moon. In Dad's view, I put an end to the big romance. When I was a toddler, Dad caught Mom in the arms of our doctor on the screened back porch of the doctor's fish camp. (Though there must have been some ambivalence about the event, because we continued to accept perch fillets from Dr. Hudson's pond.) A few years later, when the high-school PE teacher caught the doctor atop his bride and shot him, Mother cried while Dad tilted his head to the side, elevated his eyebrows, and remarked, "Live by the sword, die by the sword."

As an only child, I was the sole recipient of my parents' malignant parenting. Their drinking took place entirely in the evening and followed a rigid pattern: with each cocktail they became increasingly thin skinned, bristling at imaginary slights. When I was young, they occasionally tried to throw me into the middle of their fights ("I don't believe this! She actually bit me!"), but I developed a suave detachment ("The Band-Aids are in the cupboard behind the towels"). In a real crisis, my mother brought in our neighbor Zoe Constantine for consolation, unaware that Pop had been making the two-backed beast with Zoe since I was in fifth grade—which happened to be the same year that my mother superglued Dad to the toilet seat, so perhaps she had her suspicions.

I asked about her now, not without anxiety. "She's in bed with a bottle and the poems of Edna St. Vincent Millay," my father said. He was proud of this remark—I'd heard it before. Although my mother read a lot, she was never "in bed with a bottle." Most likely, she was out playing golf with her friend Bernardine from the typing pool over at Ajax.

My mother comes from a Southern family, though she's always lived in the North, and she has a tiny private income that has conditioned the dialogue since my childhood. Like a bazillion others of Southern origin, she is a remote beneficiary of some Atlanta pharmacist's ingenuity, Coca-Cola—not a big remittance but enough to fuel Dad's rage against entitlement. That money had much to do with his determination to keep my mother within sight of smokestacks all her life. As did his belief that everything outside the Rust Belt was fake. To him, the American Dream was a three-hundred-and-fifty-pound interior lineman from a bankrupt factory town with five-second forties, a long contract with the Colts, and a bonus for making the Pro Bowl.

In the morning, we went out to my job site, and I felt happy at once. Everything there seemed to buoy my spirits: the caked mud on the tires of a carpenter's truck, the pleasant oily smell of tools, the cool wind coming through the sage on the hill, a screaming Skil saw already at work, the smell of newly cut two-by-fours, a nail gun going off in the basement, three thermoses on an unfinished ledge.

The doctor who'd hired me wanted a marshy spot behind the house excavated for a pond, and I had my Nicaraguan, Ángel, out there with a backhoe, trying to find the spring down in the mud so that we could plumb it and spread some bentonite to keep the water from running out. So far, all we'd found was mud and buffalo skulls, which Ángel was piling to one side. I told Dad that this had once been a trap made by Indians, but he wasn't all that interested. He was drawn to the Nicaraguan, whom he considered someone real on a machine—despite the heavy Central American accent, Dad had found his Rust Belt guy out here among all the phonies in cowboy hats. And Ángel was equally attracted to Dad's all-purpose warmth. He slid back his ear protectors and settled in for a chat.

Evidently, I'd had a flat tire as I pulled up to the site, left front, and it was a motherfucker getting the spare out of a three-quarter-ton Ford, the Ford jacked up on the soft ground, and the whole muddy wheel into the bed to take to town. At the tire shop, Dad looked weird in his slacks and loosened tie, amid all the noise from impact wrenches and the compressors screaming and shutting down, but nobody seemed to notice. He gazed admiringly at the big rough kid in a skullcap running a pry bar around the rim and freeing up the tire. The kid reached inside the tire, tugging and sweating, and presented me with an obsidian arrowhead. I nearly cut myself just taking it from his hand. "Six plies of Jap snow tire and it never broke," he said. I went up front and paid for the repair.

•　◆　•

The next day, a cold, rainy day, Dad stayed at my place while I took my crew up to Martinsdale, where we'd hired a crane to drop the bed of an old railroad car onto cribbing to make a bridge over a creek. We'd brought in a stack of treated planks for the deck, and I had a welder on hand to make up the brackets, a painfully shy fellow with a neck tattoo who still had his New York accent. Five of us stood in the downpour and looked at the creek rushing around our concrete work. The rancher stopped by to tell us that if it washed out he wasn't paying for anything. When he was gone, Joey, the welder, said, "See what a big hat can do for you?"

I'd left Dad at loose ends, and I learned later that he'd driven all the way to Helena to see the state capitol and get a lap dance and then slept it off at a Holiday Inn a half mile from Last Chance Gulch.

I've been told that I come from a dysfunctional family, but I have never felt that way. When I was a kid, I viewed my parents as an anthropologist might view them and spent my time as I sometimes spend it now, trying to imagine where on earth they came from. I was conceived soon after Dad got back from Vietnam. I'm not sure he actually wanted to have children, but Mom required prompt nesting when he returned. I guess Dad was pretty wild back then. He'd been in a lot of firefights and loved every one of them, leading his platoon in a daredevil manner. He kept wallet pictures of dead VC draped over the hood of his jeep, like deer-camp photos. His days on leave had been a Saigon fornication blitz, and it fell to Mom to stop that momentum overnight. I was her solution, and from the beginning Dad viewed me skeptically.

One night, I crept down the stairs in my Dr. Denton footies

to the sound of unusually exuberant and artificial elation and, spying from the door of the kitchen, saw my father on his knees, licking pie filling from one of the beaters of our Sunbeam Mixmaster, tearful and laughing, his long wide tongue lapping at the dripping goo. The extraordinarily stern look on my mother's face above her starched apron, as he strained upward to the beater, disturbs me to this day.

I have a million of these, but disturbance, as I say, is not trauma, and besides I moved away a long time ago. I came to Montana on a hiking trip with my girlfriend after college and never went back. I've left here only once, to join a roofing crew in Walnut Creek, California, and came home scared after two months. I saw shit at parties there that it'll take me years to forget. Everyone from the foreman on down had a crystal habit. I had to pretend I was using just to get the job.

Dad returned from Helena and sat in my kitchen with his laptop to catch up on business while I met with Dee and Helen Folsom out on Skunk Creek, leaving the whir of the interstate and veering into real outback within a quarter mile. I was building the Folsoms' first house, on a piece of ground that Dee's rancher uncle had given him. Not a nice piece of ground: it'd be a midwinter snow hole and a midsummer rock pile. The Folsoms were old enough to retire, but, as I mentioned, this was their first home. They were poor people. Dee had spent forty years on a fencing crew and constantly massaged his knotty, damaged hands. Helen cooked at the high school, where generations of students had ridiculed her food. I could see that this would be a kind of delayed honeymoon house, and I wanted to get it right.

The house was in frame, and Helen stood in what would be the picture window, enchanted by not much of a view—scrub pine, a shale ledge, the top of a flagless flagpole just below the hill along the road. Her expression would not have been out of place at the Sistine Chapel or on the rim of the Grand Canyon. One hand was plunged into the pocket of her army coat while the other twirled a pair of white plastic reading glasses. Dee just paced in his coveralls, happy and worried, pinching the stub of his cigarette.

I had cut this one to the bone—crew salaries and little else. The crew—carpenter, plumber, electrician—sensed the tone of things and worked with timely efficiency. Dee had prepared the site himself with a shovel and a wheelbarrow. We had a summer place for a plastic surgeon under way at Springhill, and if I'd looked a little closer, I might have seen it bleeding materials that managed to end up at the Folsoms'.

While I was at work, Dad was wandering the neighborhood, talking to my neighbors. After a few days, he knew more of them than I did, and I would forevermore have to be told what a great guy he was. But by the time I got home, he was in his underwear with the portable phone in his lap, nursing a highball and looking disconsolate. "Your mother called me from the club," he said. "I understand there was some dustup with the manager over the sneeze shield at the salad bar. Mom said she couldn't see the condiments, and it went from there."

"From there to where?" I inquired peevishly.

"Our privileges have been suspended."

"Golf?"

"Mm, that, too. Hey, I'll sort it out."

I nuked a couple of Rock Cornish hens, and we sat down in

the living room to play checkers. Halfway through the game, my father went into the guest room and called my mother. This time she told him that she'd bought a car at what she thought was the dealer's cost. Dad shouted, "Asshole, who got the rebate? I'm asking you, goddamn it, who got the rebate?" I heard him raging about the sneeze shield then, and after he quieted down I heard him say plaintively—I think I heard this—that he no longer wished to live. I always looked forward to this particular locution, because it meant that they'd get back together soon.

I'm not lacking in affection for my parents, but they are locked into something that is so exclusive as to be hermetically sealed to everyone else, including me. Nevertheless, I'd had a bellyful by then. So when my father came back to finish the checkers game, I asked him if he'd enjoyed the lap dance.

"'Enjoy' isn't quite the word. I'm aware that the world has changed in my lifetime and I'm interested in those changes. I went to this occasion as . . . as . . . almost as an investigator."

"You might want to withhold the results of your research from Mom."

"How dare you raise your voice to me!"

"Jump you and jump you again. Checkers isn't fun if you don't pay attention."

"I was distracted by the club thing. I'm red, right?"

At some point, I knew he would confide that he and my mother were considering a divorce. They've been claiming to be contemplating divorce for half of my lifetime, and I have found myself stuck in the odd trope of opposing the idea just to please them. I don't know why they toss me into this or if only children always have this kind of veto power. I do care about them, but what they don't know, and I would never have the heart to tell them, is that the idea of their no longer being a married couple bothers me not at all. My only fear is that, separate, no one else would have them, that I'd get stuck with them one at a time or have to watch them wither away in solitude. These scenarios give me the fantods. Am I selfish? Yes and no. I'm a bachelor and hope someday to be an old bachelor.

My father picked at a bit of imaginary dust on his left shirt cuff, and I suspected that this was the opener to the divorce gambit. Cruelly, I got up and left the game half finished.

"Can you pardon me? I was slammed from daylight on. I'm all in."

"Well, sure, okay, good night. I love you, Son."

"Love you, too, Dad." And I did.

When my father came home from the war, he was jubilant about all the violence he'd seen. Happy to have survived, I suppose. Or perhaps he saw it as a game, a contest in which his platoon had triumphed. He worked furiously to build a business, but there was something peculiar about his hard work. He seemed to have no specific goal.

When I was fourteen, my mother said, "Do you know why your father works so hard?"

I thought I was about to get a virtue speech. I said, "No."

She said, "He works so hard because he's crazy." She never elaborated on this but left it in play, and it has remained with me for more than a quarter of a century.

The only time my father ever hit me was when I was fifteen and he asked if I was aware of all the things he and my mother had done for me. I said, "Do you have a chart I could point to?"

and he popped me square on the nose, which bled copiously while he ran for a box of Kleenex. His worst condemnation of me was when he'd mutter, "If you'd been in my platoon . . ." a sentence he always left unfinished.

My mother was a scientist; she worked in an infectious-disease lab until my father's financial success made her income unnecessary. Even then, she went on buying things on time, making down payments, anxiety from their poorer days leading her to believe that she wouldn't live long enough to pay off her debts, even with her Coca-Cola money. Once they were comfortable with affluence, they became party people, went to the tropics, brought back mounted fish, and listened to Spanish tapes in the car. But they were never truly comfortable away from the smoke and rust of their hometown.

The last year I lived with them, my father came to the bizarre conclusion that he lacked self-esteem, and he bought a self-help program that he was meant to listen to through headphones as he slept. From my bedroom, I could hear odd murmurings from this device attached to his sleeping head: "You are the greatest, you are the greatest. Look around you—it's a beautiful day." You can't make this shit up.

We were nearly done with the plastic surgeon's vacation home. I had a big crew there, and everyone was nervous about whether we'd have someplace to go next. We had remodels coming up, and a good shot at condominiumizing the old Fairweather Hotel in town, but nothing for sure. I met with Dr. Hadley to lay out the basement media room. He was a small man in a blazer and bow tie, bald on top but with long hair to his collar. I asked him,

"Are you sure you want this? You have beautiful views." Indeed, he had a whole cordillera stretched across his living-room window. He was gazing around the space we were inspecting, at the bottom of some temporary wooden stairs. Push brooms stood in a pile of drywall scraps in the corner. There was a smell of plaster. He lifted his eyes to engage mine, and said, "Sometimes it rains." One of the carpenters, a skinny cowboy type with a perpetual cigarette at the center of his mouth, overheard this and crinkled his forehead.

No checkers tonight. Dad was laying out his platoon diagram, a kind of spreadsheet, with all his guys, as he called them, listed. "When I can't fill this out, I'll know I have dementia," he said. It was remarkable, a big thing on butcher paper, maybe twenty-five names, with their specialties and rankings designated— riflemen, machine gunners, radiomen, grenadiers, fire-team leaders, and so on. There was, characteristically, a star beside my father's name, the CO. Some names were crossed out with Vietnam dates; some were annotated as natural-cause eliminations. It was all so orderly—even the deaths seemed orderly, once you saw them on this spreadsheet. I think this was how Dad dealt with mortality: when a former sergeant died of cirrhosis in his sixties, Dad crossed out his square on the spreadsheet with the same grim aplomb he'd used for the twenty-somethings in firefights; it was all war to him, from, as he said, "the erection to the Resurrection."

Although he complained all the time, Dad lost weight on my regimen. When he got below the magic number, Mom didn't believe my scale or my word, and we had to have him weighed at the fire station, with a fireman reading the number to her over the phone while Dad rounded up a couple of guys to show him the hook-and-ladder. He'd made it by a little over a pound.

When I came home from the plastic surgeon's house that night, Dad was packing up. He had a glass of whiskey on the nightstand, and his little tape player was belting out a nostalgic playlist: Mott the Hoople, Dusty Springfield, Captain Beefheart, Quicksilver Messenger Service—his courting songs. My God, he was heading home to Mom again!

"Got it worked out?" I said, flipping through one of the girlie magazines he'd picked up in Helena, a special on "barely legals."

"We'll see."

"Anything new?"

"Not at all. She's the only one who understands me."

"No one understands you."

"Really? I think it's you that nobody understands. Anyway, there are some preliminaries in this case that I can live with."

"Like what?"

"I can't go to the house. I have to stay at a hotel."

"And you're okay with that?"

"Why wouldn't I be? A lot of surprising stuff happens at a hotel. For all intents and purposes, I'll be home."

And now I have to figure out how to work around Dee and Helen Folsom, who are on the job site continuously and kind of in the way. One night, they camped out on the subflooring of what will be their bedroom, when we barely had the sheathing on the roof.

The crew had to shoo them away in the morning. I think the Folsoms were embarrassed, dragging the blow-up mattress out to their old sedan.

I have no real complaints about my upbringing. My parents were self-absorbed and never knew where I was, which meant that I was free, and I made good use of that freedom. I've been asked if I was damaged by my family life, and the answer is a qualified no; I know I'll never marry, and, halfway through my life, I'm unable to imagine letting anyone new stay in my house for more than a night—and preferably not a whole night. Rolling over in the morning and finding . . . let's not go there. I build houses for other people, and it works for me.

I like to be tired. In some ways, that's the point of what I do. I don't want to be thinking when I go to bed, or, if there is some residue from the day, I want it to drain out and precipitate me into nothingness. I've always enjoyed the idea of nonexistence. I view pets with extraordinary suspicion: we need to stay out of their lives. I saw a woman fish a little dog out of her purse once, and it bothered me for a year. It's not that there's anything wrong with my ability to communicate: I have a cell phone, but I only use it to call out.

The House on Sand Creek

When Monika and I were first married we rented a house on Sand Creek, sight unseen, because Monika wanted to live in the country, and nothing else was available within reach of town. Everything we had been told was true: the house was a furnished ranch house with two bedrooms, two baths, near a quiet grove of aspens. It had been repossessed from a cowboy and his wife, who had gone on to Nevada or Oregon—somewhere in the Great Basin. The man at the bank said that he was an old-time rambling buckaroo, who'd stopped making his mortgage payments because "he was looking for a quit." Monika turned to me for an explanation, but I just wanted to get the deal done and move in. "It might not be exactly to your taste," the banker said, "but nothing says you can't tweak it."

It was an absolute horror. Skinned coyote carcasses were piled on the front step, and a dead horse hung from its halter where it had been tied to the porch. Inside was a shambles, and there was one detail we couldn't understand without the help of the neighbors: shotgun blasts through the bathroom door. Apparently Mrs. Old-Time Buckaroo used to chase Mr. Old-Time Buckaroo around the house until he ran into the bathroom, locked the door, and hid in the bath. The sides of the tub were pocked with lead.

Monika, who had seen the dead horse, said that it was a shame the wife had failed and that the two of them were now in the Great Basin, living out their lives. This is a bit of an understatement—at the time Monika broke into sobs and begged to be taken away. "Is this how you treat your wife?" she turned on me. "Stop calling me your princess, you bastard." I never quite got used to these flare-ups or to Monika's sometimes misleading passion for fresh starts.

Monika was not only not a westerner; she was not even an American. She had been stranded in architecture school by the uproar in the former Yugoslavia, and by the time it was safe for her to go home, we had met and planned to marry. Which we did. And now we were in that house. Monika was commuting to architecture school, and I was running an underemployed law office that five years earlier had done thirty real-estate closings a month and now did at most two and often none. Booms in real estate came and went, like weather, except that there always seemed to be plenty of weather.

I am aware that my ability to wittily point out things like this, and to describe the house the way I am describing it, has a lot to do with the fact that Monika left soon after we'd moved in. She abandoned what she contemptuously described as "the western lifestyle" to return to her parents in Bosnia-Herzegovina. There, she found herself a nice house with no dead horses or coyotes, and a nice man and a nice baby—a twofer in the fresh-start business. Ours had been a poor excuse for a marriage, borne on an ill wind from the start.

I was still in the house, which we had painted in such a hurry that we'd rolled right over the outlets and floor moldings in uneven lines, giving one the feeling that the interior had somehow been draped in paint. For a long time, the sight of the walls kept Monika in my mind, even when womenfolk came for a visit, always short. Something—either me or the house—seemed to give them the willies.

I first met Bob when he came to congratulate me on "getting rid of that Croat." Like many other men in the area, Bob wore cowboy boots and a big hat and described himself as a former cowboy. This phenomenon interested me, and I began to put the stories together a bit. For example, Bob, a retired electrician, had not been a cowboy for at least forty-five of his sixty-two years. Further investigation suggested that his cowboy years had occurred somewhere between the sixth and seventh grades and may have lasted just under a month. I had always imagined cowboys, former and otherwise, to be laconic men, who, if they overcame their reluctance to speak at all, did so without much expression. Not Bob. Bob never shut up and his facial movements had more in common with those of Soupy Sales than John Wayne. A surprising number of his anecdotes culminated in his telling people off, especially members of his own family. "My mother's in her eighties and she keeps talking about when I was in her belly. Ever hear anything more disgusting? I finally had to tell her to shut her trap." Or "I got fed up with my son. I told him to go fuck himself. He said he'd give it his best shot. Never at a loss for words, that boy." Or "They're all driving me crazy: my wife, my mother, my son, all his noisy friends. All the guys I worked with. Too much time on their hands. They need to get a life and quit cluttering up mine."

Mail addressed to Bob was once mistakenly delivered to my

box, so I took it up to his place. It was clear that he was living alone. In time, I learned that he had been living alone for years and that all his stories of telling people off were just wishful thinking. Bob's relatives had put plenty of distance between themselves and him long ago. The only car that was ever in his driveway was his, an obsolete six-cylinder Bel Air with plenty of gravel cracks in the windshield. But at least Bob had integrity: he was mad at the world, if not yet at me. If I didn't wind sprint to my car or work on weekends, I was in for long visits. Still, something about him touched me.

Bob and I had really started to settle in—with Bob tracking my movements to make sure that I was home from work for at least ten minutes before he showed up—when Monika called me from Belgrade. She had written occasionally since leaving, but this was the first time I had spoken to her in a couple of years. I found it painful in the extreme and didn't quite keep track of the conversation, uncertain why I should care that she had money from the sale of her house or that little Karel already slept through the night and was such a happy boy. Monika must have detected my confusion because she suddenly asked, "Are you following this?" and I had to admit that I was a bit lost. She filled me in: she wanted to come back. What had happened to her new man? I asked her. "Out the window!" she said.

Monika spoke nearly perfect English, but she always managed to alter our colloquialisms slightly. My favorite was her description of a problem as "a real kink in the ointment." I tried to correct this to "fly in the ointment," but with a blank look on her beautiful face she asked me what a fly would be doing in ointment. I let it go. I had been raised to think that loving your spouse was a requirement. "Love is a job," my mother had snarled at our wedding as she gazed at Monika, who was wear-ing some sort of shocking Eastern European headdress. Thus, I loved Monika even after she left me and until the day she announced her return, a baby under her arm by someone I had never met.

On the first day of the Bozeman Sweet Pea Festival, Monika got off the plane and handed me little Karel. "For you. Have I aged? I don't seem to turn heads the way I used to." She wore some sort of gown that fit her like a giant lampshade, a grand cone that went from her neck to the ground. "Is that a dirndl?" I asked.

"No, it's a dashiki. Oh, God, you haven't changed."

I was in shock. As for little Karel, now in my arms, he was clearly black. I had an unworthy thought: Wait until Bob gets a load of this. Turned out I was wrong to worry about it because when Bob met Karel he thought he had a skin condition of some kind and expressed his sympathy.

In the parking lot, Monika said, "What are you doing with this tiny car?"

"I've been single, Monika. It was all I needed."

"Well, I'm back." She worked her way into the passenger seat while I held little Karel, who was gazing into my eyes confi-dently. "And this put-put will prove inadequate."

The feeling came back to me, from the days of our marriage, that I was doomed in life to take a lot of shit and make weak jokes in response.

We made love as soon as we got to the house. Monika bounced me around and remarked that I seemed out of it. Across her lower back was a mysterious architectural tattoo, which turned out to be Le Corbusier's plan for the High Court of Chandigarh, India. As I drifted off into postcoital tristesse, Monika raided the icebox. She was perfectly candid about her enthusiasm for food, explaining that her ex was a glutton. "Often when people come from lands of scarce resources their response to abundance is gluttony."

"A big fellow, is he?" I asked weakly.

"In every way," she said with a laugh. "You know what a Mandingo is?"

"Is it something to eat?"

"No, idiot! A Mandingo is an African warrior. You're thinking of a mango!"

"Oh. Is he an African warrior?"

"Hardly. He's a Nigerian neurosurgeon. But Olatunde has the sort of Mandingo traits that I hope Karel inherits. He's actually Yoruba."

I looked over at Karel. He didn't seem to possess any Mandingo traits. He was just a little baby waving his arms around. When Monika collapsed with jet lag, I took him out to the sofa and let him play on my chest until he fell asleep. And then I fell asleep. The last thing I saw was a bird trying to get in the window. Monika's luggage was still sitting in the living room, unopened.

Bob must have figured out that Karel did not have a skin condition because there was certainly a theme to the gifts he brought over. "He already had a baby shower in Belgrade," Monika said, but that didn't stop Bob. A children's biography of Martin Luther King Jr., James Brown's *Greatest Hits,* and a pretend leg of fried chicken made out of some rubberlike material. "He can actually teethe on it!" Bob said.

When he was gone, Monika said, "My dream was of a new life here, but this may be impossible."

"I think Bob meant well," I said.

"Ah, make no mistake: that was not Bob speaking and bringing his symbolic gifts. That was America speaking through Bob."

Meanwhile, Karel teethed contentedly on his rubber drumstick, his little chin glistening as he hummed.

As part of Monika's first assignment on her return to architecture school she began to design some alterations for our house, a wing here, a wing there: I was terrified that she would actually want me to have these things built.

"Why do we need a loggia?"

"Why do I even talk to you?"

Bob continued to visit some mornings for coffee. If he arrived before Monika left for school, she fled to her car. "Always in a hurry, that gal," Bob said. "Someday she'll be designing skyscrapers, and we'll brag we knew her back when." Whenever Bob drove Monika from the house, it fell to me to care for Karel until the babysitter arrived in her white tennis shoes and loose shorts that made the vanishing of her thighs into them a matter of urgent mystery. I loved to start the day by playing with Karel in bed. He'd sit on my stomach, and we'd play hand games that always ended with this merry little boy tipping over onto the pillows only to arise and crawl on top of me again to resume the battle with a shout. If Bob was still there, we did this on the living-room rug, scurrying around until I had rug burns on my knees. When Bob wasn't launching into some complaint about his overindulgent mother, he was wonderful with Karel. I could leave the two of them together while I dressed for work, and whatever Bob did always had Karel squealing with delight. The arrival of the babysitter, nubile Lydia, would put an end to all this: I went to work; Bob went home.

I have lived in this town for a long time, but I was raised in Bakersfield, California, a town I was longing to flee by the age of ten. I coughed up out-of-state tuition, went to law school, then settled here, at first alone and then with Monika. I mention all this because my colleague, Jay Matthews, who has lived here all his life, told me that Bob's mother could hardly be driving him crazy: she died when he was a boy. "Got to be fifty years ago."

"I must have misheard him."

"Yeah, Bob was an only child, and his mom was single. Ole Bob was a bubble and a half off plumb, even back then. That's why he's always fit right into this godforsaken town."

Life went on. Karel's father, Olatunde, called every week, sometimes talking to me and sometimes to Monika. His attempts to talk to Karel came to nothing, as Karel drooled and stared at the receiver. Olatunde spoke in measured tones in a deep voice, which, combined with his cultivated, slightly fusty British accent, seemed to come from a tomb. Nonetheless, his melancholy over the absence of his little boy could be discerned. He wished me luck with Monika and said that I was going to need it. His, he said, had run out.

Bob and Karel became so close—Karel singing in his presence and crying out in delight when he arrived—that Monika and I consulted about dispensing with the babysitter and using Bob instead. I wasn't sure about this. The babysitter was getting ready to start college and needed the money, and, besides, I was sweet on her and thought she was starting to come around, recklessly bending over to pick up Karel's toys in my presence. Monika noticed this once and started braying with sardonic and distinctly Slavic laughter. The time had come for me to take the bull by the horns. I followed Lydia to her car and told her that any fool could see how beautiful she was and I was no fool. She started but failed to reply. "You—you—you—" She got into her car and roared off. I thought it best to maintain a sphinxlike expression on my way back into the house. Monika smiled at me as I entered. "Turn you down?"

"Seems to be running okay. I can't think why she thought the ignition was going out."

Gales of laughter. "Oh, good one, Stick to your weapons."

The moment blew over, with the usual residue, but in the end I was furious with Lydia for having wiggled around the house on the assumption that I wouldn't notice. Entrapment, pure and simple. Another few steps down that trail, and Lydia could have owned my law firm. These youngsters look right through you, unless their gaze falls on something they might need. I should have held my wallet aloft with one hand while pointing at my crotch with the other, but I simply lacked the nerve. So (a) babysitter leaves, and (b) here comes Bob. The convenience and economy of this arrangement appealed even to Monika, who allowed that he was "not a bad chicken egg after all."

Obviously, we made several forays into marriage counseling, during which we turned each of our counselors into helpless referees. I always felt that these sessions were nothing more than attempts by each side to win over the counselor, with charm, cajoling, whatever it took. In the end, Monika decided that everything that had led to the idea of counseling—Freud, Jung, Judeo-Christianity—was spiritually bankrupt. Therefore, she was going to look back thousands of years and seek the help of a shaman, now resident in Missoula. This shaman, she explained, had the benefit of ten thousand years of human spiritual experience, as opposed to the Johnny-come-latelies of psychoanalysis, and she intended to partake of that knowledge. I listened thoughtfully and replied that it sounded promising so long as she didn't fuck the shaman.

Thus began our decidedly parallel lives: Monika and her shaman and her architecture, me and my law practice, Bob and Karel. Monika came home in the evening with long rolls of paper under her arm, and I with my briefcase, containing few briefs in these straitened times, to the happy home of Bob and Karel. When Bob left for the night, I held Karel's rigid little body as he wailed and reached frantically in the direction of Bob's departure. "Give him something to eat," Monika remarked on her way into the bedroom.

One afternoon, Monika and I had a rather sharp exchange in the presence of Bob and Karel. I asked innocently if it was absolutely necessary for her to keep using her boarding pass as a bookmark.

Monika said, "None of your business."

"I suppose it helps to remind you of that shithole where you grew up."

"It reminds me that they still have airplanes that go back there."

"Everyone wants to go to Yugoslavia," I said, "where shooting your neighbor is the national sport."

"Oh, you're awful. You're just so awful. My God, how truly awful you are."

Karel started to cry, and Bob took him outside. Soon I could see the chains of the swing flashing back and forth and hear Karel's delighted cries.

Monika had recently undergone an abrupt sartorial change from dark Euro-style clothing to Rocky Mountain chic: hiking boots, painter pants, bright yellow down jacket, and a wool cap with strings hanging down the sides. Now screwing a mountaineer, I thought ungenerously. Her exhaustion, I assumed, owed more to her shagging the mountain man than to anything she was doing in the world of architecture.

It should come as no surprise to anybody that the day came when Monika and I returned from work to find Bob and Karel missing. Having read *Huckleberry Finn,* she remarked that Bob had "lit out for the territory" with Karel. I don't want to overstate the ghastly nature of our response, as we were both crying— though whether at the loss of Karel or at the feeling that we deserved to lose him and Bob deserved to have him, I couldn't say. When I attempted to cheer Monika up by saying that when life gives you lemons you must make lemonade, she slapped my face. I almost fought back, and you can only imagine how that would have seemed under the circumstances.

Instead, I called the police in town. Monika called Olatunde in Yugoslavia and put me on the phone. "You tell him."

"Good morning, Doctor. It's afternoon there already? Well, I have news, well, not news exactly. One of our neighbors here has . . . kidnapped Karel." Dr. Olatunde was understandably slow in absorbing this announcement but not in any other way, and it fell to me to pick him up at the airport a day and a half later.

These were terrible hours. Monika stayed home as we awaited word from the police, her drawings laid out on the kitchen table. She showered me with reproaches, the recurrent one being that Karel would never have "slipped through her hand" if I hadn't chased the babysitter away with my ogling. Pointing at the drawings, I said, "I see the loggia stays."

"Yes, and a pergola."

"I hadn't noticed."

"There are none so blind as those who will not see."

I met Dr. Olatunde at the baggage claim though he had only a carry-on. He was the sole African among all the skiers, and he drew a bit of attention to himself for that and for the suit he wore, a nice English cut, rumpled from the long trip. He was not at all the big Mandingo glutton I had pictured but a small, precise man with a slightly receding hairline and a friendly but crisp manner. He said, "You were kind to come for me."

"You must be tired."

"Not so bad, really."

"Well, I have marvelous news for you. Karel has been found."

"Is that so?"

"I hope you don't feel the trip was wasted."

"Nothing could compare to this. Is he well?"

Bob and Karel had not gone far, at least not far enough to give plausibility to a charge of kidnapping. They were in the first motel on the way into town. Their loud music had given them away. Bob was belligerent about what he described as the hostile atmosphere of our home, and we felt that by pressing charges we would only bring his version into the public eye. Karel responded to his father, whom he could hardly have been expected to remember, much as he responded to Bob: he was always drawn to someone who looked straight at him as though making a delightful discovery. I spell this out because it was against all odds that we allowed Bob to come back again and let ourselves be compensated by Karel's squeals of delight. More and more, he stays over at Bob's anyway, which Monika and I hope will give us some room to work things out.

Grandma and Me

My grandmother lost her sight about three years ago, just before she turned ninety, and because it happened gradually, and in the context of so much other debility, she adapted very well. Grandma's love of the outdoors combined with her remarkable lucidity and optimism to keep her cheerful and realistic. And she could get on my ass about as good as she ever could. She was now greatly invested in her sense of smell, so I tried to put fresh flowers around her house, while Mrs. Devlin, her house-keeper of forty-one years, kept other things in the cottage fresh, including the flow of gossip and the newspaper under Chickie, a thirty-year-old blue-fronted parrot that had bitten me several times. When Grandma goes, Chickie is going into the disposal.

Grandma did a remarkable job of living in the present, something I'd hoped to learn from her before going broke or even crazier than I already was. I'd been away for over a decade, first as a timekeeper in a palladium mine, then dealing cards, downhill all the way. Three years in a casino left me so fucked up I was speaking in tongues, but Grandma got me back on my feet with pearls of immortal wisdom like "Pull yourself together." And while I waited for her to give me a little walking-around money, a pearl or two would come to me, too, like "Shit or get off the pot."

Grandma owned several buildings in the middle of our small town, including the old hotel where I lived. I looked after them, not exactly as a maintenance man—I don't have such trade skills—but more as an overseer, for which Grandma paid me meagerly, justifying her stinginess with the claim that I was bleeding her white. Another building housed an office-supply shop and a preschool, where I was a teaching assistant. That is, a glorified hall monitor for a bunch of dwarfs. I also tended bar two nights a week—the off nights, when tips were scarce, but it was something to do and kept me near the hooch. Grandma had bought the bar, too, back when it was frequented mainly by sheepherders. Sheep have mostly disappeared from the area since being excluded from the national forest, which they had defoliated better than Agent Orange. I didn't see much point in tending an empty bar, but Grandma required it. It was part of my "package," she said, and besides she was sure that if we closed it down, it would become a meth lab. Grandma was convinced every empty building housed a meth lab.

The preschool thing was another matter. Mrs. Hessler, the teacher, considered me her employee, and I played along with this to keep the frown off that somewhat-shapeless face she had crowned with an inappropriate platinum pixie. I regularly fed her made-up news items from imaginary newspapers, and she always bought it.

"Drone Strike on a Strip Club," for example. In return, Mrs. Hessler made me wear clothes she supplied and considered kid friendly; loud leisure suits and sweatpants, odd-lot items that gave me the feeling I was at the end of my rope.

Barring weather or a World Series game, on Sundays I'd pick up a nice little box lunch from Mustang Catering and take Grandma someplace that smelled good. I was often in rough shape on Sunday mornings, so a little fresh air helped me dry out in time for work on Monday. We'd have our picnics in fields of sage and lupine, on buffalo-grass savannas north of town, on deep beds of spruce needles, and in fields of spring wildflowers. I'd have enough of nature pretty quick, but we stayed until Grandma had had her fill; she told me it was the least I could do, and I suppose she's right.

Today's nature jaunt turned out to be one for the ages: we went to a bend in the river near Grandma's and set up our picnic under the oldest of cottonwoods, so that the eastbound current raced toward us over pale gravel. It smelled wonderful. Once out of the car, I led Grandma with a light touch on the elbow, marveling at how straight and tall she was—how queenly she looked with her thick white hair carefully piled and secured by Mrs. Devlin with a broad tortoiseshell comb. I had just settled Grandma on her folding chair and popped open our box lunch when the corpse floated by. Though facedown, he seemed formally attired, and the tumult of current at the bend was strong enough to make him ripple from end to end, while his arms seemed lofted in some oddly valedictory way, and his hair floated ahead of him. The sunlight sparkling on the water made the picture ghastly.

"Oh!" said Grandma as though she could see it.

"What?"

"That divine smell, of course! I can still smell snow in the river!"

The corpse had rotated in such a way that I could now see

the heels of its shoes and the slight ballooning of its suit coat. Just then I remembered that cheap Allegiant flight I'd taken back from Las Vegas. I'd lost so much money, I got drunk on the plane and passed out, and someone scrawled LOSER on my face in eyebrow pencil, though I didn't see it until the men's room at the Helena airport. Was I so far gone I was identifying with a corpse?

"What an awful child you were," Grandma said. "Already drinking in the sixth grade. What would have become of you if I hadn't put you in Catholic school? It was your salvation and thank goodness the voodoo wore off in time. It wasn't easy humoring those silly nuns. They never took their hands out of their sleeves the whole time you were there."

"Uh, Grandma, excuse me, but I have to see a man about a horse." I jogged along the riverbank until I was well out of ear-shot, and lighting a cigarette, I called the sheriff's office on my cell. I let the dispatcher know who I was and asked if the sheriff or one of the deputies was available. "I'll check. What's the topic?" The dispatcher's tone let me know how they felt about me at the sheriff's office.

"I'm down on the river, and a corpse just went by. Across from the dump. It's going to pass under the Harlowton Bridge in about ten minutes."

"There's no one here right now. Marvin has a speeder pulled over at the prairie dog town. Maybe he could get there."

"Next stop after that is Greycliff. Somebody'd have to sit on the bridge all day."

"Please don't raise your voice. Any distinguishing features?"

"How's 'dead' sound to you?"

I went back to find Grandma lifting her face in the direction of the sun and seeming contented. A few cottonwood leaves fluttering in a breath of wind onto the surface of the river revealed the speed of the current. Every so often people floated by on rafts, blue rafts, yellow rafts, their laughter and conversations carried along on the water like a big, happy wake following a corpse.

"Are you ready to eat?" I asked.

"In a bit, unless you're hungry now. It smells different than when we were here in August. I think something happens when the leaves begin to turn, something cidery in the air, and yesterday's rain stays in the trunks of these old trees." It had rained for about two minutes yesterday. Grandma's got all these sensations dialed in as though she's cramming the entire earth before she croaks.

I walked down to the river, took off my shoes and socks, and rolled up my pant legs. I waded in no more than a few inches when I heard my phone ring. I turned just in time to see Grandma groping for it next to where I left the box lunches. Oh, well. I kept wading and noticed three white pelicans standing among the car bodies on the far side of the river. I'd have thought they'd have gone south by now. I dug a few flat stones off the bottom and skipped them toward the middle of the river. I got five skips from a piece of bottle glass before going back to Grandma.

"That was the sheriff's office."

"Oh?"

"They wanted you to know that it was a jilted groom who jumped into Yankee Jim Canyon on Sunday. What day is today?"

"Wednesday." Must have averaged a couple miles an hour.

"Why would they think you'd care about a jilted groom jumping into Yankee Jim Canyon?"

"Idle curiosity," I said sharply.

"And the sheriff was calling just to fill you in? I don't understand one bit of that, not one bit."

I wasn't about to let Grandma force me to ruin her outing by telling her what I had seen. So I opened the box lunch, spread a napkin on her lap, and there I set her sandwich, sliced cucumbers, and almond cookie. She lifted half of the sandwich.

"What is this? Smells like deviled ham."

"It is deviled ham."

"Starving."

Must have been: she fucking gobbled it.

"I see where you had another DUI."

You didn't see that, you heard it, and I could reliably assume that Mrs. Devlin made sure of it. "Yes. Grandma, drunk at the wheel." Of course I was making light of this, but secretly I thanked God it had stayed out of the papers. When you work with young children, it takes very little to tip parents into paranoia—they are already racked with guilt over dropping their darlings off with strangers in a setting where the little tykes could easily get shot or groped.

In families like mine, grandmothers loom large as yetis. I always thought having Grandma had been a blessing for me, but still I have often wondered if it wasn't her vigor that had made my father into such a depressed boob. He was a case of arrested development who never made a dime, but Grandma supported him in fine-enough style for around here and at the far end of her apron strings. He was devoted to his aquarelles—his word. The basement was full of them. His little house has remained empty, except for the flowers, bunnies, puppies, and sunsets on every wall. Grandma says it's without a doubt a meth lab.

Perhaps I felt some of his oppression as Grandma sat bolt upright holding that half a sandwich ("I trust you washed up before handling my food") and inhaling the mighty cottonwoods, the watercress in the tiny spring seeping into the broad green and sparkling river. I thought about the drowned bridegroom sailing by, his arms fluttering like a bat. It was Grandma who'd taught me that every river has its own smell and that ours are fragrant while others stink to high heaven, catch fire, or plunge into desert holes never to be seen again.

I think that at bottom some of these reflections must have been prompted by the mention of my latest DUI, which was a frightful memory. I knew it wasn't funny. I had left the Mad Hatter at closing, perfectly well aware that I was drunk. That was why I went there, after all. From the window at the back of the bar, as the staff cleaned up, I watched the squad car circle the block until I had determined the coast was clear. I ran through the cold night air to my car and headed up the valley. I hadn't gone far when I saw the whirling red light in my rearview mirror, and there's where I made a bad decision. I pulled over and bolted out of the car and ran into a pasture, tearing my shirt and pants on a barbed-wire fence. I didn't stop running until I fell into some kind of crack in the ground and broke my arm. That light in my rearview turned out to be an ambulance headed farther up the valley. I crawled out of the crack and got back into the car to drive to the emergency room back in town. I soon attracted an actual policeman and hence the DUI, the cast on my arm, and this latest annoyance from Grandma, who may in fact be the source of my problems. I knew that thought was a tough sell which defied common sense, but it was gathering plausibility for me.

I looked across the river at the row of houses above the line of car bodies. I heard a lawn mower over the whisper of river. A tennis ball came sailing over the bank, a black dog watching as it disappeared into the river.

Grandma said, "When you were a little boy, I thought you would be president of the United States." I got that odd shriveling feeling I used to get when our parents couldn't handle us and she would have to come to our house. I decided to give her the silent treatment. She didn't notice. I watched as she took in all she could smell and hear with the same upright posture and air of satisfaction. I unexpectedly decided that I was entitled to a little liquid cheer and began tiptoeing in the direction of my car a good distance away, wasted tiptoeing, I might add, as Grandmother said, "Bye-bye."

I have no idea why starting the car and putting it in gear gave me such a gust of exhilaration that the quick stop for a couple of stiff ones seemed almost redundant. But that's what happened, and I felt all the better for it as I walked into the sheriff's office just as Deputy Crane was leaving. I caught his sleeve and asked about the corpse. I could tell by his expression that he could smell the adult beverage on my breath. "They pulled it out of the water at the Reed Point Bridge. I'm headed there now."

"Oh, let me ride along."

"What's the matter with you?"

Deputy Crane would have to get up earlier in the morning if he wanted to be rid of me. By the time he pulled out of town, I was hot on his trail. The interstate followed the river, and we sped along doing seventy-five, the river intermittently visible on my left. Thus far the bridegroom had outrun us.

Pulling off the interstate and down into a riverside trailer park, I was convinced that euphoria was the rarest of all prizes, and being as good as anyone at cherishing mine, I started to fear that seeing the corpse up close might be a buzzkill. A small crowd had formed at the riverbank, and the squad car was parked close by. I pulled up next to the deputy, who got out and, spotting me, said, "Jesus Christ." The small crowd parted at the sight of the uniform, and I pushed through in its wake, rudely asked to stop shoving. There within the circle of gawkers was the dead bridegroom. Either his wedding clothes were too small for him or he was seriously waterlogged. I don't know why they laid him out on a picnic table. The well-trimmed mustache seemed misplaced on the broad moon face whose wide-open eyes were giving me such a bad feeling. The gawkers would look at the face, then at one another searching for some explanation. People with sideburns that long were inevitably from the wrong side of the tracks, where me and my family, excepting Grandma, had all lived. I couldn't say why I felt a corpse shouldn't have a mustache and long sideburns. It seemed about time to buck up with some more artificial elation. But first I thought it only right to inform this group that it was I who had first spotted our friend floating past. This fell on deaf ears. I looked around me with a bleak, ironic smile undaunted by their indignation.

Somebody at the Mad Hatter had told me there was going to be midget wrestling at the Waterhole. There was a van parked in front with the logo SUPPORT MIDGET VIOLENCE, but no midgets in sight unless they were asleep inside. Two horses stood tied to the hitching rack in front by the trough and beside them four pickup trucks with so much mud on the windshields that the drivers could only have seen through the wiper arcs. Between two of the trucks was a blood-red Porsche Carrera with New

Mexico plates and a King Charles spaniel at the wheel. I was able to get what I wanted without giving the others the impression that I cared to mingle. The bartender was a compulsive counter wiper, and when I got up, the tip I left there disappeared. He pretended to find the bills under the rag as I departed, giving the entire crowd a laugh at my expense as I pushed through the doors. I thought of going back and raising hell but found the Porsche unlocked and released the spaniel instead. It was dark, and all I could think of was one word, "Grandma!" The dog headed off through the houses with their lighted windows as I was swept by uneasiness.

Something was making me drive this fast. I was trying my best to reckon where those little units of time had gone. Whatever trouble I was headed for, it didn't feel like it was entirely my fault, just because someone decided to send a corpse through my day. If he'd lived on Grandma's side of town, he would have enjoyed more options with no sideburns to maintain.

It was not easy to find our picnic site in the dark, and I wouldn't have been sure I'd found it if I hadn't spotted the remains of the box lunch. I ate the other deviled-ham sandwich, the hard-boiled egg, the spicy pickle, and the cookie, and staring at the large expanse of the river, breathing mostly with my abdominal muscles, I tried to collect my thoughts and ward off hysteria.

The chair was gone. So, she didn't jump in the river. Can't have more than one corpse a day. Somebody must have found Grandma and taken her home. This thought gave me an especially sharp pain, as it suggested one more person looking down on me, the oaf who left his blind grandmother on the riverbank.

I drove back across the Harlowton Bridge, through town heading for Snob Hollow, where Grandmother lived. My watch has a luminous dial, but I was afraid to look, fearing yet another buzzkill. By the time I stopped in front of Grandma's, I was having palpitations. I rifled the backseat in search of the minis sometimes scattered there but found only a mocking handful of empties. I stared through the windshield at the pair of juniper hedges leading to the door. My mind was so inflamed that when I got out of the car I thought I saw a face. I approached the front door and knocked, and then knocked again. Blood rushed to my head when I heard something within.

Mrs. Devlin was fastening her terry-cloth wrapper at the neck. She was no girl herself, and those big teeth and accusing eyes only subtracted from any impression of innocence. She had led a blameless life and wouldn't say shit if she had a mouthful, but when backed by Grandma's authority she could be dangerous.

"You," she said.

"Just checking in on Grandma."

Then in the dark behind Mrs. Devlin I heard Grandma ask, "Is that him?"

"Yes, it is, Adeline."

"Mrs. Devlin, kindly slap his face for me." It sure stung.

I imagined saying, *Try this one on for size,* before throwing Mrs. Devlin a roundhouse, but of course I just stood there as the door was slammed in my face. I headed back downtown, which in the dark looked abandoned, with so few lights that their silhouettes showed against the night sky, the blank face of the derelict mercantile, the bell cupola of the fire station with its mantle of cold stars. I returned to my room at the hotel, and the view of the mountains through the empty lobby, the old billiard table on which a century ago some surgeon treated the victim of a gunfight, the smells of mahogany and matted carpet, the dimmed lights gleaming off the souvenir cabinet. On my wave of booze and self-pity, one more nobody for the rest of the world to kick around. I pictured myself as the last survivor of my family, except for Grandma, who was left to contemplate what she had achieved over the generations. The thought lulled me into a nice sleep. I awakened to the sound of the breakfast dishes clattering in the restaurant, and for me a brand-new chance for success. As usual, whether I made the most of it or not, it would be fun just to see what happened, because, say what you will, I'm a glass-half-full kind of guy.

There wasn't time to eat before going to work, Mrs. Hessler being a Nazi about punctuality. I was careful to avoid a long look at myself as I brushed my teeth and glanced at my watch. I pulled on one of my work shirts, the one that says YOUR COMPANY NAME HERE at the top, YOUR LOGO HERE in the middle, and ONE CHILD AT A TIME at the bottom. Mrs. Hessler had gotten them in some close-out sale and expected to see them.

When I first went to work for Mrs. Hessler, it was just after my casino years and, knowing about my résumé, she got me to teach her Texas Hold'em. She was pretty good but soon got overconfident and went off for a gambler's weekend to Vegas and lost her ass. Naturally she blamed me. That set the tone. I told her that in a world where sperm donors are expected to pay child support, anything could happen.

Hooray for me! I was actually early. I let myself into the playroom and realized I had never cleaned up on Friday. I had been in some haste to get to the Mad Hatter, and so now, with so little strength, I would have to put everything in order before Hessler let me know by her silence how unhappy she was with me, her drone. *Back to the barracoon, darky!* I told her I'd read that some archbishop staying at a five-star hotel in the Seychelles got his ass scorched on a rogue bidet. She didn't even crack a smile. Chutes and Ladders was all over the floor, and I got dizzy picking up all the pieces. Moronic instruments for tiny mites—drums, tambourines, ocarinas—all would have to go on the music shelf. The GOD MADE ME SPECIAL poster had broken free of its thumbtacks. I didn't remember so much chaos on Friday—motivational ribbons and certificates, birthday crowns, star badges, alphabet stickers all over the room—but then my mind had been elsewhere.

Frau Hessler made the rounds of the refrigerator, counted out the snacks in a loud voice, put the removable mop heads back in the closet, gave her own YOUR COMPANY HERE shirt a good stretch, and greeted the first mother at the door. It was on. They came in a wave of noise as Hessler and I checked each other's faces for the required cheer. I had mine on good but felt like my teeth were drying out. Two mothers asked for the containers of their breast milk to be labeled and were quite abrupt telling me that Post-its would fall off in the fridge. The room was full of children, nearly babies, little boys and girls thematically dressed according to the expectations of their parents, little princesses and tiny cowboys, some still in pajamas. Hessler always seemed to know exactly what to do and began creating order. I dove into the sock-puppet bins, trying to find one that felt right, pawing through the Bible-themed puppets, the monster puppets, the animal puppets. I was fixated on getting one I was comfortable with, since I'd ended up with Saint John the Baptist the previous week, and Hessler rebuked me for failing to come up with relevant Bible quotes. Realizing I was running out of time by Hessler standards, I just snatched one randomly and found myself wearing an African American fireman and wiggling the stick that operated the hand holding the hose, all for the sake of a surly four-year-old named Roger. Roger was not amused and after long silence called me poopoo head. I offered up some goofy laughter, and Roger repeated the remark. "In ten years, Roger," I muttered, "you'll be sniffing airplane glue from a sandwich bag." I dropped the fireman on the bench and moved on to nicer children. I made it until time-out, when I left the playhouse for a cigarette. A cold wind stirred the last leaves on the old burr oaks at the corner. Up on the hill, where Grandma's house stood, the sun was already shining. Mrs. Devlin would be setting out her midmorning tea, and Grandma was sure to feel that things were in perfect order.

Hubcaps

By late afternoon, Owen's parents were usually having their first cocktails. His mother gave hers some thought, looking upon it as a special treat, while his father served himself "a stiff one" in a more matter-of-fact way, his every movement expressing a conviction that he had a right to this stuff, no matter how disagreeable or lugubrious or romantic it might soon make him. He made a special point of not asking permission as he poured, with a workmanlike concentration on not spilling a drop. Owen's mother held her drink between the tips of her fingers; his father held his in his fist. Owen could see solemnity descend on his father's brow with the first sip, while his mother often looked apprehensive about the possible hysteria to come. Owen remembered a Saturday night when his father had air-paddled backward, collapsing into the kitchen trash can and terrifying the family boxer, Gertrude. Gertrude had bitten Owen's father the first time she saw him drunk and now viewed him with a detachment that was similar to Owen's.

In any event, the cocktails were Owen's cue to head for the baseball diamond that the three Kershaw boys and their father had built in the pasture across from their house, with the help of any neighborhood kids who'd wanted to pitch in—clearing brush, laying out the baselines and boundaries, forming the pitcher's mound, or driving in the posts for the backstop. Doug, the eldest Kershaw boy, was already an accomplished player, with a Marty Marion infielder's mitt and a pair of cleats. Terry, the middle son, was focused on developing his paper route and would likely be a millionaire by thirty. Ben, the youngest and sweetest, was disabled and mentally handicapped, but he loved baseball above all things; he had a statistician's capacity for memorizing numbers and had learned to field a ball with one crippled hand and to make a respectable throw with the other. To Owen, Ben's attributes were nothing remarkable: he had his challenges; Ben had others.

It was rare to have full teams, and occasional lone outfielders started at center field and prepared to run. Eventually, Ben was moved off first base and into the outfield. With his short arms, he couldn't keep his foot on the bag and reach far enough for bad throws. Double plays came along only about three times a summer, and no one wanted to put them at risk. So long as Ben could identify with a renowned player who had played his position—in this case, Hoot Evers—he was happy to occupy it, and physically he did better with flies than with grounders.

Owen was happy with his George Kell spot at third base, and he didn't intend to relinquish it. He was a poor hitter—he was trying to graduate from choking the bat, though he was still not strong enough to hold it at the grip—but his ability to cover stinging grounders close to the foul line was considered compensation for his small production at the plate. He had learned to commit late to the ball's trajectory—grounders often changed angles, thanks to the field's irregularities—and he went fairly early when they chose up sides. Chuck Wood went late, despite being the most muscular boy there, as he always swung for the fence in wan hope of a home run and was widely considered a showboater. Ben was a polished bunter and could run like the wind, assuring his team of at least one man on base. He was picked early, sometimes first, but never got to be captain, because in the hand-over-hand-on-the-bat ritual for choosing sides, his hand wouldn't fit anywhere below the label. In the beginning, Mrs. Kershaw had stuck around to make sure that he was treated fairly, announcing, "If Ben doesn't play, nobody plays." But now he belonged, and she restricted her supervision to meeting him as he got off the school bus and casting an authoritarian glance through the other passengers' windows.

After a game, the equipment was stored on the back porch of the Kershaw house, where Terry ran his newspaper operation and often recruited the players to help him fold for the evening delivery. The Kershaws' small black schipperke dog, Smudge, watched from a corner. Doug put a few drops of neat's-foot oil in the pocket of his mitt, folded a ball into it, and placed it on the broad shelf that held shin guards, a catcher's mask, and a cracked Hillerich & Bradsby thirty-four-inch bat that Mr. Kershaw thought could be glued. It had been a mistake to go from oak to maple, he said. Eventually, Mrs. Kershaw would appear, mopping her hands on her apron before making an announcement: "Kershaw dinner. All other players begone." Owen and the other boys would rush out, with ceremonial doorway collisions, looking up at the sky through the trees: still light enough to play.

Owen would walk home, reflecting on the game, his hits, if he'd had any, his errors and fielding accomplishments. His parents dined late and by candlelight, in an atmosphere that was disquieting to Owen and at odds with thoughts about baseball.

He eventually gave up on family dinners altogether and fed himself on cold cereal. Sometimes he arrived home in time for an argument, his father booming over his mother's more penetrating vehemence. There were times when his parents seemed to be entertaining themselves this way, and times when they seemed to draw blood. Owen would flip his glove onto the hall bench and slip upstairs to his room and his growing collection of hubcaps. He'd still never been caught. He had once been on probation with the Kershaws, though: Doug, hiding in the bushes with a flashlight, had caught him soaping their windows on Halloween, but winter had absolved him, and by baseball season he was back in their good graces. He still didn't know why he had done it. The Kershaws' was the only house he'd pranked, and it was the home of people he cherished. He'd wanted contact with them, but it had come out wrong.

Owen sat with Ben on the school bus every morning. Half asleep, his lunch box on his lap, he listened to Ben ramble on in his disjointed way about the baseball standings, his mouth falling open between assertions—"If Jerry Priddy didn't hold the bat so high, he could hit the ball farther"—and his crooked arms mimicking the moves he described: George Kell's signature scoop at third or Phil Rizzuto's stretch to loosen his sleeve after throwing someone out. Only Ben, whose bed was like a pass between two mountains of *Baseball Digest* back issues, would have remembered that Priddy had torn up Rizzuto's fan letters. Yet in almost every other way, he was slow and easily influenced by anyone who took the trouble: Mike Terrell lost a year of Kershaw baseball for sending Ben on a snipe hunt.

The MacIlhatten twins, Janet and Janice, sat at the back of the bus, two horsey, scheming freshmen who dressed alike, enjoyed pretending to be each other, and amused themselves by playing tricks on Ben, hiding his hat or talking him out of the Mars bar in his lunch box. They laughed at his blank stare or repeated everything he said until he sat silent in defeat. Idle malice was their game, and, because they were superior students, they got little resistance from adults. Not entirely pretty themselves, they were brutal to Patty Seitz and Sandy Collins, two unattractive girls unlucky enough to ride the same bus, who quietly absorbed the twins' commentary on their skin, their hair, their Mary Jane shoes, and their Mickey Mouse lunch boxes. Only Stanley Ayotte, who was often suspended, except during football season, when he was a star, stood up to the twins, and to their intervening mother, actually calling them bitches. They flirted with Stanley anyway, though he ignored it.

Owen felt the twins' contemplation of his friendship with Ben: they were watching. At school, they disappeared down the corridor and forgot about him, but on the bus at the end of the day they resumed their focus. His rapt absorption in Ben's recitation of baseball statistics seemed to annoy them, but, because they understood nothing about the subject, he had been safe so far.

The school knew about Ben's love of sports. His schoolwork was managed with compassion, but water boy for the football team was the best the teachers could come up with on the field. Still, it was a job he loved, running out in front of the crowded bleachers with a tray of water-filled paper cups.

•　•　•

Church. Owen hated church and fidgeted his way from beginning to end. Or maybe not all of it, not the part where he stared at some girl like Cathy Hansen, the plumber's beautiful daughter. The moment when Cathy turned from the Communion rail, her hands clasped in front of her face in spiritual rapture, took Owen to a dazed and elevated place. He wondered how such a girl could stand to listen to a priest drone on about how to get to heaven. Cathy must have registered his attention. After Mass, she sometimes tried to exchange a pleasantry, but Owen could only impersonate disdain from his reddening face, his agony noticed with amusement by his mother, when she wasn't gazing down the sidewalk in search of a good spot for a cigarette. After contemplating the suffering of Christ, she needed a bit of relief. Owen's father had slipped an Ellery Queen novel into the covers of a daily missal; he kept his eye on the page, presenting a picture of piety. He saw his presence at the weekly service as an expression of his solidarity with the community, sitting, standing, or kneeling following cues provided by the parishioners around him.

The slow drive home after church was a trial for Owen, who could picture the game already under way on the Kershaws' diamond. Slow because they had to creep past the Ingrams' driveway. Old Bradley Ingram had married the much-younger Julie, who claimed to have been a Radio City dancer but was suspected of having been a stripper at the downtown Gaiety Burlesque House. Now they were separated. Bradley had moved into the Sheraton, and Julie was still in their home, receiving, it was said, all-night visitors. Julie did not mingle locally, and so no information could be gotten from her. The best Owen's parents could do was check out her driveway on the way home from church.

His father stopped the car so that they could peer between the now-unkempt box hedges. His mother said, "It's a Buick Roadmaster."

"I can't see the plates. I don't have my glasses."

"They're Monroe."

"That tells us nothing."

"Really?" His mother blew smoke at the ceiling of their Studebaker. "Last week it was a Cadillac."

"She's coming down in the world."

"Not by much," his mother said, and they drove on.

Owen was required to stay at the table for Sunday lunch, which went on until the middle of the afternoon. Usually, he missed the game.

In the hardwood forest, a shallow swamp immersed the trunks and roots of the trees near the lake. Owen and Ben hunted turtles among the waterweeds and pale aquatic flowers. The turtles sunned themselves on low branches hanging over the water, in shafts of light spotted with dancing dragonflies. Ever alert, the creatures tumbled into the swamp at the first sound, as though wiped from the branches by an unseen hand. The wild surroundings made Ben exuberant. He bent saplings to watch them recoil or shinnied up trees, and he returned home carrying things that interested him—strands of waterweed, bleached muskrat skulls, or the jack-in-the-pulpits he brought to his mother to fend off her irritation at having to wash another load of muddy clothes. Once, Owen caught two of the less-vigilant turtles, the size of fifty-cent pieces, with poignant little feet constantly trying to get somewhere that only they knew. Owen loved their tiny perfection, the flexible undersides of their shells, the ridges down their topside that he could detect with his thumbnail. Their necks were striped yellow, and they stretched them upward in their striving. Owen made a false bottom for his lunch box with ventilation holes so that he could always have them with him, despite the rule against taking pets to school or on the school bus. He fed them flies from a bottle cap. Only Ben knew where they were.

One afternoon, Owen came back from the swamp to find the flashing beacon of the town's fire truck illuminating the faces of curious neighbors outside his house. He ran up the short length of his driveway in time to see his mother addressing a small crowd as she stood beside two firemen in obsolete leather helmets with brass eagles fixed to their fronts. She looked slightly disheveled in a housedress and golf-club windbreaker, and she spoke in the lofty voice she used when she had been drinking, the one meant to fend off all questions: "Let he who has never had a kitchen grease fire cast the first stone!" She laughed. "Blame the television. Watching *The Guiding Light*. Mea culpa. A soufflé." Owen felt the complete bafflement of the neighborhood as he listened. Then her tone flattened. "Look, the fire's gone. Good night, one and all."

Owen's father's car nosed up to the group. His father jumped out, tie loosened, radiating authority. He pushed straight through to the firefighters without glancing at his wife. "Handled?" The shorter of the two nodded quickly. His father spoke to the neighbors: "Looks like not much. I'll get the details, I'm sure." Most had wandered off toward their own homes by then, the

Kershaws among the last to go. Owen's father turned to his wife, who was staring listlessly at the ground, placed his broad hand on the small of her back, and moved her through the front door, which he closed behind him, leaving Owen alone in the yard.

When Owen went in, his parents were sitting at opposite sides of the kitchen table, the *Free Press* spread out in front of them. The brown plastic Philco murmured a Van Patrick interview with Birdie Tebbetts: it was the seventh-inning stretch in the Indians game. Owen's father motioned to him to have a seat, which he did while trying to get the drift of the interview. His mother didn't look up, except to access the flip lid on her silver ashtray. She held a Parliament between her thumb and middle finger, delicately tapping the ash free with her forefinger. His father flicked the ash from his Old Gold with his thumbnail at the butt of the cigarette and made no particular effort to see that it landed in the heavy glass ashtray by his wrist. Commenting on what he had just read, his father said, "Let's blow 'em up before they blow us up!"

"Who's this?" his mother said, but got no answer. Instead, she turned to Owen. "Your father and I are going to take a break from each other."

"Oh, yeah?"

"We thought you'd want to know."

"Sure."

His father lifted his head to glance at Owen, then returned to the paper. Owen knew better than to say a single word, unless it was about the weather. He wanted his parents to be distracted, so that he could fit in more baseball and get any kind of haircut he liked, but he worried about things falling apart entirely.

He was unable to picture what might lie beyond that. School, of course, out there like a black cloud.

His mother said, "Ma said she'd take me in."

At this, his father raised his head from the paper. "For God's sake, Alice, no one is 'taking you in.' You're not homeless."

"Why don't *you* go someplace, and I'll stay here? Maybe someone will take you in."

"I'll tell you why: I've got a business to run." His business, which dispatched plumbers and electricians to emergencies, was called Don't Get Mad, Get Egan and made the sort of living known as decent. With tradesmen on retainer, he worked from an office, a hole-in-the-wall above a florist's shop. An answering service gave the impression that it was a bigger operation than it was.

"Ma will think you've failed."

"Well, you tell Ma I haven't failed."

"No, you tell her, sport."

"I'm not calling your mother to tell her that I haven't failed. That doesn't make sense. Owen, where have you been? You look like you've been in the swamp."

"I've been in the swamp."

"Would you like to add anything to that?"

"No."

His mother stubbed out her cigarette and said, "I think you owe your father a more complete answer, young man."

"It's nothing more than a little old swamp," Owen said. "Mind turning that up? It's the top of the eighth."

Nobody was going anywhere except back to the newspaper.

•　•　•

Mr. Kershaw was an agricultural chemist for the state—a white-collar position that was much respected locally—but, despite his sophisticated education and job, he was a country boy through and through, with all the practical and improvisatory skills he'd acquired growing up on a subsistence farm. He wore bib overalls on the weekends and had a passion for Native American history. He was interested in anything from the remote past. He had a closet full of Civil War muskets that had been passed down through his family and a cutlass given by a slave on the Underground Railroad to a forebear who had run a safe house on the route to Canada. This same forebear, by family legend, while pretending to help find a runaway, had pushed a Virginia slave hunter out of a rowboat and held him off with an oar until he drowned.

When baseball was rained out one Saturday, Mr. Kershaw took Owen aside. "How's everything at your house?"

"Great," Owen said suspiciously, assuming he was being asked about the grease fire in the kitchen.

Mr. Kershaw looked at him closely and said, "Now, Owen, after it rains I hunt arrowheads. The rain washes away the soil around them, and if you're lucky you can see them. My boys don't care, but maybe you'd like to come along."

They drove a few miles to a farm that belonged to a friend of Mr. Kershaw's. The long plowed rows in front of the farmhouse stretched to a line of trees that shielded the fields from wind off the lake. A depression, not quite plowed in, ran diagonally across the main field, from corner to corner.

"That was a creek, Owen. The Potawatomi hunted and

camped along it. Their palisades were right over there, where you see the stacks of the electric plant. So you go down the left side of the old creek, and I'll go down the right. If you have anything at all on your mind, you will never find an arrowhead."

The two walked in close sight of each other, staring at the ground. From time to time, Mr. Kershaw stooped to examine something, while Owen strained to catch sight of an arrowhead among the stones. At length, Mr. Kershaw summoned him to look at a broken point. Owen was amazed to see how its symmetrical flakes distinguished it from an ordinary stone. When Mr. Kershaw called him over again, he had an arrowhead in his hand, perfect as a jewel. "Bird point," Mr. Kershaw said, and Owen stared in possessive longing. Mr. Kershaw dropped it into his shirt pocket with a smile. "Don't think and you'll find one," he said.

Owen resumed the search with greater intensity as they approached the row of trees, whose tops were ignited by lake light. Sticking out of a clod was a pale white object that Owen picked up and gazed at without recognition. "What've you got there?" Mr. Kershaw called. "Bring it here." Owen crossed the depression and handed it to Mr. Kershaw. "Oh, you lucky boy. It's a"—he shook dirt from it—"French trade pipe. Indians got them from the trappers such a long time ago. Want to swap for my arrowhead?"

"Which is worth more?"

Mr. Kershaw laughed. "Probably your trade pipe, but that's a good question. So good, in fact, that I'll give you my arrowhead. Perhaps I'll find another." He reached into his shirt pocket, removed the arrowhead, and dropped it, warm, into Owen's palm, where its glittering perfection nearly overwhelmed him.

The ground had dried, and by the time Owen got back to the diamond the other boys were choosing up sides. Mike Stallings was captain of one team and Bobby Waldron captain of the other. Owen wanted to put his finds in a safe place; he ran toward his house, a hand pressed over the lumps of arrowhead and clay pipe in his shirt pocket, the late sun starting to flash from the windows of the neighborhood, a lake freighter moaning as it passed to the east.

The early football game with Flat Rock a week later was played under lights and in the mud from another afternoon rain. It was a bloody affair from the start, with poorly understood game plans and pent-up, random excitement among the players. At the end of the first quarter, Ben dashed out with his tray of water, tripped, and fell in a melee of paper cups. The stands erupted in laughter. Owen ran onto the field and squatted beside Ben to pick up the mess, stacking wet cups while Ben stood by, helpless and ashamed. The players waited, hands on hips, while Ben and Owen carried the remains back to the sidelines. The game resumed, and Owen wandered behind the bleachers, hoping that Flat Rock would kick the home team's asses and give the handful of visitors something to cheer about. He headed over to the parking lot, thinking he might spot some Oldsmobile spinner hubcaps to steal for his collection but settled for a set of Pontiac baby moons, which he stashed in the bushes to be picked up later. The car didn't look quite the same with its greasy wheel studs exposed, and he really wanted to stop there, but then he saw Bradley Ingram's Thunderbird and soon had all four of its dog-dish ten-inch caps.

On the bus the next morning, the twins were arguing with each other, a welcome change, as it kept their attention away from others. Ben watched them with delight, despite all their teasing. The twins were as knowledgeable about radio hits as Ben was about baseball, and he was drawn to their statistical world. Also, he had begun to notice girls. These days he often sat at the back of the bus by the twins, who seemed to regard him as a trophy stolen from Owen. They sensed that Owen's popularity was falling, and they enjoyed seeing him sitting by himself. On good days now, Ben was their playmate, their mascot. They alone—thanks to their status—could make liking Ben fashionable. Owen used his new privacy to peek into the false bottom of his lunch box and check on the well-being of his turtles. He liked finding his bottle cap empty of flies. The safety patrol, an unsmiling senior with angry acne and an attitude that went with the official white belt across his chest, had been steadily expanding his list of prohibitions from standing while the bus was in motion to eating from lunch boxes and arm wrestling. He had never bothered Owen but appeared to watch him in expectation of an infraction. Owen watched him back.

The low autumn light left barely enough time for a few innings after school. The chalk on the base paths had faded into the underlying dirt, and a ring of weeds had formed around third base. Horse chestnuts were strewn across the road between the Kershaws' house and the diamond. Somehow, partial teams were fielded, though even the meagerest grounders ended up in the outfield, to be run down by Stanley Ayotte, who was proud of his arm and managed to rifle them back. Shortstop had been eliminated for lack of candidates. The score ran up quickly.

Owen's father appeared and boomed that an umpire was

needed. He hung his suit coat on the backstop, tugged his tie to one side, stepped behind the catcher, folded his arms behind him, and bent forward for the next pitch. There was no next pitch. The players saw his condition, and the game dissolved. As Owen started to walk home with his father, Mr. Kershaw, observant, came out his front door and gave them a curt wave. Owen tried to think of hubcaps he didn't have yet while his father strode along, looking far ahead into some empty place toward home.

On the school bus the next day, Owen fielded questions about "the ump" and sat quietly, sensing the small movements of the turtles in the bottom of his lunch box, which was otherwise filled with the random sorts of things his mother put in there— Hostess Twinkies, not particularly fresh fruit, packaged peanut butter and crackers. Ben was sitting on the broad bench seat at the back, between the twins, who tied things in his hair and pretended to help him with his homework while enjoying his incomprehension. He must have begun to feel rewarded by his limitations. The twins whispered to each other and to Ben and made his face red with the things they said. Then Ben told the twins about Owen's turtles, and the twins told the safety patrol, who towered over Owen's seat and asked to see his lunch box.

"Why do you want to see it?"

"Give it to me."

"No."

The safety patrol worked his way forward to the driver and said something, then returned. "Give it to me or I'm putting you off the bus."

Owen slowly handed the lunch box to him. The safety patrol undid the catch, opened the lid, and dumped the food. Then he pried out the false bottom and looked in. "You know the rules," he said. He gingerly lifted the turtles out of the box, leaned toward an open window, and threw them out. Owen jumped up to see them burst on the pavement. He fell back into his seat and pulled his coat over his head.

"You knew the rules," the safety patrol said.

Life went on as though nothing had happened, and nothing really had happened. Ben was the twins' plaything for several months, and then something occurred that no one wanted to talk about—if one twin was asked about it, the question was referred to the other—and Ben had to transfer to a special school, one where he couldn't come and go as he pleased, or maybe it was worse than that, since he was never seen at home again or in town or on the football field with his water tray. Owen continued to attend the football games, not to watch but to wander the darkened parking lot, building his hubcap collection. As time went on, it wasn't only the games: any public event would do.

On a Dirt Road

I'd have thought we would have met the Jewells sooner, since we all had the same commute down the long dirt road to the interstate and thence to town and jobs; to say they never reached out would be an understatement. The first year they didn't so much as wave to either Ann or me, a courtesy conspicuously hard to avoid given that passing on our road is virtually a windshield-to-windshield affair, and an even slightly averted gaze is a very strong bit of semaphore. That we could see their faces in extraordinary detail, his round and pink with rimless glasses, hers an old Bohemian look with stringy hair parted in the middle, hardly seemed to matter. He looked sharply toward us while she just stared away.

"It's just fine with me," Ann said. "We don't spend nearly enough time with the friends we already have."

"Oh, baby, we need new ones."

"No, not really. We've got good friends."

"Like the vaunted Clearys?" I was egging her on.

"That wasn't great, I'll admit," she said. "Maybe they need another chance." This was a reference to a dinner celebrating the Clearys' seventeenth wedding anniversary. The big party on an odd year was their idea of a joke. They had us wearing paper hats and twirling noisemakers, all part of their bullying cheer, which made us feel they were making fun of us. I wouldn't have put it past a guy like Craig Cleary, regional super-salesman and fireworks mogul, with a Saddam Hussein mustache that somehow matched the black bangs his dour wife wore down to her eyebrows. Before we even went, I had told Ann that I'd rather go to town and watch haircuts, but she pronounced the whole thing clever. "Cleary's an oxygen thief," I pleaded. "You can hardly breathe around him."

Unneighborly though they were, the Jewells had the fascination of mystery, but that was likely due to the extent of their remodeling project. For half a year, tradesmen were parked all around their house, the familiar plumber and electrician, but also the wildly expensive Prairie Kitchens people must have been there for two months, with those long slabs of polished black granite in the front yard lying under a tarp that blew off regularly and was just as regularly replaced. "It's granite," I said. "Stop worrying about it."

Ann said, "Could they be building a restaurant?"

The Jewells would keep us wondering, and I thought we agreed about the Clearys. So after a perfectly pleasant ride home through the tunnel of cottonwood one night, I met Ann's announcement of the Clearys' invitation that we meet them at Rascal's for pizza with regrettable thoughtlessness: "No fucking way," I think is what I said. Or "Fuck no." Or, "Is this a fucking joke?" Something like that. As I say, thoughtless. Ann didn't take it well.

"If memory serves, you were the one clamoring to get out more."

"I wasn't 'clamoring.' What's more, these people aren't promising." All I wanted was my chair and the six o'clock news, not pizza peppered with Craig Cleary's rapid-fire hints as to how I might turn my career around.

"You're not even a little tempted?"

"No."

"But I accepted!" I was thunderstruck and all too mindful of how lovely she looked as she primped for this pizza outing in town, a wholly inauspicious occasion to which she seemed excitedly committed. She wore the flowered silk skirt with the delicate uneven hem that she knew to be my favorite and the linen shirt with pleats, another of my favorites, both of which had been hibernating in her closet. All these preparations for pizza with two boors? When I caught her taking a final glance in the hall mirror, I detected distinct approval. As she left, she chortled, "I hope you don't feel stuck!"

"We have two cars," I said cheerfully.

I admit that I was aware of our isolation and in a way glad to see her take the lead in freshening things up. But we'd been through at least one so-called social occasion with the Clearys, and I thought our disapproval was solid. I remember asking Ann on the way home, "How about the 'Moroccan cuisine'? We should have called them on it: 'Moroccan? Moroccan how?'"

Ann had said, "But exactly." At that time.

So finding myself at loose ends because of the Clearys of all people came as a surprise. I pulled open the door to the refrigerator hoping to ignite my appetite, but I got no farther than lifting a piece of Black Diamond cheddar to my scrutiny before returning it and closing the door. I went into the mudroom and looked at my car through the window, trying to think of something I could do with it. I really wasn't used to Ann going off like this on her own. I have a way of extolling peace and quiet in theory without enjoying it in practice and end up fending off the idea that I've been abandoned. As I've grown older, I've begun listing my more regrettable traits, and this one has always made the cut. I think the list was supposed to help me improve myself, but it's turned out to be just another list alongside yard chores, oil changes, and storm windows.

I've been out of the legislature for over a year, and it has not been the best thing in the world for our relationship, though I just hate to use that word. I served one term and made my values plain to the voters—respect for the two-parent household, predator control, and reduced death taxes for the family farm. When I ran for a second term, fringe groups twisted everything I'd said, and the net result was this Assiniboin half-breed named Michelle Red Moon Gillespie cleaned my clock, leaving her wigwam for the capitol in Helena while I, unwilling to resume my job as a travel agent, headed home to try to figure out what was next. I kept my office in town on the theory that something would come along, but nothing did. It allowed me at least to keep Ann at bay while I tried to think, and we went on referring to it as "my job." Eventually, my weakened state was something she could smell, and once or twice I caught her regarding me in a way I never saw when she was frisking around the Governor's Ball or any other time when I was a senator. We talked about the early days of our marriage, before the travel agency, before state politics, before we learned there would not be children. We were going to get the fuck out of Montana and buy a schooner. We even flew to Marina del Rey to look at it parked there among thousands of other boats that never went anywhere. I said, "You know, I just can't see it."

Ann said, "You're not serious! I've heard nothing but schooner for the last five years!"

"It was only a dream."

"I'll give you dream. Don't do this to me again."

The captain came out of the cabin in a cloud of marijuana smoke to ask if we were interested. He said he was tired of life at sea and was going to carry the anchor inland until someone asked him what it was. There he would settle down, find himself a gal of Scandinavian heritage, and raise a family. He kept looking hungrily at Ann, then back at me with an expression that said, *What's she doing with you?*

We flew home, and Ann began tap-dancing lessons. One day when I'd forgotten, she told me to flush the toilet immediately, adding, "In this matter, timeliness counts. I can't be expected to review your diet at this remove." That was one of the low points and yet another hint that my idleness was so complete that I no longer remembered to flush the toilet.

By way of placating my instantaneous loneliness in Ann's absence, I decided to visit the Jewells and find out why anyone would get so involved in remodeling such a plain house, one probably built on the cheap to judge by the rusty stovepipe sticking out the top. Their place was so close, I almost didn't need to drive, though I did so very slowly, without listening to the radio or anything else as I thought about why I was doing this at all. I figured that it was a bit like having a drink, just a matter of changing gears. I didn't know why Ann would want to join the Clearys. Was she that bored? Did I bore her? I certainly wasn't entertaining myself. So going to visit the Jewells was not just a matter of breaking the ice with inscrutable neighbors but, frankly, to get myself out of our settled cottage with its old trees and vines, even for a half-mile journey to what looked like remodeling hell a mile down the road. Would the Jewells peek at me through a crack of their front door and ask what I wanted? Would they pretend they weren't at home? Either way it would be more interesting than killing time while I waited for Ann to return. A pleasant jolt of the unfamiliar ought to have been within my capacities. I might cook it up as an enchanting tidbit for Ann.

I felt newly alive as I looked for a place to park in front of the Jewells' house amid the building supplies, camper shell, cat travel crates, cement mixer. Two things struck me: the drawn curtains and pirate flag fluttering from the pole in the front yard. Also, the manufacturer's stickers on the plate-glass windows had not been removed. As I passed the upended canoe going to the door, several cats ran out, one climbing the only tree in the yard. When I knocked, the door opened so quickly as to confirm that I'd been observed.

"How did you find a place to park in all that junk?"

Jewell's teeth were big for his face, or he was just too thin for them, but his smile was intense and welcoming all the same. We were nearly the same height, so his eager proximity was especially notable. I found myself leaning back. He was very glad to see me!

"I thought we'd never meet!" he cried. "Bruce."

"Well, here I am!" I exclaimed, sounding exceptionally stupid. "Bruce."

"You can say that again!" Was Jewell being ironic? The all-knowing look you get when you buy rimless glasses seemed at odds with his guileless enthusiasm. I was confused. "We don't allow smoking," he added. For just a moment I thought, Jewell was fucking with me, but the thought passed as I followed him into the house, his windmilling arms leading the way. That he was barefoot was not so remarkable given that he was at home, but it seemed at odds with his somewhat-spiffy attire, slacks and smoking jacket. Bruce was a little younger than me, and painted toenails might have been a generational thing I missed.

"What's with the pirate flag?"

"Oh, Nell and I have a kind of game. I pretend I'm a pirate, and she's a royal prisoner." Jewell shifted into a guttural "pirate" voice: "You look after the old lady and I shall see to the daughters."

"Is that Blind Pew?" I asked.

"Oh God, no. Anyway, at first we were going to be cowboys— here's my study—and then astronauts. At the moment, it's pirates, but who knows. Nell, thank goodness, has a private income. Being a programmer was more a matter of my personal dignity, but oh well, what's the use of that? Life is short, don't you agree, might as well enjoy it."

Opening the door to the study, Jewell called out, Ed McMahon style, "Heeeeeeere's, Nell!" And indeed there she was in a prospect of piled Lego pieces, with a large picture of the finished model thumbtacked to the wall next to her: the Leaning Tower of Pisa. "She's already done Big Ben. So, she's ready to move up the Architecture Series. This one got a great review in Eurobricks, didn't it, Nell?" Her face had no expression of any kind, and she was wearing a wash dress of the sort seen in WPA photographs. "We got sidetracked by the Royal Baby series when Kate's little Prince George of Cambridge was commemorated with a fifty-five brick pram."

"I want a baby!" boomed Nell.

Jewell seemed not to have heard and introduced us. Nell struggled to respond. There was something wrong with Nell, big-time. Retarded, I think, but healthy otherwise and rather pretty. She stood up and smiled, quite a nice smile, and said with extraordinary deliberation, "Hullo."

Jewell said, "Why don't I just leave you two for a moment and let you get acquainted."

I instinctively turned as though to follow Jewell out the door, but it was gently closed in my face. Nell said, "We don't serve drinks in here."

"Ah."

"But we do have healthful snacks."

"Thank you, but I'm okay."

"This puzzle is very time-consuming."

She had a gentle, crooning voice that, once I absorbed its strangeness, was so soothing as to be almost hypnotic. She told me the puzzle didn't really interest her and that before her accident she had seen the real Tower of Pisa and that hadn't interested her, either. I began to ask what sort of accident, to which she answered preemptively, "bicycle," before going on to tell how on Tuesday she got lost in the woods behind the house and that it didn't bother her but it bothered "Bruce" and, because it had, she was sad all day, until "Bruce" made her pancakes with blueberry syrup and after that they were fine about the woods and what she was doing there.

The door opened and Jewell, now shod—they looked like bowling shoes—entered briskly and said, "Just that little bit past name and face makes everyone more comfortable. So you're Hoyt, right? Okay, Hoyt, I was going to throw something together for Nell and me. Care to join us? Not promising a lot because the kitchen is a work in progress, to say the very least."

This is when lightning struck. I glanced at Jewell in his suspenders and bowling shoes, and at Nell in her clean Depression shift, and said, "Why don't we run down to Rascal's and split a pizza? My treat."

Before Bruce could answer, Nell clapped her hands and bayed, "I love pizza!"

"You really want to take us on, Hoyt? We've only just met, and we can be a handful. Nell is very active, aren't you, Nell?"

I had enough on my hands to understand why I had cooked up the invitation at all. My hands were already pretty full trying to figure out what I could have been thinking in the first place. I tried to sell myself the idea that this would be a rescue operation to save Ann from the wearisome Clearys, but that still left me with the original bafflement as to why she wanted to meet them at all. Nevertheless, everything would be quite clear when the Jewells sat down at the table. The introductions would be interesting, and Nell versus the pizza menu could be a real hoot, since Rascal's had about a hundred toppings.

Nell made me promise to help her with the puzzle later, and when I agreed she looked at me quite pointedly and said that she was not a vegetable. I assured Nell that indeed she was not, and Jewell smiled his assent. We stood around for a bit while he set the burglar alarms, an exercise I failed to understand. The Jewells must have come from someplace where this was necessary. Their clothing seemed rural, backwoods almost, but had something of the costume about it. "Pizza!" said Jewell. "What an idea! Nell, when was the last time we had pizza?"

"Two Thanksgivings ago," said Nell sternly.

"Did we enjoy it?" asked Jewell.

Nell said, "How should I know?"

I wanted to get in on this somehow and asserted that you could get turkey as a topping at Rascal's, but the two just gazed at me thoughtfully as though the meaning of this would come to them if they were patient.

In any case, we'd have to hurry along if we were going to catch Ann and the Clearys. Afterward, once she got her face out of the pizza, she could pitch in on the jigsaw puzzle. Ha! These were brave thoughts: I still couldn't believe she'd prefer dinner with the Clearys to codependent nattering with me in our enchanted cottage with its vine-crowded windows.

We took my car; in fact I didn't see one at the Jewells'. En route, I let them in on the setup: "My wife, Ann, is dining with the Clearys, and I thought it might be fun to join them as a kind of surprise and give you a chance to meet not only Ann but the Clearys, Craig and Bonny, because Craig runs an international fireworks company right from his house, and Bonny heads up the county commissioners, in case you need some rules bent."

Nell said, "Can I play the radio?"

"We're talking, Sweet Pea, can't you see that?"

Nell looked puzzled. "I can hear you talking . . ."

"Hush, now," Jewell said to her rather more firmly. We were at highway speed when Nell rolled down the window and stuck her head out, the wind inflating her cheeks. Our mail and several documents I'd left in the backseat were now whirling around the inside of the car. Jewell raced to batten them down, but Nell just kept hanging her head out, her hair streaming all the way past the rear window. "Guy clipped her and kept going. Forget about the helmet. Shattered like an egg. We're talking former

Miss Utah runner-up." I thought about this and then sought to change the subject.

"What's your business . . . ?"

"Bruce. I sold my original business and ten-thirty-oned it into self-storage. Now my job is limited to welcoming receipts."

"Your original business was?"

"Nutritional supplements, weight-loss products, essential oils, pet vitamins, the usual. I ran it right here in town. Now it's in a portfolio somewhere, probably Bahrain." Bruce pulled Nell back into her seat by her shirt collar and rolled up the window. She slumped and stared at the dark radio dial.

"Where is your car?"

"Do we have a car?"

Nell said, "We have a car. Ours is a sedan."

What would have unnerved me otherwise, I welcomed: Wait'll I load this duo onto Ann and the Clearys. "Why can't she listen to the radio."

"She can listen to the radio but not while we're talking. We've covered the main stuff. Now she can listen. There's a time and a place for everything." I rejoiced at this clodhopper's philosophy.

Nell turned the radio on, dialing around until she found a classical station and the mournful sound of an oboe, which seemed to settle her down. As though speaking only to herself, she said that she had never been to Bahrain, either in a sedan or any other way. "It's across the ocean," barked Jewell.

Nell said, "A truck hit me."

"Poor Nell."

"A small red Japanese truck with Idaho plates and a woman driver."

"See what bubbles up?" said Jewell.

Nell said, "Handel Oboe Concerto in G Minor," and raised the volume, cupping her hand over the knob so that no one would be able to interfere. Her brows raised, eyes bright, mouth wide open, she was in awe.

Jewell said, "As discussed."

After listening to the music intently for several minutes, Nell said, "Bruce only likes stupid hillbillies. I take him for what he is."

I was confused: Nell was mentally challenged, underappreciated, and had a killer body. A guy could get into a world of hurt with such mixed signals. I concentrated on the road and reflected that nothing would alleviate my present anxieties like a bulletproof spell of adultery. The ex-Miss-Utah-runner-up thing had an enticing ring of prestige as well, and I was up for leaning into her Tower of Pisa problem.

"What are you, anyway?" she asked her husband.

I pulled into the parking lot of Rascal's Pizzeria and found a slot between a rusted-out Pontiac GTO and a home-oxygen supply van with a kayak rack on top. A light rain had begun to fall, and when Nell got out, she danced around, head thrown back, tongue wiggling and palms up. It was crazy but kind of infectious. Jewell caught her eye, raised a warning finger, and her arms dropped to her sides. Then Bruce pivoted toward the front door. "We surf the toppings." Nell and I followed, and I was startled when she sought my hand, like a child. I thought I'd extract it, then thought I'd just let it ride and watch for Ann's reaction. Even in the shift, Nell was eye-catching and would remain so until her behavior was observed.

Looking around the half-filled room, I said, "Let me see if I can spot them." Rascal's had turned into something of a sports bar, with armatured TV screens hung all around the room, speakers blaring. Servers in the lavender Rascal's uniform hunched over beers while keeping eyes on the screens, some of which showed a demolition derby in Wyoming; one was playing an interview with A-Rod as to his health, and yet another displayed a girl weeping in some jungle setting, holding a revolver. I regarded each of these as a distraction, ground clutter keeping me from finding my wife. Jewell was right in front of me, thumbs in his suspenders. "What say we eat?"

"Sure, Bruce, grab a table. We can always move."

"Not once I tuck into a family size. I could eat a horse."

"I'm soooooo hungry!" cried Nell.

They weren't here, and I was very abruptly frantic. I kept checking my watch as though it could tell me something. I made sure the ring and vibrate features were both activated on my cell phone, probably taking too much time doing so, since before I knew it both the waitress and the Jewells were eyeing me impatiently. I ordered a small house pizza automatically, just to dispel the awkwardness.

"Not even going to check out the toppings?" asked Jewell.

"Got it," said the waitress and sped off.

Jewell said, "You all right?"

"Me? Sure. It's just that I—"

"Maybe she ran away with the circus! Ha-ha-ha!"

"Yeah, that must be it," I mumbled, instantly aware of what must have been my disquieting delivery. In any case, they saw nothing funny and gazed at me quietly, Nell with her own fervor and concern. "The circus," I added.

Why was I so preoccupied? Because I had been deceived by my wife and she had invested some serious planning in this deceit. To what end? To meet someone who was not me and as

I awaited a pizza I would have enormous trouble choking down while sitting with two idiots. These were not happy thoughts.

Then it hit me! The Clearys were too good for a pizza joint, and they had changed restaurants. No doubt, one of their children would be happy to tell me which one they had chosen. I excused myself and went outside with the smokers and called the Clearys' house. Craig Cleary answered. "Oh, Craig, hi, Hoyt here. Wasn't tonight the night Ann and I were to meet you at Rascal's?"

"I don't eat at Rascal's. Is that where you are?"

"No big deal. We'll just grab something to go."

"Rascal's! How's Ann taking this?"

"I think she's fascinated in a kind of ironic way."

"Fascinated! What's fascinating at Rascal's?"

I struggled, finally blurting, "The toppings." I disliked this treatment by Craig, and so I repeated firmly, as though training a dog, "The toppings, goddamn it!"

When I got back to the table, Jewell remarked, "Your face could turn wine into vinegar." I took it in stride. I had to. My head was spinning. There was a numb spot on my leg, and my mouth felt like it had been years since my last cleaning. There was only one thing to do: get home before Ann.

"Why is the food taking so long?"

Jewell asked, "First time ordering a pizza, pal?"

"I just found out on the phone that Ann sprained her ankle—"

"Oh, how?"

"Gopher hole."

"A gopher hole!"

"Jesus Christ, do you have to challenge everything?"

"Oh. Oh. Oh. Say, I don't like the way this is heading at all."

"People, people," Nell implored, "let's just simmer on down."

My head was full of a picture of my wife, random and danger-ous as a Scud missile. I told the waitress about my emergency, and we soon had the pizzas, packed to go. I grabbed a menu from the counter. Neither of the Jewells spoke as I drove hell-bent back up the dirt road, trees rushing through the side win-dows, nor when I shoved their pizzas across the seat at them as I parked in front of the darkened house. Jewell said, "Thanks, neighbor," as he got out. "Thanks, a bunch." Nell already in flight across the pea rock that served as a lawn. I was soon home with a drink in hand and thinking, perhaps too much, about Ann with someone else, intimate, of course, but also covered with sweat. How much did I want to know? I seemed to be doing all right with bourbon and abstraction at least not having seen her yet. Fortunately, there was a built-in time frame, since last call at Rascal's would dictate the faux chronology. In this sense, I felt I had my ducks in a row and relaxed for the time being, perusing the Rascal's menu.

As part of financing her education, Ann had served in the navy, where I have no doubt she was the darling of the fleet. When we were courting, I could hardly avoid colliding with one of her amatory enthusiasms, especially the one called Shelley, with his collar-length hair and crew-neck sweaters. Shelley was no seaman; Ann believed him to be a filmmaker. It turned out he was a drug dealer, which remained unclear to Ann until formal charges had been filed. I don't know how that would have turned out if Shelley hadn't gone to prison, where he was rehabilitated as a nurse. He's now at a regional hospital outside Omaha. I refilled my drink and started killing moths to pass the time. At the edge of my consciousness, the mystery of Ann's whereabouts reared its head as often as I could chase it away. I couldn't tell if the whiskey was helping or not; on the one hand, it seemed to numb me to the escalating misery; on the other hand, it made the drama of it more florid. I was like a dog trapped in a hot car. The temptation was to drink more and throw the matter into greater relief on the theory, masquerading as fact, that I would thereby handle the situation with more equanimity, or at least not start a fight that could only enlarge my suffering while making sure Ann shared it. In the end, I realized it wouldn't pay to be drunk, and I dumped my latest refill, taking up instead some microwave popcorn, which I ate from a bowl in the armchair I had positioned to face the front door. I pictured this as a prosecutorial touch, which it might well have been if I'd had any guts. I was still at some remove from recognizing that I was terrified of the truth, and when I thought of the way Ann used emery boards as bookmarks, I felt myself choking with emotion.

Ann came in the door with a blaze of energy and a wildly insincere "Honey, I'm home!" She was a little taken aback to find me hunkered down in the armchair, bowl of popcorn and pizza menu in my lap. And there must have been something in my tone when I asked her about the evening, since she paused with the coat halfway off her shoulders. I could have pressed my face to her crotch and busted her on the spot, but this was not my way. "It was okay," she said. "How good could it have been with the Clearys?"

"Did you stuff yourself?"

She paused before saying, "I've never been that excited about pizza."

"Mozzarella and pepperoni? The usual?"

"Yep."

I raised the menu to my eyes. "Didn't feel like trying the sundried tomatoes, anchovies, porcini mushrooms, prosciutto, eggplant—"

"Where'd you get the menu?"

"Rascal's. I thought I'd join you."

Ann finished hanging her coat and came over to where I sat with the bowl.

"Did you put butter on this?"

I felt the shift like a breath.

"No."

Ann took a single piece of popcorn and raised it to her mouth.

"So, how shall we leave it?"

A Long View to the West

The wind funneled down the river valley between the two mountain ranges, picking up speed where the interstate hit its first long straightaway in thirty miles. Clay's car lot was right on the frontage road, where land was cheap and the wind made its uninterrupted rush whatever the season of the year. Before winter had quite arrived to thicken his blood, while the cattle trucks were still throwing up whirlwinds of cottonwood leaves, the wait between customers seemed endless. He couldn't even listen to the radio anymore. In the snowy dead of winter it was easier somehow. Now, face close to the window, and one hand leaning against the recycled acoustic tile that lined the walls, he stared down at the roofs and hoods of used vehicles in search of a human form.

When, just before lunch, a rancher came in about a five-year-old three-quarter-ton Dodge that Clay had sold him, Clay was glad even to receive a complaint. Barely over five feet tall in his canvas vest and railroad cap, the rancher held a pair of fencing pliers as an invitation to mayhem. He shouted, "It's a lemon!" Clay, trying to lighten the mood, said, "The space shuttle was six billion, and it's a lemon." But he ended up getting sucked into a retroactive guarantee just to keep the guy's business. With my luck, thought Clay, I'll end up throwing a short block into it, or a rear end. Once the rancher, a friend of Clay's father, had the repair deal in hand, he asked, "How's the old man? Gonna pull through?"

"He's just about dead," said Clay emphatically, and went back into the shack with its telephone, cash drawer, and long view of the vehicle lot. At the end of the frontage road, where it met Main Street, a newspaper tumbling through plastered itself against the boarded-up frozen-yogurt stand. The metal sign on wheels in front of the tire-repair shop was flapping back and forth. The Dodge pulled back onto the road and went by the shack. The rancher, barely able to see over the wheel, gave Clay a wave, and Clay smiled broadly saying, "Eat shit!" behind his teeth.

It was really no longer a hospital, just a place providing emergency care until an ambulance or helicopter could take you to Billings. Three nurses and a doctor were on call. Clay got his father admitted there on the strength of being one of three ranchers who had founded the little hospital when it actually served the rural population then flourishing. It had the advantage of being close to home, with views that meant something to the old man, like the one of the big spring where they'd watered cattle for a century. There was not a lot to be done for him, at least not here. About all anyone could do was listen to his stories, and that seemed enough. Clay of course had heard them all, so there remained only to notice the thickening of detail with each retelling, assuming he could stand to hear his father express yet again his love for the life he'd lived while Clay pondered his own peaked existence at the lot. Should you interrupt the telling, the hard look would return, the face of a man who, throughout his life, had called all the shots that really mattered. Seeing his father in the bed, Clay could hardly help thinking about the ease that lay ahead for him and his sister, even as guilt tore at him. Times had changed all right, but that didn't excuse much.

Weekdays Clay listened for as long as he could; and on weekends his sister, Karen, came over from Powderville, sometimes with one of her kids. There were three boys, but two were too wild for that long a ride. Karen said that while she was gone they always got up to something obnoxious if their dad couldn't find time to come in off the place and kick their asses.

The hospital sat right in the middle of the old Matador pasture, where the longhorns coming up from Texas had recovered from the long trail. Clay's great-grandfather had been one of the cowboys, and the story was that when they first arrived the Indian burials were still in the trees, and the ground was covered with stone tepee rings. A picture of that first roundup crew, with the reps from five outfits lined up in front on their horses, was Bill's most cherished possession, and he fretted constantly about its safekeeping when he was gone. He seemed to feel that no one in his family cared anything about it. That was probably true. Either that or they were sick of hearing about it.

It had begun to rain, and with the rain came the smell of open country. Karen was supposed to have been there already, and Clay really wanted to get back to the lot. No matter how often intuition betrayed him, he could still convince himself that someone was going to come along and buy a car today. Apart from that he felt a little angry, but at what he wasn't so sure, maybe everything.

"I don't know what's keeping her," he said to his father.

"Probably had to wait for Lewis to get out of school or find someplace to stash them two other little shits."

His father couldn't see as far as the door. So when Karen appeared there, she was able to summon Clay discreetly. For a small brunette, in her jeans and boots and hoodie she could be as emphatic as a trooper telling you to pull over. She was proud to be married to a cowboy.

"I've got to take Lewis in for a shot. He got bit by a skunk and, now, the poor little guy is going to have to have that series. So you need to hold the fort."

"My God, Karen, I can't stay anymore. I've been here all morning." He couldn't say he'd been fucked over by that sawed-off rancher just half an hour past breakfast, because Karen had zero sympathy so far as his job was concerned.

Karen said, "You're going to have to," and just walked on out. By the time it had occurred to him to offer to take Lewis for the shot, his sister was gone and his father was awake. What good had it been, the old man herding thousands of cattle over all those years only to wind up with his arms like Popsicle sticks and pissing through a tube. Nothing to show for his trouble but stories his son would have to hear all over again, with no relief but the chance of picking up something new about Leo the Illegal or O.C. or Robert Wood or some horse plowed under way back when. Sometimes during these tales, Clay would think about pole dancers or money pouring out of a slot machine or some decent soul appreciating something he'd done, such as that time he acquired the nearly new fire engine the government had bought because the Indians on the Rez didn't want it, since they already had a bunch just like it they hadn't gotten around to wrecking. The town enjoyed a lot of use out of that engine, even though no one seemed to remember who found it for them, or even that day the big red beauty first rolled down the street, sirens blazing and blinding chrome all over it. So much for quiet acts of heroism. Maybe it was time to start drawing attention to himself. A Ford dealership in Great Falls was having a Christian fund-raiser with TV stars on Saturday, and something like that might well be in his future. Or just toot his own horn down at the chamber of commerce.

It was the last Mother's Day before World War II. You and Karen was just little bitty. Your ma and me drove into the ranch yard, and Leo, the illegal who worked for me then (*Here we go,* thinks Clay), said some old fellow had arrived about sundown on a wild horse and rolled out his bedroll under the loading chute, put his head on his saddle, and gone to sleep. I had this feeling that it was old Robert Wood, and sure enough it was. *(Yep!)* Of course I caught him before he fell asleep, just caught his eye to tell him I would see him in the a.m. I pretty much knew what he was after. *(So do I.)* He had a band of mares up on the mesa behind our mares, and they were running out with wild horses there. Folks from town had come out from time to time to chase them around, and they was absolutely wild. I had been hoping for the chance to gather them for Robert when we had enough hands, because it wasn't going to be easy at all. *(And what a bitch it would turn out to be.)*

Clay's only defense against these onslaughts was the things he couldn't say aloud.

Several months before this, Robert went out into the sagebrush to catch his red roan stud, which was running with some draft horses by the springs. He came with nothing but a little pan of oats and a lariat. *(Wait'll you see how good this trick works.)* Just as he got his stud caught, one of the draft horses bites the stud, and Robert gets hung up in the rope and dragged. Your uncle O. C. Drury was plowing up wheat stubble about two miles away and saw the dust cloud from where Robert was being hauled. At his age, Robert really never should have lived, but he did. He was in the hospital all winter.

I ran into him after he'd healed some, and he said to me in his kind of whiny voice, "Bill, I been laid up. Can you carry me to the place?" I went with him into his little shack of a cabin, and he stripped down to his long underwear. He pulled back the covers of his bed, and there was a great big nest of mice, just full of little pink babies. He carefully moved them to one side and got in next to them, pulled up the covers, and nodded thanks for the lift. *(Set your watches for hantavirus.)*

Gradually, I heard rumors that he was back at work pulling up his poor fence and halfway cowproofing it. He brought back his black baldies and his bulls. He was even seen crawling around the cockleburs packing a sprayer with a full tank and a rag tied across his face. He had always lived and worked alone and was still on the place where he was born. *(Same dog bit me.)*

Robert was an old-time spade-bit horseman. His horses were quick and bronc-y, and the only safe place around them was on their backs. But they were quiet in a herd of cattle and had the lightest noses in Montana. O. C. Drury hauled cattle as a sideline, and he hated to haul Robert's calves. Invariably, he'd arrive in the ranch yard mid-October, and Robert would complain, "O.C., I'm so shorthanded just now. Would you catch up that bay and help me bring these cattle in?" O.C. would feel obliged, and he'd crawl on the old bay or the old sorrel, both of which would know right away it wasn't Robert Wood. So one false move, and the bronc ride was on. *(Nice way to treat someone helping you out.)*

So I let Robert sleep through the night, and by the time I woke, just before sunup, I could smell his fire and coffee. Then in a bit I could hear Leo's voice, and I knew the two of them were working on a plan. I threw on the lights and got dressed, went into the kitchen, and started cooking. I knew I didn't want to put on a breakfast for everyone. I was buying time, and I was still hoping I could talk Robert out of his dangerous plan to bring these horses off the mesa with such a small crew. Leo came in with Robert, who had to be helped up the steps, and we shared a big breakfast, and then we smoked and shot the shit. Leo was a little Indian-looking feller from Sonora, with black bangs over his face. You couldn't joke with him, because he was always serious, but he could work like nobody's business and make any kind of a horse do like he said, even the ones you'd rather not get on. *(Of course he didn't have a sense of humor. Wasn't nothing around there that was funny.)*

Robert had an old-fashioned, long-nosed face, and you could see a little blue vein in the thin skin of his forehead. He was a puncher who had outlived his time. *(Sound familiar?)* He hated farming and especially alfalfa, which he thought was the enemy of the Old West. I suppose he was seventy-five. The hat he wore was just the way it came out of the box—no crease, no nothing. He wore it year-round. He said a straw hat was a farmer's hat. He said that was what you wore when you went out to view the alfalfa.

We always laid our plans at breakfast, except if I was sitting on the john writing out the day's work on a matchbook cover. Robert wanted us all to go up the switchback together all the way to the mesa. "When we get there," he said, "I'll ride around to the crack." The crack was a deep washout, and Robert didn't want the horses to get past it and escape. Instead, he'd hide in the brush and keep them from getting there. Once they were out on the flat, we'd just ride on past them and turn them down toward my corrals.

That crack was deep and steep, and personally I didn't think Robert was going to be able to turn them there. I felt sure this herd of canners would jump the crack even if it meant breaking their necks and no horse or rider would consider following them. If it had been me, I'd just fog them off toward the neighbors' and gather them up when we had us a big-enough crew. *(Why take a knife to a gunfight?)* But Robert didn't think a lot of our horsemanship after all his years on the N Bar and Niobrara. So I thought better of voicing my doubts.

He looked pretty stove up leading his sorrel mare out of the pen behind the scales and tied her to a plank of the chute, just his kind of horse, sickle hocked, good withers, short pasterns, low crouped, and coon footed, a real mutt of a cow horse you wouldn't take to a halter class. *(In short, the whole reason God invented cars.)* Robert looked barely strong enough to throw his old Miles City saddle up on her or reach over to pull the Kelly Brothers grazer into her mouth. He led her around to the front of the chute, threw one rein up around the horn, and looped the other around the corner post. She had her nostrils blowed out and white all around her eyes, but then all his horses looked half loco.

Robert limped around to the holding pen, squeaked open

that old gate, went inside, crawled up the chute, out the end, and sorta fell onto his horse. She snorted, backed away stretching out that one rein until he could reach down and retrieve it, plait them both through the fingers of his left hand, which he lifted a tiny bit, and the mare sat down on her hocks and backed across the ranch yard. Robert lifted his hand, and she stopped, straightened up, and looked around for some work to do.

Karen came in with Lewis, who wanted to talk about his rabies shot, but Karen raised a finger to her lips, and now all three of us had to hear this damn thing all over again. Lewis at least had a coloring book, and Karen could tap around on her smartphone. I was dying for a cigarette.

Ramrod straight as we go single file up the trail, Robert had his boots plumb home in iron oxbows; he turned to look us over. It wasn't long before we were on top. Leo loped out to the west and made a little dust. His small form sank and then nearly disappeared as he made a big ride around the horses. They had wheeled up to watch him and only began to disperse and feed as the circle he made came to seem too grand to concern them. I was able to ride straight back to the far side of the mesa, and by the time I got there, Leo was closing in my direction and those horses, two miles off, had already begun to drift away.

We rode straight at them, and in two jumps they were smoking. Our horses caught their wildness and for a minute or two were pretty hard to handle, kicking out behind and trying to run slap through their bridles until we got the best of them. *(I admit this is actually scary.)* The mares had such a cloud of dust behind them it just seemed to drift off into that day's weather, like from a grass fire. We'd seen Robert just float out of there to remind us how coarse broke we had our ponies.

Robert was nowhere in sight, and there was no possible way to turn them down the road the way we had planned. We knew the mares had winded him somewhere because they suddenly slowed down and blew out their nostrils. The crack, which was big enough to be an earthquake fault, was the place to turn them, so long as they didn't try to jump it. All we could do then would be to throw them down the slope and let them play hell with the farming on all those little ranches along the river. What a mess. *(Here comes the part I still like hearing even if I sometimes wish I could have been there.)*

Then, everything changed. Way past the crack, Robert broke out of the brush on his horse. Hell, we didn't even know he was in there, and Leo on the back of his sweaty gelding just looked at me. The mare came out in a flurry, greasewood stobs racking off in the air around her. Those wild horses froze. Either they would leap that crack and fly past him, or Robert could jump it himself and turn them down toward the house. I couldn't see doing much of anything to save this wad of cayuses, Roman noses, and big feet. Back at the time of the Boer War, some remount outfit had turned draft studs to put some size on them, but it turned up in all the wrong places. Leo looked like they hurt his eyes.

They boiled back toward us, and we whooped and hollered at them. Leo took down his slicker and got them bunched up once more toward the trail, where they didn't want to go, but Robert kept yelling for us to drive them. They advanced his way like a bright cyclone; and just before they broke around him, Robert spurred his horse straight at the huge crack like he was riding into hell, but the mare just burned a hole in the wind, and when she reached that yawning gap, she just curved up, into the air, Robert easing back into the saddle with his stirrups pushed out in front, the mare's legs reaching toward the far shore. I saw them land, but Leo had his eyes covered.

I guess when the wild horses challenged Robert to raise them, he just raised them out of their chairs, because as he leaned up in his saddle, deep slack of reins hanging under the sorrel's neck, taking time to count them, they were just the quietest most well-behaved herd of critters, ready to jog on home to my corrals. When we had them locked in, Robert said, "There, got that out of the way. I was afraid we might have trouble with them." He rode over to where he left his bedroll and said to me, "Mind if I ask your Mexican to cheek this mare while I slide off? She's bad to paw at you when you get down. Man'd rather piss down her shoulder than go through that."

In the hall, Clay admired some of Lewis's coloring before following Karen to the cemetery to pick out a plot, leaving Lewis in the car with an electronic game he played with his thumbs. They strolled through the old part with a kind of Boot Hill of wild old-timers, before they hit some of the kids they'd gone to school with, Charlie Derby (gored by a rodeo bull), Milly Makkinen, homecoming queen (overdose), and so on.

They selected a plot near two trees and a long view to the west. "Well," said Karen, "at least we got that out of the way." Efficiency was always her tonic; Clay felt rotten. He stopped to see his father before he locked up at the car shack. He was surprised to find him back so soon. Clay tried to make light of it. He said, "So, I interrupted something? What're you doing?" He wished he hadn't asked.

"Dying. What's it look like?"

Clay didn't know what to say, so he said, "And you're okay with that?"

"How should I know? I've never done it before."

Clay was surprised to feel so shaken. He'd known when he'd brought his father here that it was the end of the trail, but hearing him admit it reminded Clay that he was more frightened than his father was. Soon he would be gone and the stories with him. Maybe he'd be able to remember them during hard times or, really, whenever he needed them. Maybe he needed them now.

The Casserole

We waited under the cottonwoods for the ferry to come back across the Missouri River. But the heat still throbbed from the metal of our car, and it turned out to be better to stand close to the water. The river seemed so big, its incongruous whisper belying its steady speed. Clouds of swallows chased insects over the water, and doves rested in the shadows. My wife kept touching her forehead with a Kleenex and staring across at the ferry, as if to hurry its return. We could see the ferryman chatting with his passengers, which only increased her agitation. We were heading from our home in Livingston to Ellie's family ranch to celebrate our twenty-fifth wedding anniversary. Twenty-five years and no children: her parents had stopped interrogating us about that. They assumed that it was a physical problem that some clinic could solve, but we didn't want children. We lacked the courage to tell them that. We both liked children; we just didn't want any ourselves. There were children everywhere, and we saw no reason to start our own brand. Young couples plunge into parenthood, and about half the time they end up with some ghastly problem on their hands. We thought we'd leave that to others. But my in-laws were elderly, and they had the usual views of hereditary landowners: they longed for an heir. They had acquired their land from my wife's grandfather and, with it, a belief in family values that did not stand up to scrutiny, since most ranches these days were the scene of bitter inheritance battles. But even if my wife had had siblings, she would not have been part of this sort of trouble, as she had never—at least, not since adolescence—wanted to pursue ranch life, rural life, agricultural life. She would have said to a sibling, *Take it! It's all yours. I'm out of here.* There would have been an element of posturing in this, because she was very attached to the land; she just didn't want to own it or do anything with it. Neither did I.

The thing was that we were quite poor. We were both grade-school teachers, and owning a house had been the extent of our indulgences. We loved our house and our work and were suitably grateful for both, though Ellie felt that if I hadn't been so hell-bent on retiring the mortgage we might have done a few more things for fun. My in-laws couldn't believe that we had no interest in owning a ranch that was worth millions. But they wouldn't have allowed us to sell it. We'd be stuck with it if we went along with them, which we weren't about to do, and so now they were stuck with it: cows, farming equipment, fences—the whole enchilada. And they were getting old.

The ranch was going to eat them alive, and they knew it. The fences would fall down; the cows would get out; the neighbors, old friends, would start to think of them as a problem. Once across this river, we'd be heading for a very sad story.

Well, not that sad. They'd had their day, and it was almost over. That's how it is for everybody. They liked to be seen as heroic strivers, alone on the unforgiving prairie, but they could have handed the ranch over, no strings attached, and headed for Arizona; after the sale, there would have been plenty for everybody. I had an extensive collection of West Coast jazz records, including the usual suspects, Gerry Mulligan, Chet Baker, Stan Getz, and so on—not everybody has Wardell Gray and Buddy Collette, but I did—and if I'd had a bit more dough I could have added a room on to our house specifically to house this collection, with an appropriate sound system. But when I complained about things like this to Ellie, she just said, "Cue the violins."

It looked as though our appallingly high-mileage compact car was going to be the only one going on the ferry. My wife and I sat in the front, while the backseat was filled with her belongings, as was the trunk. I had no idea why she'd felt called upon to bring this exalted volume of luggage, unless it was to store things on the ranch that were cluttering up our little house. I could have asked, but I just didn't feel like it.

"I think he's turning around," Ellie said, and I came out of my trance. The cable groaned next to us, and, across the river, I could see the ferry finally moving our way. Ellie was looking forward to this visit. I certainly was not. The ranch was where she had grown up, a nature lover. Despite all its deficiencies, it was her place on earth.

We watched the ferry tack across the Missouri, tugging at an angle to the cable, then landing with a broad thump on the ramp. The ferryman, who was far too young for the wide red suspenders he affected, motioned us forward, and I drove our piece-of-shit car onto the dock.

While we crossed, my wife stood on the ferry deck, looking out at the river, smiling and sighing at the swallows circling the current. I told her that they were just after the bugs. She said she understood that, but they looked beautiful whatever they were doing, all right? I've long had trouble with people picking out some detail of the landscape and pretending it's the whole story, as though, in this case, the blue light around those speeding birds could do anything to mask the desolation of the country north of the river, a land I traverse holding my nose.

"Aren't you going to get out of the car?" she asked.

"Who's supposed to drive it off the ferry?"

I looked away from my wife and turned on the radio: no signal. I thought about her peculiar cheer today. I supposed it was the prospect of seeing her mother and father, of revisiting the scenes of her childhood, which she had done often enough to prove the utter heroism of my patience. Though, in recent times, we had talked less and less, which begged the question: What was there to talk about? We worked and we saved. We saved quite a bit more than Ellie would have, had she been in charge of things. What was becoming a comfortable nest egg would have disappeared in jaunts to Belize or some other place, where Ellie could show more of the body she was so proud of to anyone and everyone. She once had the nerve to point out that all this saving up for old age was remarkable for someone who had so much contempt for the elderly. I said, "Ha-ha-ha." She was going to have to settle for wiggling her butt in the school corridors until the inevitable day when the damn thing sagged.

At last we landed, and I drove off. Ellie was having a lively chat with the ferryman, and she took her time getting back in the car. I stared straight through the windshield until she got around to it. When she climbed in, with a sort of bounce, she exclaimed, "He grew up on the neighbor's place, the Showalters'. He's a Showalter. Graduated from Winnett, where I went."

"Ah, so."

The ranch was no more than half an hour from the ferry.

Ellie's excitement grew along the route. Here is a sampler of her exclamations:

- · "Look at all the antelope! There must be a hundred of them!"
- · "Oh, I can smell the sage now!"
- · "This road looks like a silver ribbon!"
- · "Those are all red-tailed hawks, just riding that thermal!"
- · "Larkspur!"
- · "What a grass year! Can you imagine what Dad's calves will look like?"

To this last, I said, "No." I honestly thought she was getting manic as we approached the ranch. Ellie is an enthusiast, but this went well beyond her usual behavior. I don't know if she detected my concern, but she seemed to catch herself and clam up; she was talking less, but I could still feel her glee from my position at the wheel. I wondered if the situation called for a pill.

I drove under the ranch gate, with its iron brand hanging overhead—two inverted Vs, known in the graceful local vernacular as the squaw tits. Dad, as I had long felt obliged to call him, and his wife, Mom, stood at the edge of the yard, framed from behind by their bitter little clapboard house. Dad was in full regalia: Stetson hat, leather vest, cowboy boots, and—this was new—a six-gun. Mom was dressed more conventionally, except for the lace-up boots with her wash dress and the lunch pail she was holding. Believe me, it was Methuselah and his bride at the Grand Ole Opry.

There was something about their expressions that I didn't like. It was my turn to keep busy as I tried to elicit signs of life from this tableau, which now included my somber wife. Dad helped me unload Ellie's considerable luggage, and, once it was all out on the ground, Mom handed me the lunch pail. "What's this?" I asked.

"Something to eat on the way home. A casserole."

I turned to Ellie. Tears filled her eyes. I felt that this could have been handled in another way—without Dad's hand on the gun and so forth. I think, at times like this, your first concern is to hang on to a shred of dignity. If I had a leg to stand on, it was that Ellie was upset and I was not. What kind of idiot puts a casserole in a lunch pail?

After I got back on the ferry, the thought that I was headed . . . home—well, I was not entirely comfortable with this thought, and I didn't enjoy the ferryman staring at me, either, or asking if someone had shot my dog. I just stared out at the river, hardly a ripple in it, and miles to go before the next bend.

Motherlode

In the hotel mirror, Dave adjusted the Stetson he so disliked before pulling on the windbreaker with the cattle-vaccine logo. He was a moderately successful young man, one of many working for a syndicate of cattle geneticists in Oklahoma, employers he had never met. He had earned his credentials from an online agricultural portal, the way other people became ministers, and was astonishingly uneducated in every respect, though clever in keeping an eye out for opportunity. He had spent the night in Jordan at the Garfield, ideal for meeting his local ranch clients, and awoke early enough to be the first customer in the café, where, on the front step, an old dog slept with a canceled postage stamp stuck to his butt. By the time Dave had ordered breakfast, several ranchers had taken tables and were greeting him with a familiar wave. Then the man from Utah, whom he'd met at the hotel, the one who said he'd come to Jordan to see the comets, appeared in the doorway, looking around the room. He was small and intense, middle-aged in elastic-top pants and flashy sneakers. He caught the notice of several of the ranchers. Dave had asked the elderly desk clerk about the comets. The clerk said, "I don't know what he's talking about and I've lived here all my life. He doesn't even have a car." Though he'd already ordered,

Dave pretended to study the menu to keep from being noticed, but it was too late: the man was looming over him, laughing so hard his eyes shrunk to points and his gums showing. "Don't worry. I'll get my own table," he said, his fingers drumming the back of Dave's chair. It gave Dave an odd sense of being assessed.

The door to the café kept clattering open and shut with annoying bells on a string. Dave enjoyed all the comradely greetings and gentle needling, and even felt connected to the scene, if loosely. Only this fellow, sitting alone, seemed entirely set apart. But he kept attracting glances from the other diners. The cook pushed plate after plate across his high counter as the waitress struggled to keep up. It was a lot to do, but it lent her star quality among the diners, who teased her with personal questions or air-pinched her bottom as she went past.

Dave kept on studying the menu to avoid the stranger's gaze and then resorted to making notes about this and that on the pad from his shirt pocket.

The waitress, a yellow pencil stuck in her chignon, arrived with his bacon and eggs. Dave gave her a welcoming smile in the hope that when he looked that way again, the man would be gone. But there he was still, now giving Dave a facetious military salute, then holding his nose against some imaginary stink. The meaning of these gestures eluded Dave, who was disquieted by the suggestion that he and this stranger knew each other. He ate and went to the counter to pay, so quickly the waitress came out from the kitchen still wiping her hands on a dishcloth and said, "Everything okay, Dave?"

"Yes, very good, thanks."

"Put it away in an awful hurry. Out to Larsen's?"

"No, I was there yesterday. Bred heifers. They held everything back."

"They're big on next year. I wonder if it does them any good."

"Well, they're still in business, ain't they? No, I'm headed for Jorgensen's. Big day."

Two of the ranchers, done eating, leaned in their chairs, their Stetsons back on their heads while they picked their teeth with the corners of the menus. As Dave pushed his wallet into his back pocket he realized he was being followed to the door. He didn't turn until halfway across the parking lot. When he did, the gun was in his belly, and his new friend was in his face. "Ray. Where's your ride?"

"You robbing me?"

"I just need a lift, amigo."

Ray got in the front seat of Dave's car, tucked the gun into his pants, and pulled his shirt over it, a blue terry-cloth shirt with a large breast pocket full of ballpoint pens. The top flap of the pocket liner was courtesy of "Powell Savings, Modesto, CA."

"Nice car. What're all the files in back?"

"Breeding records, cattle-breeding records."

"Mind?" Without awaiting an answer, he picked up Dave's cell phone and began tapping in a number. In a moment, his voice changed to an intimate murmur. "I'm here, or almost here," he said, covering the mouthpiece as he pointed to the intersection: "Take that one right there." Dave turned east at the intersection. "I got it wrote down someplace, east two hundred, north thirteen, but give it to me again, my angel. Or I can call you as we get closer . . . No cell service! Starting where? Never mind, a friend's giving me a lift"—again he covered the mouthpiece— "your name?"

"David."

"From?"

"Reed Point."

"Yeah, great guy, Dave, I knew back in Reed Place."

"Reed Point."

"I mean, Reed Point. Left the Quattro for an oil change, and Dave said he was headed this way. Wouldn't even let me split the gas . . . So, okay, just leaving Jordan now. How much longer is that gonna be, Morsel? . . . Two hours! Are you kidding? . . . Yeah, right, okay, got it, I'm just anxious to see you, baby, not being short with you at all."

Ray turned away and murmured softly, lovingly, and then lifting his eyes to the empty miles of sagebrush, snapped shut the phone and sighed. "Two fucking hours." Except for the gun in his pants, Ray could have been any other impatient lovebird. He turned the radio on: *Swap Shop* was playing: "Broken refrigerator suitable for a smoker." Babies bawling in the background. He turned it off. Dave was trying to guess if he was a fugitive, someone Dave could bring to justice for a reward or just the fame, which might be good for business. He had tried every other promotional gambit, including refrigerator magnets with his face beside the slogan DON'T GO BUST SHIPPING DRIES.

"Wanna pick up the tempo here? You're driving like my grandma."

"This is not a great road. Deer jump out all the time. My cousin had one come through the windshield on him."

"Fuckin' pin it or I'll take the wheel and drive it like I stole it."

David sped up slightly. This seemed to placate Ray, who slumped against the side window and stared at the passing landscape. An old pickup went by the other way with a dead animal in back, one upright leg trailing an American flag.

"Ray, do you feel like telling me what this is all about?"

"Sure, Dave, it's all about you doing exactly as you're told."

"I see. And I'm taking you somewhere, am I?"

"Uh-huh, and waiting around as needed. Jesus Christ, if this isn't the ugliest country I ever seen."

"How did you pick me?"

"I didn't pick you, I picked your car. You were a throw-in. If I hadn't a took you along you'd of had to report it stolen. This way you still got it. It's a win-win. The other lucky thing for you is you're now my partner."

The road followed Big Dry Creek, open range with occasional buttes, mostly to the north. "I guess this is the prairie out here, huh, Dave? It's got a few things going for it: no blood on the ground, no chalk outlines, no police tape. Let's hear it for the prairie!" Ray gaped around in dismay, then with rising irritation sought something that pleased him on the radio. After nearly two hours, passed mostly in silence, a light tail-dragger aircraft with red-and-white-banded wings overtook them and landed about a quarter of a mile down the road. The pilot climbed out and shuffled their way. Dave rolled down the window to reveal a weathered angular face in a cowboy hat, sweat stained above the brim. "You missed your turn. Mile back turn north on the two-track." Ray seemed to be trying to convey a greeting that showed all his teeth but was ignored by the pilot. "Nice little Piper J-3 Cub," Ray said, again ignored.

The pilot strode back to the plane and taxied straight down the road. Once airborne again, he banked sharply over a five-strand barbed-wire fence, startling seven cows and their calves, which ran into the sage scattering clouds of pollen and meadowlarks.

Ray said, "Old fellow back at the hotel said there's supposed to be a lot of dinosaurs around here." He gazed at the pale light of a gas well on a far ridge.

"That's what they say."

"What d'you suppose one of them is worth, like a whole *Tyrannosaurus rex*?"

Dave just looked at Ray. They were coming on the two-track. It was barely manageable in an ordinary sedan. Dave couldn't imagine how it was negotiated in winter or spring, when the way was full of the notorious local gumbo. He'd delivered a Charolais bull somewhere nearby one fall, and it was bad enough then. Plus, the bull tore up his trailer, and he'd lost money on the deal.

"So, Dave, now we're about to arrive I should tell you what the gun is for. I'm here to meet a girl, but I don't know how it's gonna turn out. I may need to bail, and you're my getaway. The story is, my car is in for maintenance. But you're staying until we see how this is going, so you can carry me out of here if necessary."

"Let's say I understand, but what does this all depend on?"

"It depends on whether I like the girl or not, whether we're compatible and want to start a family business. I have a lot I'd like to pass on to the next generation. Plus, I got a deal for her that's even more important than the ro-mance."

The next bend revealed the house, a two-story ranch building barely hanging on to its last few chips of paint. "He must have landed in that field!" said Dave while Ray gazed at the Montana state flag popping on an iron flagpole.

"Oro y plata." He chuckled. "Perfect. Now, Davey, I need you

to bone up on the situation here. This is Weldon Case's cattle ranch, and it runs from here for the next forty miles or so of bad road that leads right into the Bakken oil field, which is where all the *oro y plata* is at the moment. I'm guessing that was Weldon in the airplane. I met his daughter Morsel through a dating service. Well, we haven't actually met in person, but we're about to. Morsel thinks she loves me, so we're just gonna have to see about that. If she decides otherwise, she still may want to do the business deal. All you need to know is that Morsel thinks I'm an Audi dealer from Simi Valley, California. She's going on one photograph of me standing in front of a flagship Audi. You decide you want to help, you may see more walkin'-around money than you're used to. If you don't, well, you've already seen how I make my wishes come true." He patted the bulge of blue terry cloth.

Dave pulled up under the gaze of Weldon Case. Before turning off the engine, he saw Weldon call out over his shoulder to the house. Dave rolled down the windows, and the prairie wind rushed in. Weldon stared at the two visitors, returning their nearly simultaneous greetings with a mere nod. "It's the cowboy way," muttered Ray through a forced smile. "Or either he's retarded. Dave, ask him if he remembers falling from his high chair."

As they got out of the car, Morsel appeared on the front step and called out in a penetrating contralto, "Which one is he?" Dave emerged from the driver's side affecting a formality he associated with chauffeurs. A small trash pile next to the porch featured a couple of spent Odor-Eaters. Ray climbed out gingerly, hiding himself with the door as long as he could, before raising his hand and tilting his head coyly and finally calling to Morsel, "You're looking at him." Noting that the gun was now barely concealed, Dave quickly diverted attention by shaking Weldon's hand. It was like seizing a plank. He told Weldon he was pleased to meet him, and Weldon said, "Likewise." Dave lied about his own name, "Dave" all right, but the last name belonged to a rodeo clown two doors down from his mother's house. He had never done such a thing in his life.

"Oh, Christ," she yelled. "Is this what I get?" It was hard to say whether this was positive or not. Morsel was a scale model of her father, lean, wind weathered, and, if anything, less feminine. She raced forward to embrace Ray, whose chronic look of suave detachment was briefly interrupted by fear. A tooth was not there, as well as a small piece of her ear. "Oh, Ray!"

Weldon looked at Dave with a sour expression, and Dave, still in his chauffeur mind-set, acknowledged him formally as he fell into reverie about the money Ray had alluded to. But then Dave could see Weldon was about to speak. "Morsel has made some peach cobbler," he said in a lusterless tone. "It was her ma's recipe. Her ma is dead." Ray put on a ghastly look of sympathy that persuaded Morsel, who squeezed his arm. "Started in her liver and just took off," she explained. Dave, by now comfortable with his new alias, thought, I never knew "Ma" but good riddance. Going into the house, Weldon asked him if he enjoyed shooting coyotes.

"I just drive Ray around." And observing Ray tuning in, he continued obligingly, "And whatever Ray wants I guess is what we do . . . whatever he's into." But to himself he said, *Good luck hitting anything with that shit pistol.*

He didn't volunteer that he enjoyed popping the bastards out his car window, his favorite gun the .25-06 with the Swarovski rangefinder scope and tripod he bought at Hill Country Customs. Dave lived with his mother and had always liked telling her of the great shots he'd made, like the five hundred yarder on Tin Can Hill with only the car hood for a rest, no sandbags or tripod. So much for his uncle Maury's opinion: "It don't shoot flat, throw the fuckin' thing away."

Dave, who also liked brutally fattening food, thought Morsel quite the cook. Ray, however, was a surprisingly picky eater, sticking with the salad, discreetly lifting each leaf until the dressing ran off. Weldon watched him with hardly a word, but Morsel grew ever more manic, jiggling with laughter and enthusiasm at each lighthearted remark. In fact, it was necessary to dial down the subjects—to heart attacks, highway wrecks, cancer, and the like—just to keep her from guffawing at everything. Weldon planted his hands flat on the table, rose partway, and announced he was going to use the tractor to tow the plane around back. Dave, preoccupied with the mountain of tuna casserole between him and the cobbler, hardly heard him. Ray, small and disoriented beside Morsel, shot a glance around the table looking for something else he could eat.

"Daddy don't say much," said Morsel.

"I can't say much," said Ray, "not with him here. Dave, you cut us a little slack?"

Dave, using his napkin to conceal a mouthful of food, managed to say, "Sure, Ray, of course." Once on his feet, he made a lunge for the cobbler, but dropping the napkin he decided just to finish chewing what he already had.

"See you in the room," Ray said sharply, twisting his chin toward the door.

Weldon had shown them where they'd sleep by flicking the door open without ceremony when they'd first walked past it. There were two iron bedsteads and a dresser atop which sat Dave's and Ray's belongings, the latter consisting of a JanSport backpack with the straps cut off. Dave was much the better equipped, with an actual overnight bag and Dopp kit. He had left the cattle receipts and breeding documents in the car. He flopped immediately onto the bed, hands behind his head, then got up abruptly and went to the door. He looked out and listened for a long moment and, easing it shut, darted for the dresser to root through Ray's things. Among them he found several rolls of cash in rubber bands; generic Viagra from India; California lottery tickets; a passport in the name of Raymond Coelho; a lady's wallet, aqua in color and containing one Louise Coelho's driver's license, as well as her debit card issued by the Food Processors Credit Union of Modesto; a few Turlock grocery receipts; a bag of trail mix; and of course the gun. Dave lifted it carefully with the tips of his fingers. He was startled by its lightness. Turning it over in his hand he saw that it was a fake. At first he couldn't believe his eyes, but he was compelled to acknowledge that there was no hole in the barrel. A toy. Carefully returning it to where it was, he fluffed the sides of the backpack and leaped to his bunk to begin feigning sleep. He was supposed to be at Jorgensen's by now, with his arm up some cow's ass. But opportunity was in the air. He'd need to get rid of the smile if he wanted to look like he was asleep.

It wasn't long before Ray came in, making no attempt to be quiet, singing "Now Is the Hour" in a flat and aggressive tone that hardly suited the lyrics, "'Sunset glow fades in the west, /

Night o'er the valley is creeping! / Birds cuddle down in their nest, / Soon all the world will be sleeping.' But not you, huh, Dave? Yeah, you're awake, I can tell. We hope you enjoyed Morsel's rendition of the song, lyrics by Hugo Winterhalter."

At length, Dave gave up his pretense and said, "Sounds like you got the job."

"Maybe so. But here's what I know for sure: I'm starving."

"Must be, Ray. You ate like a bird."

"Couldn't be helped. That kind of food just grips the chambers of my heart like an octopus. But right behind the house they got a vegetable garden. How about you slip out and pick me some. I've already been told to stay out of the garden. But don't touch the tomatoes; they're not ripe."

"What else is there?"

"Greens and root vegetables."

"I'm not going out there."

"Oh, yes you are."

Ray wasted no time reaching for his JanSport to draw the gun.

"Here's a meal that'll really stick to your ribs," he said.

"I'm not picking vegetables for you or, technically speaking, stealing them for you. Forget it."

"Wow. Is this a mood swing?"

"Call it what you want. Otherwise, it's shoot or shut up."

"As you might guess, I prefer not to wake up the whole house."

"And the body'd be a problem for you."

"Very well, very well." Ray went to his pack and put the gun away. "But you may not be so lucky next time."

"What-ever."

Dave rolled over to sleep, but his greedy thoughts went on

unwillingly. He had planned to head out in the morning. He was expected at ranches all around Jordan. As it was, he'd have to explain himself at Jorgensen's. He had a living to make, and were it not for his morbid curiosity about Ray and Morsel, to say nothing of the possible business deal, he might have snuck out in time to grab a room in Jordan for the night. But the rolls of money in Ray's pack were definitely real, and his hints of more to come made him wonder how anxious he was to go back to work.

"Ray, you awake?"

"I might be. What d'you want, asshole?"

"I just have something I want to get off my chest."

"Make it quick, I need my z's."

"Sure, Ray, try this one on for size: the gun's a toy."

"The gun's a what?"

"A fake. And, Ray, looks to me like you might be one, too."

"Where's the fuckin' light switch? I'm not taking this shit."

"Careful you don't stub your toe jumping off the bed like that."

"Might be time to clip your wings, sonny."

"Ray, I'm here for you. But I'm not an idiot. Just take a moment so we can agree about your so-called gun, and then we can have some straight talk."

Ray found the lamp and paced the squeaking floorboards. "I gotta take a leak," he said, heading out to the porch. "Be right back." Dave wondered whether he'd been too harsh, sensing defeat in Ray's parting remark. Dave could see him silhouetted in the moonlight in the doorway, a silver arc splashing onto the lawn, head thrown back in what Dave took to be a posture of despair. Surely, he could squeeze this guy for something.

By the time Ray walked back in he was already confessing. ". . . an appraiser in Modesto, California, where I was raised. I did some community theater there, played Prince Oh-So-True in a children's production of *The Cave of Inky Blackness,* and thought I was going places. Next came *Twelve Angry Men*— I was one of them—which is where the pistol came from. Then I was the hangman in *Motherlode.* Got married, had a baby girl, lost my job, got another one, went to Hawaii as a steward on a yacht belonging to a movie star who was working a snow-cone stand a year before the yacht, the coke, the babes, and the Dom Pérignon. I'd had to sign a nondisclosure agreement. Eventually, I got into a fight with the movie star and got kicked off the boat at Diamond Head, just rowed me to shore in a dinghy. I hiked all the way to the crater, where I used the restroom to clean up and got some chow off the lunch wagon before catching a tour bus into Honolulu. I tried to sell the celebrity-drug-fueled-orgy story to a local paper, but that went nowhere because of the thing I'd signed. Everything I sign costs me money. About this time, my wife's uncle's walnut farm went bust. He took a loan out on the real estate, and I sold my car, a rust-free '78 Trans Am, handling package, W72 performance motor, solar gold with a Martinique-blue interior—we're talking mint. We bought a bunch of FEMA trailers off the Katrina deal and hauled them to California. But of course we lost our asses. So the uncle gases himself in his garage, and my wife throws me out. I moved into a hotel for migrants and started using the computers at the Stanislaus County Library, sleeping at the McHenry Mansion, where one of the tour guides was someone I used to fuck in high school. She slipped me into one of the canopy beds for naps. Online is where I met Morsel. We shared about our lives. I shared I had fallen on hard times. She shared she was coining it selling bootleg OxyContin in the Bakken oil field. It was a long shot: Montana. Fresh start. New me. But, hey. I took the bus to Billings and thumbed the rest of the way. By the time I made it to Jordan I had nothing left. The clerk at that fleabag almost wouldn't let me have a room. I told him I was there for the comets. I don't know where I come up with that. I had to make a move. Well, now you know. So, what happens next? You bust me with Morsel? You turn me in? I can't marry her anyway. I don't need bigamy on my sheet."

"You pretty sure on the business end of this thing?" Dave asked with surprising coldness. He could see things going his way.

"A hundred percent, but Morsel's got issues with other folks already being in it. There's some risk, but when isn't there with stakes like this."

"Like what kind of risk?"

"Death threats, the usual. Heard them all my life. But think about it, Dave. I'm not in if you're not. You really want to return to what you were doing? We'd both be back in that hotel with the comets."

Ray was soon snoring. Dave was intrigued that these revelations, not to mention the matter of the "gun," had failed to disturb Ray's sleep. Dave meanwhile was wide awake, and he began to realize why: the nagging awareness of his own life. So many risks! He felt that Ray was a success despite the wealth of evidence to the contrary. What had Dave accomplished? High school. What could have been more painful? Yet, he suffered no more than anyone else. So even in that he was unexceptional.

There was only generic anguish, persecution, and lockdown. He didn't have sex with a mansion tour guide. His experience came on the promise of marriage to a fat girl. Then there was the National Guard. Fort Harrison in the winter. Cleaning billets. A commanding officer who told the recruits that "the president of the United States is a pencil-wristed twat." Inventorying ammunition. Unskilled maintenance on UH-60 Black Hawks. "Human resource" assistant. Praying for deployment against worldwide towelheads. Girlfriend fatter every time he went home. Meaner, too. Threatening him with a baby. And he was still buying his dope from the same guy at the body shop who was his dealer in eighth grade. Never enough money and coveralls with so much cow shit he had to change Laundromats every two weeks.

It was perhaps surprising he'd come up with anything at all, but he did: Bovine Deluxe, LLC, a crash course in artificially inseminating cattle. Dave took to it like a duck to water: driving around the countryside (would have been more fun in Ray's Trans Am) with a special skill set, detecting and synchronizing estrus, handling frozen semen, keeping breeding records, all easily learnable; and Dave brought art to it. Though he had no idea where that gift had come from, he was a genius preg tester. Straight or stoned, his rate of accuracy, as proved in spring calves, was renowned. His excitement began as soon as he put on the coveralls, pulled on the glove lubed up with OB goo, before even approaching the chute. With the tail held high in his left hand, he'd push his right all the way in against the cow's attempt to expel it, shoveling out the manure to clear the way, over the cervix before grasping the uterus, now that he was in nearly up to his shoulder. Dave could detect a pregnancy at two months, when the calf was smaller than a mouse. He liked the compliments that came from being able to tell the rancher how far along the cow was, anywhere from two to seven months, according to Dave's informal system: mouse, rat, cat, fat cat, raccoon, Chihuahua, beagle. He'd continue until he'd gone through the whole herd or until his arm was exhausted. Then he had only to toss the glove, write up the invoice, and look for food and a room.

Perfect. Except for the dough.

Morsel made breakfast for the men—eggs with biscuits and gravy. At the table, Dave was still assessing Ray's claim of reaching his last dime back at Jordan, which didn't square with the rolls of bills in his pack. And Dave was watching Weldon watching Ray as breakfast was served. Morsel just leaned against the stove. "Anyone want to go to Billings Saturday and see the cage fights?" she said at last, moving from the stove to the table with a dish towel. Dave alone looked up and smiled; no one answered her. Ray was probing the food with his fork, still under Weldon's scrutiny. The salt-encrusted sweat stain on Weldon's black Stetson went halfway up the crown. It was downright unappetizing in Dave's view and definitely not befitting any customer for top-drawer bull semen. Nor did he look like a man whose daughter was selling dope at the Bakken, either.

At last Weldon spoke as though calling out to his livestock.

"What'd you say your name was?"

"Ray."

"Well, Ray, why don't you stick that fork all the way in and eat like a man?"

"I'll do my best, Mr. Case, but I will eat nothing with a central nervous system."

"Daddy, leave Ray alone. There'll be plenty of time to get acquainted and find out what Ray enjoys eating."

Weldon continued to eat without seeming to hear Morsel. Meanwhile, Dave was making a hog of himself and hoping he could finish Ray's breakfast, though Ray by now had seen the light and was eating the biscuits from which he had skimmed the gravy with the edge of his fork. He looked like he was under orders to clean his plate until Morsel brought him some canned pineapple slices. Ray looked up at her with what Dave thought was genuine affection. She said, "It's all you can eat around here," but the moment Dave stuck his fork back in the food, she raised a hand in his face and said, "I mean: that's all you can eat!" and laughed. Dave noticed her cold blue eyes, and for the first time he thought he understood her.

She smiled at Ray and said, "Daddy, you feel like showing Ray 'n' 'em the trick." Weldon ceased his rhythmic lip pursing.

"Oh, Morsel," he said coyly, pinching the bridge of his nose with thumb and forefinger.

"C'mon, Daddy, give you a dollar."

"Okay Mor', put on the music." A huge sigh of good-humored defeat. Morsel went over to a low cupboard next to the pie safe and pulled out a small plastic record player and a 45, which proved to be a scratchy version of "Cool, Clear Water" by the Sons of the Pioneers. At first gently swaying to the mournful dehydration tune, Weldon seemed to come to life as Morsel placed a peanut in front of him and the lyrics began, luring a poor desert rat named Dan to an imaginary spring. Weldon took off his hat and set it upside down beside him, revealing the thinnest comb-over across a snow-white pate. Then he picked up the peanut and with sinuous movements balanced it on his nose. It remained there until near the end of the record, when Dan the desert rat hallucinates green water and trees, whereupon the peanut dropped to the table, and Weldon just stared at it in disappointment. When the record ended, he replaced his hat, stood without a word, and, dropping his napkin on his chair, left the room. For a moment it was quiet. Dave felt he'd never seen anything like it.

"Daddy's pretty hard on himself when he don't make it to the end of the record. But," she said glumly, thumbing hair off her forehead as she cleared the dishes and went into the living room to straighten up, "me and Ray thought you ought to see what dementia looks like. It ain't pretty and it's expensive." Soon they heard Weldon's airplane cranking up, and Morsel called from the living room, "Daddy's always looking for them cows."

Dave had taken care to copy the information in Ray's passport onto the back of a matchbook cover, which he tore off, rolled into a cylinder, and stashed inside a bottle of aspirin. And there it stayed until Ray and Morsel headed to Billings for the cage fights. She'd left Dave directions to the Indian small-pox burials, in case he wanted to pass the time hunting for beads. But at this point, by failing to flee in his own car, Dave admitted to himself that he had become fully invested in Ray's scheme. So he seized the chance to use his cell phone and 411 connect to call Ray's home in Modesto and chat with his wife or, as she presently claimed to be, his widow. It took two tries a couple of hours apart. On the first, he got her answering machine, "You know the drill: leave it at the beep." On the second, he got Mrs. Ray. He had hardly identified himself as an account assistant with the Internal Revenue Service when she interrupted him to state in a voice firm, clear, and untouched by grief that Ray was dead. "That's what I told the last guy, and that's what I'm telling you." She said he had been embezzling from a credit union before he left a suicide note and disappeared.

"I'm doing home health care. Whatever he stole he kept. Killing himself was the one good idea he come up with in the last thirty years. At least it's prevented the government from garnishing my wages, what little they are. I been all through this with the other guy that called. Have to wait for his death to be confirmed or else I can't get benefits. If I know Ray, he's on the bottom of the Tuolumne River just to fuck with me. I wish I could have seen him one last time to tell him his water skis and croquet set went to Goodwill. If the bank hadn't taken back his airplane, there wouldn't have been even that little bit of equity I got to keep me from losing my house and sleeping in my motherfuckin' car. Too bad you didn't meet Ray. He was an A-to-Z crumb bum."

"I'm terribly sorry to hear about your husband," said Dave mechanically.

"I don't think the government is 'terribly sorry' to hear about anything. You reading this off a card?"

"No, this is just a follow-up to make sure your file stays active until you receive the benefits you're entitled to."

"I already have the big one: picturing Ray in hell with his ass *en fuego.*"

"Ah, speak a bit of Spanish, Mrs. Coelho?" said Dave, who would have rather heard mention of some *oro y plata.*

"Everybody in Modesto speaks 'a bit of Spanish.' Where you been all your life?"

"Washington, D.C., ma'am," said Dave indignantly.

"That explains it," said Mrs. Ray Coelho, and hung up.

Dave could now see why Ray was without transportation when they met. Wouldn't want to leave a paper trail renting cars or riding on airplanes. He got all he needed done on the library computers in Modesto, where he and Morsel, two crooks, had found each other and planned a merger.

Apart from the burial grounds there was nothing to do around there. He wasn't interested in that option until he discovered the liquor cabinet, and by then it was almost early evening. He found a bottle labeled HOOPOE SCHNAPPS with a picture of a bird, and he gave it a try. It went straight to his head. After several swigs, he failed to figure out the bird, but that didn't keep him from getting very happy. The label said the stuff was made from mirabelles, and Dave thought, Fuck, I hope that's good. Then as his confidence built, he reflected, Hey, I'm totally into mirabelles.

As he headed for the burial grounds, Dave, tottering a bit, decided he was glad to have left the Hoopoe schnapps back at the house. Rounding the equipment shed, he nearly ran into Weldon, who walked by without speaking or even seeing him, it seemed. Right behind the ranch buildings a cow trail led into the prairie, then wound toward a hillside spring that didn't quite reach the surface, evident only from the patch of greenery. Just below that was the spot Morsel had told him about, pockmarked with anthills. The ants, she'd claimed, would bring the beads to the surface, but still you had to hunt for them. Dave muttered, "I want some beads."

He sat down among the mounds and was soon bitten through his pants. He jumped to his feet and swept the ants away, then crouched, peering and picking at the hills. This soon seemed futile, and his thighs ached from squatting; but then he found a speck of sky blue in the dirt, a bead. He clasped it tightly while stirring with his free hand and flicking away ants. He gave no thought to the bodies in the ground beneath him and continued this until dark, by which time his palm was full of Indian beads, and his head of drunken exaltation.

As he crossed the equipment shed, barely able to see his way, he was startled by the silhouette of Weldon's Stetson and then of the old man's face very near his own, gazing at him before speaking in a low voice. "You been in the graves, ain't you?"

"Yes, just looking for beads."

"You ought not to have done that, feller."

"Oh? But Morsel said—"

"Look up there at the stars."

"I don't understand."

Weldon Case reached high over his head. "That's the crow riding the water snake." He turned back into the dark. Dave was frightened. He went to the cabin and got into bed as quickly as he could, anxious now for the alcohol to fade. He pulled the blanket up under his chin despite the warmth of the night and watched a moth batting against the windowpane at the sight of the moon. When he was nearly asleep, he saw the lights of Morsel's car wheel across the ceiling, before going dark. He listened for the car doors, but it was nearly ten minutes before they opened and closed. He rolled over against the wall and pretended to be asleep but watching as the door latch was carefully lifted from without.

Once the reverberation of the screen-door spring had ended, there was whispering. He perceived a dim shadow cross his face, someone peering down at him, and then another whisper. Soon their muffled copulation filled the room, then paused long enough for a window to be opened before resuming. Dave listened more and more intently, comfortable in his pretended sleep, until Ray said in a clear voice, "Dave, you want some of this?"

Dave stuck to his feigning until Morsel laughed, got up, and left with her clothes under her arm. "Night, Dave. Sweet Dreams."

The door shut, and after a moment, Ray spoke. "What could I do, Dave? She was after my weenie like a chicken after a June bug." Snorts and, soon after, snoring.

In the doorway of the house, taking in the early sun and smoking a cigarette, was Morsel in an old flannel shirt over what looked like a body stocking that produced a lazily winking camel toe. As Dave stepped up, her eyes followed her father crossing the yard very slowly toward them. "Look," she said, "he's wetting his pants. When he ain't wetting his pants, he walks pretty fast. It's just something he enjoys."

Weldon came up and looked at Dave, trying to remember him. He said, "This ain't much of a place to live. My folks moved us out here. We had a nice little ranch at Coal Banks Landing on the Missouri, but one day it fell in the river. Morsel, I'm uncomfortable."

"Go inside, Daddy, I'll get you a change."

Once the door shut behind them, Dave said, "Why in the world do you let him fly that plane?"

"It's all he knows. He flew in the war, and he's dusted crops. He'll probably kill himself in the damn thing. Good."

"What's he do up there?"

"Looks for his cows."

"I didn't know he had any."

"He don't. He hadn't had cows in forever. But he looks for 'em long as he's got fuel, then he comes down and says the damn things was brushed up to where you couldn't see 'em."

"I'm glad you go along with him. That's sure thoughtful."

"I don't know about that, but I gotta tell you this: I can't make heads or tails of your friend Ray. He was coming on to me the whole time at the cage fights, then he whips out a picture of his ex-wife and tells me she's the greatest piece of ass he ever had."

"Aw, gee. What'd you say to that?"

"I said, 'Ray, she must've had one snappin' pussy, because she's got a face that would stop a clock.' I punched him in the shoulder and told him he hadn't seen nothing yet. What'd you say your name was?"

"I'm Dave."

"Well, Dave, Ray says you mean to throw in with us. Is that a fact?"

"I'm sure giving it some thought."

"You look like a team player to me. I guess that bitch he's married to will help out on that end. Long as I never have to see her."

Sometimes Dave could tell that Ray couldn't remember his

name, either. He'd say "pal" or "pard" or, in a pinch, "old-timer," which seemed especially strange to someone in his twenties. Then when the name came back to him, he'd overuse it. "Dave, what're we gonna do today." "Dave, what's that you just put in your mouth?" "I had an uncle named Dave." And so forth. But the morning that Morsel slipped out of their room carrying her clothes, he summoned it right away: "Dave, you at all interested in getting rich?"

"I'm doing my best, Ray!"

"I'm talking about taking it up a notch, and I'm fixing to run out of hints."

"I'm a certified artificial inseminator," said Dave, loftily. If he had not already scented the bait, he'd have been home days before. But this was a big step, and he knew it was a moment in time.

At least on the phone she couldn't throw stuff at him.

"The phone is ringing off the hook. Your ranchers wanting to know when you'll get there."

"Ma, I know, but I been tied up. Tell them not to get their panties in a wad. I'll be there."

"David," she screeched, "I'm not your secretary!"

"Ma, listen to me, Ma, I got tied up. I'm sparing you the details right now, but trust me."

"How can I trust you with the phone ringing every ten seconds?"

"Ma, I can't listen to this shit, I'm under pressure. Pull the fucking thing out of the wall."

"Pressure? You've never been under pressure in your life!"

He hung up on her. He knew he couldn't live with her anymore. She needed to take her pacemaker and get a room.

Morsel was able to get a custodial order in Miles City based on the danger to community presented by Weldon and his airplane. Ray had so much trouble muscling him into Morsel's sedan for the ride to assisted living that Dave's hulking frame had to be enlisted to bind Weldon, who tossed off some antique curses before collapsing in defeat. But the God he called down on them didn't count for much anymore. At dinner that night, Morsel was still a little blue, despite the toasts, somewhat vague, to a limitless future. Dave smiled along with them, his inquiring looks met by giddy winks from Morsel and Ray. Nevertheless, he felt happy and accepted, at last convinced he was going somewhere. Exchanging a nod, they let him know that he was a "courier." He smiled around the room in bafflement. Ray unwound one of his wads. Dave was going to California.

"Make sure you drive the limit," said Ray. "I'll meanwhile get to know the airplane. Take 'er down to the oil fields. Anyway, it's important to know your customers." He and Morsel saw him off from the front stoop. They looked like a real couple.

"Customers for what exactly?" Dave immediately regretted his question. Not a problem, as no one answered him anyway.

"And I'll keep the home fires burning," said Morsel without taking the cigarette from her mouth. David had a perfectly good idea what he might be going to California for and recognized the advantage of preserving his ignorance, no guiltier than the

United States Postal Service. "Your Honor, I had no idea what was in the trunk and I am prepared to affirm that under oath or take a lie-detector test, at your discretion," he rehearsed.

Dave drove straight through, or nearly so, stopping only briefly in Idaho, Utah, and Nevada to walk among cows. His manner with cattle was so familiar that none ran from him but gathered around in benign expectation. Dave sighed and jumped back in the car. He declined to be swayed by second thoughts.

It was late when he drove into Modesto, and he was tired. He checked into a Super 8 and awoke to the hot light of a California morning as it shone through the window onto his face. He ate downstairs and then checked out. The directions he unfolded in his car proved quite exact: within ten minutes he was pulling around the house into the side drive and backing into the open garage.

A woman in a bathrobe emerged from the back door and walked past his window without a word. He popped the trunk and sat quietly as he heard her load then shut it. She stopped at his window, pulling the bathrobe up close around her throat. She wasn't hard to look at, but Dave could see you wouldn't want to argue with her. "Tell Ray I said be careful. I've heard from two IRS guys already." Dave said nothing at all.

Dave was so cautious, the trip back took longer. He overnighted at the Garfield again so as to arrive in daylight, getting up twice during the night to check on the car. In the morning, he was reluctant to eat at the café, where some of his former clientele might be sitting around picking their teeth and speculating about fall calves or six-weight steers. He was now so close that he worried about everything from misreading the gas gauge to getting a flat. He even imagined the trunk flying open for no reason. He headed toward the ranch on an empty stomach, knowing Morsel would take care of that. He flew past fields of cattle with hardly a glance.

No one seemed around to offer the hearty greeting and meal he was counting on. On the wire running from the house to the bunkhouse, a hawk flew off reluctantly as though it had had the place to itself. Dave got out and went into the house. Dirty dishes sat on the dining-room table, light from the television flickered without sound from the living room. When Dave walked in he saw the television was tuned to the shopping network, a close-up of a hand modeling a gold diamond-studded bracelet. Then he saw Morsel on the floor with the remote still in her hand.

Dave felt an icy calm. Ray had done this. Dave patted his pocket for the car keys and walked out of the house, stopping on the porch to survey everything in front of him. Then he went around to the shop. Where the airplane had usually been parked, in its two shallow ruts, Ray was lying with a pool of blood extending from his mouth like a speech balloon without words. He'd lost a shoe. The plane was gone.

Dave felt trapped between the two bodies, as if there was no safe way back to the car. When he got to it, a man was there waiting. He was about Dave's age, lean and respectable looking in clean khakis and a Shale Services ball cap. "I must have over-slept," he said. "How long have you been here?" He touched his teeth with his thumbnail as he spoke.

"Oh, just a few minutes."

"Keys."

"Oh right, yes, I have them here." Dave patted his pocket again.

"Get the trunk for me, please." Dave offered him the keys.

"No, you."

"Not a problem."

Dave bent to insert the key, but his hand was shaking so that at first he missed the lock. The lid rose to reveal the contents of the trunk. Dave never felt a thing.

An Old Man Who Liked to Fish

The Smiths were a very old couple, whose lifelong habits of exercise and outdoor living and careful diet had resulted in their seeming tiny—tiny, pale, and almost totemic—as they spread a picnic tablecloth on my front lawn and arranged their luncheon. Since I live with reckless inattention to what I eat, I watched with fascination as they set out apples, cheese, red wine, and the kind of artisanal bread that looks like something found in the road. The Smiths were the last friends of my parents still alive. And to the degree we spend our lives trying to understand our parents, I always looked forward to Edward and Emily's visits as a pleasant forensic exercise.

Edward was a renowned fisherman, much admired by my father, and me, but given his present frailty, it was surprising that he thought he could still wade our rocky streams. He had a set rule of no wading staff before the first heart attack, and as he had yet to suffer one, he continued picking his way along, peering for rises, and if he ran into speedy water in a narrow place, he'd find a stick on the shore to help him through it. My father, by contrast, had always used a staff, an elegant blackthorn with a silver head that was supposed to have belonged to Calvin Coolidge.

Emily had been an avid golfer and considered fishing to be an inferior pursuit, with no score and thus no accountability. Therefore, she never followed Edward along the stream, instead taking up a place among the cottonwoods, where, with her binoculars, she quietly waited for something to happen in the canopy, hopeful of seeing a new bird for the list she kept in her head. She had done this for so many years that she felt empowered to report the rise and fall of entire species, extrapolating from her observations in the cottonwoods. This year she announced the decline of tanagers; last year, it was the rise of Audubon's warblers. Lately, she would too often describe her sighting of Kirtland's warbler, which occurred thirty years ago on Great Abaco. Not a good sign. At the last iteration, I must have looked blankly, because she said "wood warbler" in a sharp tone. Still, her birding represented mainly an accommodation of Edward, enabling her to stay close by while he fished, though he had never made a secret of his disdain for golf, golfers, and golf courses.

I fished with Edward for an hour or so, just to be sure that he could manage. He lovingly strung up his little straw-colored Paul Young rod, pulling line from the noisy old pewter-colored Hardy reel. Holding the rod at arm's length, sighting down the length of it, he announced, "Not a set after forty years." But I could see the leftward set from where I stood ten feet away. His casts, on the other hand, were straight as ever: tight, probing expressions of a tidy stream craft, such simplicity and precision. They took me all the way back to my boyhood, when from a high bank on the Pere Marquette, at my father's urging, I had first observed Edward with utter rapture at seeing it all done so well. Now watching him hook an aerial cutthroat from a seam along cottonwood roots, I concluded he would be just fine on his own. He gave me a wink and cupped the fish in his hand, vital as a spark, before he let it go. I could see the fish dart around in the clear water, trying to find its direction before racing to midstream and disappearing. Edward held the barbless fly up to the light, blew it dry, and shot out a new cast. "I'm sorry your father isn't here to enjoy this," he said, keeping an eye on his fly as it bobbed down the current.

"So am I."

"We had quite a river list. He was the last of the old gang, except for me and the wives." Edward laughed. "The Big Fellow is starting to get the range."

"My dad was a great fisherman, wasn't he?"

"Oh, not really, but nobody loved it more." My father and I hadn't gotten along, so I was surprised to find myself feeling defensive about his prowess as a fisherman. But it was true: his style of aggression was ill suited to field sports. He had played football in college, and I could recall feeling that baseball, my sport, was a little too subtle for him. And slow.

Edward promised that when the sun got far enough to the west to put glare on the water, he'd head back up to the house, and meanwhile he hoped that I would be patient with Emily. She had begun to slip further, something that I had noticed but not much worried about, because she could still be talked out of the most peculiar of her fixations. I had seen the very old—my aunt Margaret, for example—slide into dementia good-naturedly, even enjoying some of its comic effects or treating the misapprehensions as amusing curiosities. But Emily demanded to be believed, and so perhaps her progression had not been so pleasant. Edward did say that they'd had to light the flower beds at home when she began to see things there that frightened her.

Edward said, "Well, I'm going to keep moving. I want to get to the logjam while there's still good light." He looked down at the bright water curling around his legs. "Amazing this all finds its way to the sea."

Edward wasn't seen again. That's not quite accurate: his body turned up, what was left of it, in a city park in Billings, on the banks of the Yellowstone. It had gone down the West Fork of the Boulder; down the Boulder to the Yellowstone, past the town Captain Clark had named Big Timber for the cottonwoods on the banks; down the Yellowstone through sheep towns, cow towns, refinery towns; and finally to Two Moon Park in Billings, where it was found by a homeless man, Eldon Pomfret of Magnolia Springs, Alabama. In a sense, Edward had gotten off easy.

At sundown, Emily came out of her birding lair and asked, "Have you seen Edward?" She had binoculars in one hand and a birding book in the other, and her eyes were wide. I was still in the studio, and her inquiry startled me.

"Maybe he stayed for the evening rise or—"

"I wonder if you should go look for him. He doesn't see well in the dark. It will be dark soon, won't it? What time is it, anyway?"

"I don't have my watch, but I'll walk up and see how he's getting along."

"Don't bother him if there are bugs on the water. He gets furious. What time did you say it was?"

"I left my watch on the dresser."

"What difference does it make? We can tell by the sun."

"Okay, here I go."

"And if he's intent, please don't disturb him."

"I won't."

"He gets furious."

When I got back, I sat with Emily on the sun porch waiting for the sheriff. She was weeping. "He's with that woman."

"What woman, Emily?"

"The one with those huge hats. Francine. I thought that was over."

I refrained from noting that Edward would have had no means of conveyance to "Francine." Perhaps, she knew more than I thought and was escaping into this story. As time went on, "Francine" came to seem something portentous. Emily hung on to the idea even after the sheriff arrived, who seemed to us old folks an overgrown child, bursting out of his uniform. He listened patiently as Emily explained all about Francine. He nodded and blinked throughout.

"She met him in the lobby of the Alexis Hotel in Seattle and lured him to her room. That was back in the Reagan years, and she has turned up several times since."

"Ma'am," said the sheriff—and I remember thinking that this big, pink, kindly, bland child of an officer was the right person to say "ma'am" as slowly as he did—"Ma'am, I can't really comment on that other lady, but this creek comes straight off the mountain, and we're a long way from town." Emily watched him closely as he made his case. She was quiet for a moment.

"He's dead, isn't he. I knew this would happen." Emily turned to me. "I suppose that settles it." I couldn't think of one thing to do except wrinkle my brow in affected consternation. "Well," said Emily. "I hope she's happy now."

Prairie Girl

When the old brothel—known as the Butt Hut—closed down, years ago, the house it had occupied was advertised in the paper: "Home on the river: eight bedrooms, eight baths, no kitchen. Changing times force sale." The madam, Miriam Lawler, an overweight elder in the wash dresses of a ranch wife, beloved by her many friends, and famous for having crashed into the drive-up window of the bank with her old Cadillac, died and was buried at an exuberant funeral, and all but one of the girls dispersed. Throughout the long years that the institution had persevered, the girls had been a constantly changing guard in our lively old cow town. Who were they? Some were professionals from as far away as New Orleans and St. Louis. A surprising number were country schoolteachers, off for the summer. Some, from around the state, worked a day or two a week but were otherwise embedded in conventional lives. When one of them married a local, the couple usually moved away, and over time our town lost a good many useful men—cowboys, carpenters, electricians. This pattern seemed to land most heavily on our tradespeople and worked a subtle hardship on the community. But it was supposed by the pious to be a sacrifice for the greater good.

Mary Elizabeth Foley was the one girl who stayed on after the Butt Hut closed. She retained a pew at the Lutheran church, just as she had while working for Miriam. No one sat with her at first, but gradually people moved over, with expressions of extraordinary virtue. The worldly old pastor must have cited some Christian duty. It fell to Mrs. Gladstone Gander—not her real name but a moniker bestowed by others with less money—to ask the aggressive but traditional local question: "Where are you from?"

Mary Elizabeth replied, "What business is it of yours?"

Where was the meekness appropriate to a woman with her past? It was outrageous. From then on, the energy that ought to have been spent on listening to the service was dedicated to beaming malice at Mary Elizabeth Foley. Even the men joined in, though it was unlikely that they had entirely relinquished their lewd fantasies. Soon she had the pew to herself all over again and greeted it each Sunday with happy surprise, like someone finding an empty parking spot right in front of the entrance to Walmart.

The rest of the town was suspicious of Lutherans, anyway, and would have been more so if Gladstone Gander—not his real name—hadn't been president of the bank that was the only lending institution in town, and if his wife had not been the recognized power behind the throne. Mary Elizabeth was a depositor at the bank and would have enjoyed modest deference on that basis, but everything changed when she eloped with Arnold, the son and only child of the banker and his wife, whose actual names were Paul and Meredith Tanner.

Since it was a small town, and functioned reliably as a Greek chorus, the Tanners had never been free of the pressure of being the parents of Arnold, a gay man. Now that Arnold had married, appearances were much improved, or would be once time had burnished Mary Elizabeth's history. In town, there were two explanations for the marriage. The first held that Mary Elizabeth Foley had converted Arnold by using tricks she had learned at the Butt Hut. The second was that she intended to take over the bank. Only the second was true, and the poor Tanners never saw it coming. But it wouldn't have worked if Arnold and Mary Elizabeth hadn't been in love.

Mary Elizabeth was an ambitious woman, but she was not cynical. In Arnold she saw an educated lost soul. She had great sympathy for lost souls, since she thought of herself as one, too. She lacked Arnold's fatalism, however, and briefly thought that she could bring him around with her many skills. Once she realized the futility of that, she found new ways to love him and was uplifted to discover their power. She delighted in watching him arrange the clothes hanging in his closet and guessing at his system. He had ways with soft-boiled eggs, picture hanging, checkbook balancing, and envelope slitting that she found adorable. She could watch him stalking around the house with his flyswatter in a state of absorbed rapture. He brushed her hair every morning and played intelligent music on the radio. He had the better newspapers mailed in. Mary Elizabeth was not a social climber, but she did appreciate her ascent from vulgarity and survival. They slept together like two spoons in a drawer, and if she put her hands on him suggestively and he seemed to like it, she didn't care what he was imagining. She had been trained to accept the privacy of every dream world.

When they returned from their elopement, in Searchlight, Nevada, the Tanners welcomed them warmly. After a preamble of Polonian blather, Paul Tanner said, "Mrs. Tanner and I are both pleased and cautiously optimistic going forward. But, Mary, wouldn't your father have preferred to give you a big, beautiful wedding?"

"Possibly."

"I don't mean to pry, but who, exactly, is your father?"

"What business is it of yours?"

This could have been a nasty moment, but the Tanners' eagerness to sweep Junior's proclivities under the rug resulted in their pulling their punches, which was much harder on Mrs. Tanner, who was bellicose by nature, than on her husband. At times like this, she gave out a look that suggested that she was simply awaiting a better day.

The luxury of sleeping with someone threatened Arnold's punctilious habits. It was his first experience of sustained intimacy, and it had its consequences, which weren't necessarily bad but were quite disruptive. Arnold was a homely man, and one local view had it that his homeliness was what had driven him into the arms of men. He had big ears and curly hair that seemed to gather at the very top of his head. He had rather darty eyes except when he was with Mary Elizabeth or when he was issuing instructions at the bank. His previous love had been the only lawyer in town who had much of a standing outside of town, and whatever went on between them did so with fastidious discretion. Their circumstances made it certain that they would never have any fun.

"Where is he now?" Mary asked.

"San Juan Capistrano."

"And that was the end of your affair?"

"Here."

"You know I don't mind." And she didn't. The sea of predators who had rolled through the Butt Hut had seen to that.

"I'd like to be a good husband."

Arnold was the vice president of the family bank and dressed like a city banker, in dark suits, rep ties, and cordovan wing tips. He had a severe, businesslike demeanor at work that put all communications, with staff and customers alike, on a formal basis. He and Mary Elizabeth lived thirteen blocks from the bank, and Arnold walked to work, rain or shine. If the former, he carried an umbrella, which was an extremely unusual object in town. Everyone knew what an umbrella was, of course, but it seemed so remarkable in this context that, on rainy days, it was as though the umbrella, not Arnold, was the one going to work. In any case, what anyone might have had to say about Arnold in town, no one said to his face. People were confused, too, by the motorcycle he rode on weekends. He did a fifty-yard wheelie down Main Street on a Saturday night that really had them scratching their heads. When Mary asked him to wear a helmet, he replied, "But then they won't know who it is."

The last thing Paul Tanner did before he died was send Mary off to be trained in banking skills. She'd told him that she wanted to work. She went to a loan-officer and mortgage-broker boot camp and returned to town well versed in the differences between F.H.A., V.A., and conventional forward mortgages, as well as reverse mortgages and loan models. And she was going to have a baby. Arnold said, "I hope he's a nice fellow."

"We don't even know if it's a boy or a girl!"

"I mean, the father."

"Sweetheart, that was a joke."

"Okay, but who is he?"

Mary said, "What business is it of yours?" But she quickly softened and said, "You, Arnold, don't you see?"

Paul Tanner died in his sleep, of an embolism—or something like that. Arnold wasn't sure. He and his father had never been close and had viewed each other with detachment since Arnold was in kindergarten. Paul had been so anxious to see Mary's baby that Arnold concluded that his father's hopes were skipping a generation and was more pissed off than ever. But now Arnold was president of the bank, which was merely a titular change, as he had run the place for years and run it well, with a caution that allowed it to avoid some of the ruinous expansions that had recently swept the banking community. With Paul gone, Mrs. Tanner was slap in the middle of their lives, and Mary knew from the beginning that Mama was going to need a major tune-up if they were to live in peace.

It happened when Mary's water broke and labor commenced. Arnold promptly took her to the hospital and sat by her bed, grimacing at every contraction. His mother arrived in a rush and with a bustle and consumption of space that indicated that she intended to be in charge. After she had removed her coat and scarf, tossed them over the back of a chair, and bent to pull the rubbers from her red shoes, she made a point of seeming to discover Mary and said, "Breathe."

"I'll breathe when I want to breathe."

"Of course you will, and no one is at their best going into labor." Mrs. Tanner went to the window and raised her arms above her head. "I'm about to become a grandma!"

Arnold and Mary glanced at each other: it was ambiguous. Was Mrs. Tanner happy to become a grandmother? Hard to say. Mary groaned through another contraction unnoticed by Mrs. Tanner, who was still at the window, craning around and forecasting the weather. Arnold was keeping track of the contractions with his wristwatch while Mary dutifully gave a passing thought to the stranger at the loan-officer school who was about to become a father. She hoped that Arnold was having a fond thought for his friend in San Juan Capistrano and that the arriving child would help to sort out all these disparate threads. Family-wise, Mrs. Tanner already stood for the past, and it was urgent that she bugger off ASAP. Arnold knew of Mary's aversion to his mother and had survived several of Mary's attempts to bar her from their home. "We can't just throw her under the bus," he said. This was an early use of the expression, and Mary took it too literally, encouraged that Arnold thought such an option was in play.

Mrs. Tanner turned from the window, beaming at everything and animadverting about the "new life." Arnold winced at these remarks as sharply as he did at Mary's contractions. Mary was just disconcerted by the number of unreciprocated statements, more bugling than dialogue. Arnold held her hand, and then leaned across so that he could hold both of her hands, while Mrs. Tanner strode the linoleum. He loved to hold Mary's hands: they were so strong. He thought of them as farmer's hands.

Mary owed her hard hands and a confidant horsemanship to her childhood on a ranch a mile and a quarter from the Canadian border, a remote place yet well within reach of the bank that had seized it and thrown Mary and her family into poverty. The president of the United States had told them to borrow, borrow, borrow for their business; thus, the bank had gotten the swather, the baler, the rock windrower, the tractor, the front-end loader, the self-propelled bale wagon, and eight broke horses and their tack, while the family had hit the road. Mary used to say that "bank" was just another four-letter word, but eventually she'd put that behind her, too.

"Mrs. Tanner," Mary said, "I seem to be oversensitive tonight. Could you stop talking?"

"Is it a problem?"

"'Is it a problem?'" Mary repeated. Arnold's face was in his hands. "Mrs. Tanner, it is a huge problem. This is a time when people want a little peace, and you just won't shut up. I'm about to have a baby, and you seem rambunctious."

Mrs. Tanner reassembled her winter clothes and departed. Mary looked at Arnold and said, "I'm sorry, Arnie."

The boy was born at two o'clock in the morning. Mary was exhausted and so was Arnold, who was both elated and confused but truly loving to his bedraggled wife. They had never chosen a name for the baby, thinking that it was presumptuous to do so before seeing whether it was a boy or a girl. They agreed that a list of gender-based alternatives was somehow corny. But Mary's suggestion, based on a sudden recollection of the aspirant at loan-officer school, startled Arnold.

"Pedro? I don't think I'd be comfortable with that, Mary."

They settled on Peter, which left Mary with her glimmer of rationale and pleased Arnold, who liked old-fashioned names. Mary's affectionate name for him, however, would always be Pedro. And, without question, he had a Pedro look to him.

Mary bought a horse and, as Peter grew, Arnold spent more and more time in San Juan Capistrano; the day came when he told Mary that he would not be coming back. As foreseen as that must have been, they both wept discreetly to avoid alarming Peter, who was in the next room. They tried to discuss how Arnold would spend time with Peter, but the future looked so fractured that they were forced to trust to their love and intentions.

"Will I always be able to see Peter?" Arnold sobbed. Mary was crying, too. But she knew where to put her pain. She had her boy to think of, and where to put pain was a skill she'd learned early on.

"The house is yours, of course," Arnold said with a brave, generous smile that suggested he was unaware that he was speaking to a loan officer who had already begun to do the numbers in her head. She couldn't help it. It was her latest version of tough.

"Thank you, Arnold."

"And my owning the bank with my mother means that your job is assured."

Mary loved Arnold, but this airy way of dispensing justice hurried her agenda.

"Don't you find that a little informal?"

"You must mean divorce."

"I'm not the one going to San Juan Capistrano. You are."

"No doubt we'll have to get something written up."

"This is a no-fault state. When couples split the sheets, they split them fifty-fifty." Mary laughed heartily. "I could keep you on at the bank, Arnold, but not from California."

He'd let Mary see his origins, and Mary had reminded him of hers. Arnold sighed in concession.

His mother was not pleased when she learned of her new partnership. Her mouth fell open as Mary explained the arrangement, but Mary reached across the conference-room table and gently lifted it shut. News of all this was greeted warmly as it shot around the bank.

Mary learned more about banking every day. Mrs. Tanner, despite her claims at the beauty parlor, however, knew nothing except how she had come to acquire what equity she had, and she spent more and more of her time and money on increasingly futile cosmetic surgery. As a figurehead at board meetings, she wore costumes and an imitation youth that contrasted with the professionalism of Mary Elizabeth Tanner, who ran the bank with evenhanded authority. Over time, there came to be nothing disreputable about Mary whatsoever. Wonderful how dollars did that, and Mary had a little gold dollar sign on a chain around her pretty neck.

Considering the hoops he had to jump through, Arnold did his very best to be Peter's father, virtually commuting from California. This was even more remarkable once he had sold his share of the bank to Mary, since this occasioned a rupture with his own mother. Peter was consoled by the fact that his parents were now sleeping together once a month, and Arnold called him Pedro at intimate moments. He never let on to his friend in California how much he enjoyed these interludes of snuggling with Mary.

Peter was already a star at little-guy soccer. Mrs. Tanner came to the games, and Peter ran straight to Grandma after each game, which softened the smirk on her well-stretched face. Finally, Arnold and his mother reconciled, under the leafless cottonwoods shadowing the battered playing field, during a 3–1 win over the Red Devils of Reed Point, Montana. All the fight went out of Mrs. Tanner, who never made another board meeting but spent her life estate as she saw fit, letting her face sag and reading bodice rippers on her porch, from which she could watch the neighbors during the warm months, and by the pool in San Juan Capistrano during the cold.

Arnold got out of banking and into business, at which he did well. Arnold always did well: no one was more serious about work. Peter had a girlfriend, Mary's hair was going gray, and Arnold's domestic arrangements were stable most of the time, except during the winter, when his mother interfered.

"She's driving me nuts," Arnold complained to Mary.

"You'll have to stand it," Mary said. "She's lonely, she's old, and she's your mother."

"Can't Peter do winter sports? What about basketball?"

When Mrs. Tanner's advancing dementia and prying nature made Arnold's companion, T.O.—tired of her referring to him as a "houseboy"—threaten to leave, Arnold popped her into assisted living, and that was that. Mrs. Tanner did not go easily; as T.O., a burly Oklahoman, drawled, "She hung on like a bulldog in a thunderstorm."

"She's my mother!" Arnold cried without much feeling.

Before Peter left for college, Mary decided to take him to see the place where she had grown up. This was a reward, in a sense, because Peter had always asked about it. No doubt he had heard rumors concerning his mother, and he wanted to confirm her ranch origins. This was straightforward curiosity, as Peter was the furthest thing from insecure. Well brought up and popular,

he was the first in his family to trail neither his past nor his proclivities like a lead ball.

They set out in the middle of June, in Mary's big Lincoln,
heading for the great, nearly empty stretches of northern Montana, where underpopulated counties would deny the government's right to tax them, attempt to secede from the Union,
and issue their own money in the form of scrip. Some radical-
ized soothsayer would arise—a crop duster, a diesel mechanic,
a gunsmith—then fade away, and the region would go back to
sparse agriculture, a cow every hundred acres, a trailer house
with a basketball backboard and a muddy truck. Minds spun in
the solitude.

Peter said, "Where is everybody?"

"Gone."

"Is that what you did, Mom?"

"I had to. We lost the place to the bank. I liked it where I was.
I had horses."

"Don't you wish you'd gone to college?"

"I got an education, Peter, that's what matters. And now I can
send you to college. Maybe you can go to college in California,
near Pop."

"Where did your brothers go?" Mary understood that Peter
would have liked to have a bigger family.

"Here and there. They didn't stay in touch."

"Did you ever try to find them?"

Mary didn't say anything for a moment. "I did, but they didn't
want to stay in touch with me."

"What? Why's that?"

"They had their reasons."

"Like what?" Peter could be demanding.

"They didn't like what I did for a living."

"What's wrong with working at the bank?"

She thought for a moment. "Well, a bank took away our home."

Peter said, "I still think it's totally weird. They'd better not be there."

Mary glanced over from the wheel, smiled a bit, and said, "It was a long time ago, Peter."

She watched him as he looked out the window at the prairie. She thought that he was beautiful, and that was enough. It didn't hurt that the car was big and smelled new and hugged the narrow road with authority. She said to herself, as she had since she was a girl:

"I can do this."

The Good Samaritan

Szabo didn't like to call the land he owned and lived on a ranch—a word that was now widely abused by developers. He preferred to call it his property, or "the property," but it did require a good bit of physical effort from him in the small window of time after he finished at the office, raced home, and got on the tractor or, if he was hauling a load of irrigation dams, on the ATV. Sometimes he was so eager to get started that he left his car running. His activity on the property, which had led, over the years, to arthroscopic surgery on his left knee, one vertebral fusion, and mild hearing loss, thanks to his diesel tractor, yielded very little income at all and some years not even that—a fact that he did not care to dwell on.

He produced racehorse-quality alfalfa hay for a handful of grateful buyers, who privately thought he was nuts but were careful to treat his operation with respect, because almost no one else was still producing the small bales that they needed to feed their own follies. They were, most of them, habitués of small rural tracks in places such as Lewistown or Miles City, owners of one horse, whose exercise rider was either a daughter or a neighbor girl who put herself in the way of serious injury as the price of the owner's dream. Hadn't Seattle Slew made kings of a couple of hapless bozos?

Szabo was not nuts. He had long understood that he needed to do something with his hands to compensate for the work that he did indoors, and it was not going to be golf or woodworking. He wanted to grow something and sell it, and he wanted to use the property to do this. In fact, the work that he now did indoors had begun as manual labor. He had machined precision parts for wind generators for a company that subcontracted all the components, a company that sold an idea and actually made nothing. Szabo had long known that this approach was the wave of the future, without understanding that it was the wave of his future. He had worked very hard, and his hard work had led him into the cerebral ether of his new workplace: now, at forty-five, he took orders in an office in a pleasant town in Montana, while his esteemed products were all manufactured in other countries. It was still a small, if prosperous, business, and it would likely stay small, because of Szabo's enthusiasm for what he declined to call his ranch.

It wasn't that he was proud of the John Deere tractor that he was still paying for and that he circled with a grease gun and washed down like a teenager's car. He wasn't proud of it: he loved it. There were times when he stood by his kitchen window with his first cup of coffee and gazed at the gleaming machine in the morning light. Even the unblemished hills of his property looked better through its windshield. The fact that he couldn't wait to climb into it was the cause of the accident.

The hay, swathed, lay in windrows, slowly drying in the Saturday-morning sun. Szabo had gone out to the meadows in his bathrobe to probe the hay for moisture and knew that it

was close to ready for baling. The beloved tractor was parked
at the foot of the driveway, as though a Le Mans start would be
required once the hour came around and the moisture in the
tender shoots of alfalfa had subsided, so that the hay would not
spoil in the stacks. Szabo, now in jeans, tennis shoes, hooded
sweatshirt, and baseball cap, felt the significance of each step
as he walked toward the tractor, marveling at the sunlight on
its green paint, its tires nearly his own height, its baler pert and
ready. He reached for the handhold next to the door of the cab,
stepped onto the ridged footstep, and pulled himself up, raising
his left hand to open the door. Here his foot slid off the step,
leaving him briefly dangling from the handhold. A searing pain
informed him that he had done something awful to his shoulder.
Releasing his grip, he fell to the driveway in a heap. The usually
ambrosial smell of tractor fuel repelled him, and the towering
green shape above him now seemed reproachful. Gravel pressed
into his cheek.

As he lay in recovery, the morphine drip only prolonged his
obsession with the unbaled hay, since it allowed him to forget
about his shoulder, which he had come to think of not as his
but as a kind of alien planet fastened to his torso, which glowed
red like Mars, whirling with agony, as soon as the morphine ran
low. It was a fine line: when he wheedled extra narcotic, his singing caused complaints, and he got dialed back down to the red
planet. Within a day, he grew practical and managed to call his
secretary.

"Melinda, I'm going to have to find somebody for the property. I've got hay down and—"

"A ranch hand?"

"But just for a month or so."

"Why don't I call around?"

"That's the idea. But not too long commitment-wise, okay? I may have to overpay for such a limited time."

"It is what it is," Melinda remarked, producing a mystification in Szabo that he ascribed to the morphine.

"Yes, sure," Szabo said. "But time is of the essence."

"You can say that again. Things are piling up. The guy in Germany calls every day."

"I mean with the hay."

Melinda was remarkably efficient, and she knew everyone in town. Her steadiness was indispensable to Szabo, who kept her salary well above temptation from other employers. By the next day, she had found a few prospects for him.

The most promising one, an experienced ranch hand from Wyoming, wore a monitoring ankle bracelet that he declined to explain, so he was eliminated. The next most promising, a disgruntled nursery worker, wanted permanent employment, so Szabo crossed him off the list, ignoring Melinda's suggestion that he just fire him when he was through. That left a man called Barney, overqualified and looking for other work but happy to take something temporary. He told Melinda that he was extremely well educated but "identified with the workingman" and thought a month or so in Szabo's bunkhouse would do him a world of good. Szabo called Barney's references from his hospital bed. He managed to reach only one, the wife of a dentist who ran a llama operation in Bozeman. Barney was completely reliable, she said, and meticulous: he had reshingled the toolshed and restacked their large woodpile in an intricate pattern—almost like a church window—and swept the sidewalk. "You could eat off it!" she said. Szabo got the feeling that Mrs. Dentist had been day-drinking. Her final remark confused him. "Nobody ever did a better job than Barney!" she said, laughing wildly. "He drove us right up the wall!"

Szabo took a leap of faith and hired him over the phone. The news seemed not to excite Barney. "When do you want me to start?" he droned. After the call, Szabo gazed at his phone for a moment, then flipped it shut. His arm in a sling, his shoulder radiating signals with every beat of his heart, he returned to his office and stirred the things on his desk with his left hand. Eventually, he had pushed the papers into two piles: "urgent" and "not urgent." Then there was a painful reshuffle into "urgent," "not that urgent," and "not urgent." Melinda stood next to him. "Does that make sense?" he asked.

Melinda said, "I think so."

"I'm going home."

Barney, who looked to be about forty, with a pronounced widow's peak in his blondish hair and a deep dimple in his chin, was a quick study, though it took Szabo a while to figure out how much of his instruction the man was absorbing. Barney was remarkably without affect, gazing at Szabo as he spoke as if marveling at the physical apparatus that permitted Szabo's chin to move so smoothly. At first, Szabo was annoyed by this, and when Barney's arm rose slowly to his mouth to place a tooth-pick there, he had a momentary urge to ask him to refrain from chewing it while he was listening. It was the sense of a concealed smirk behind the toothpick that bothered Szabo the most. But once he'd observed Barney's efficiency, Szabo quickly trained himself not to indulge such thoughts. Some of the hay had been rained on, but Barney raked it dry, and soon the shiny green tractor was flying around the meadows making beautiful bales for the racehorses of Montana. This gave Szabo something of a heartache, but he praised Barney for the job he had done so well. Barney replied, "That's not enough hay to pay for the fuel."

Szabo tried to ride his old gelding, Moon, a tall chestnut half-thoroughbred he had been riding for thirteen of the horse's sixteen years. One armed, he had to be helped into the saddle. He could get the bridle over Moon's head and pull himself up from the saddle horn, barely, but the jogging aroused the pain in his shoulder so sharply that he quickly gave up. Barney looked on without expression.

Szabo said, "I really need to ride him regularly. He's getting old."

"I'll ride him."

"That would be nice, but it's not necessary."

"I'll ride him. There's not much else to do."

Barney rode confidently but without grace of any kind. Moon's long trot produced a lurching sway in Barney's torso, exaggerated by the suspenders he always wore, that was hard for Szabo to watch. And it was clear from Moon's sidelong glances that he, too, was wondering what kind of burden he was carrying. But the sight of Barney's lurching exercise rides seemed a small price to pay for the skilled work he provided: repairing fences, servicing stock waterers, pruning the orchard, and even doing some painting on the outbuildings. One day, as he rode Moon down the driveway, Barney said to Szabo, who had just pulled up, "By the time you get the sling off, I'll have your horse safe for you to ride." From the window of his car, Szabo said, resisting the impulse to raise his voice, "As I recall, he's been safe for me to ride since he was a three-year-old colt." Barney just looked down and smiled.

When Barney restacked the woodpile, Szabo decided to treat it as an absolute surprise. He stood before the remarkable lattice of firewood and, while his mind wandered, praised it lavishly. He was reluctant to admit to himself that he was trying to get on Barney's good side. "It's one of a kind," he said.

Szabo's mother lived in a ground-floor apartment across the street from a pleasant assisted-living facility. She had stayed in her own apartment because she smoked cigarettes, which was also what seemed to have preserved her vitality over her many years. Further, she didn't want to risk the family silver in an institution, or her real treasure: a painting that had come down through her family for nearly a century, a night stampede by the cowboy artist Charlie Russell, one of very few Russell night pictures in existence, which would likely fetch a couple of million dollars at auction. The old people across the street would just take it down and spill food on it, she said. When Szabo was growing up as an only child, his mother's strong opinions, her decisive nature, had made him feel oppressed; now those qualities were what he most liked, even loved, about her. He recognized that when he was irresolute it was in response to his upbringing, but caution, in general, paid off for him.

Barney enjoyed tobacco, too, smoke and smokeless. One afternoon, Szabo sent a shoebox of pictures and two much-annotated family cookbooks to his mother by way of Barney, who was heading into town to pick up a fuel filter for the tractor. Later, Szabo cried out more than once, "I have only myself to blame!"

In a matter of weeks, Szabo was able to discard the sling and to exercise his shoulder with light weights and elastic strips that he held with one foot while feebly pulling and releasing, sweat pouring down his face. The next morning, three bird-watchers entered the property without stopping at the house for permission and were all but assaulted by Barney, who chased them to their car, hurling vulgar epithets until they disappeared down the road with their life lists and binoculars.

"But, Barney, I don't mind them coming around," Szabo said.

"Did they have permission, yes or no?"

There was no time for Szabo to explain that this didn't matter to him, as Barney had gone back to work. At what, Szabo was unsure, but he seemed busy.

Szabo had to be in Denver by the afternoon. He took an overnight bag and drove to town, past Barney, lurching from side to side on Moon, who bore, Szabo thought, a fresh look of resignation. He stopped on the way to the airport to see his mother, who sat in her living room doing sudoku in front of a muted television, a cigarette hanging out of the corner of her mouth. On a stand next to her chair, her cockatiel, Toni, hunched in the drifting smoke.

"I'm off to Denver till tomorrow, Ma. I'll have my cell if you need anything." She looked up, put down her stub of pencil, and moved the cigarette from her mouth to the ashtray.

"Nothing to worry about here. I've got a million things to do."

"Well, in case you think of something while I'm—"

"Lunch with Barney, maybe drive around."

"Okay!" Luckily his mother couldn't see his face.

Melinda had things well in hand, had even reduced some of the piles on his desk by thoughtful intervention where his specific attention was less than necessary. She was a vigorous mother of four, barely forty years old, happily married to a highway patrolman she'd grown up with. They were unironic enthusiasts for all the mass pleasures the culture offered: television, NASCAR, cruises, Disney World, sports, celebrity gossip, and local politics. Szabo often wished that he could be as well adjusted as Melinda's family, but he would have had to be medicated to pursue her list of pleasures. And yet she was not just an employee but a cherished friend.

It was a tested friendship with a peculiar intimacy: Szabo's former wife, Karen, an accomplished ironist, had made several stays at the Rimrock Foundation for what ended up as a successful treatment for alcoholism—successful in that she had given up alcohol altogether. Unfortunately, she had replaced it with other compulsions, including an online-trading habit that had bankrupted Szabo for a time. Once it was clear that Szabo was broke, she had divorced him, sold the house, remarried, and moved to San Diego, where she was, by the reports of their grown son, David, happy and not at all compulsive. What does this say about me? Szabo wondered obsessively. Maybe she was now on a short leash. Szabo had met her husband, Cliff: stocky, bald, and authoritarian—a forensic accountant, busy and prosperous in the SoCal free-for-all. His dour affect seemed to subdue Karen. In any case, Szabo had loved her, hadn't wanted a divorce, and had felt disgraced at undergoing bankruptcy in a town of this size. He'd sunk into depression and discovered that there was no other illness so brutal, so profound, so inescapable, that made an enemy of consciousness itself. Nevertheless, he had plodded to the office, day after day, an alarming, ashen figure, and there he had fallen into the hands of Melinda, who dragged him to family picnics and to the dentist, forged his signature whenever necessary, placed him between her and her husband at high-school basketball games as though he might otherwise tip over, taught him to cheer for her children, and occasionally fed him at her house in the uproar of family life. When, once, as she stood by his desk in the office, he raised a hand to her breast, she amiably removed it and redirected his attention to his work. By inches, she had restored his old self, and solvency seemed to follow. He began to see himself as someone who had returned from the brink. He liked making money. He liked visiting his little group of suppliers in faraway places. He liked having Melinda as a friend, and her husband, Mike, the highway patrolman, too. Mike was the same straight-ahead type as his wife: he once gave Szabo a well-deserved speeding ticket. Now Szabo's only argument with his ex-wife's contentment in San Diego was that it seemed to prove to David that it had been Szabo who drove her crazy.

As Szabo headed away from the Denver airport, he could see its marvelous shape at the edge of the prairie, like a great nomads' camp—a gathering of the tents of chieftains, more expressive of a world on the move than anything Szabo had ever seen. You flew into one of these tents, got food, a car, something to read, then headed out on your own smaller journey to the rapture of traffic, a rented room with a TV and a "continental" breakfast. It was an ectoplasmic world of circulating souls.

On a sunny day, with satellite radio and an efficient midsize Korean sedan, the two-hour drive to the prison that had held his son for the past couple of years flew by. Szabo was able to think about his projects for the ranch—a new snow fence for the driveway, a mouseproof tin liner for Moon's grain bin, a rain gauge that wouldn't freeze and crack, a bird feeder that excluded grackles and jays—nearly the whole trip. But toward the end of the drive his head filled with the disquieting static of remorse, self-blame, and sadness, and a short-lived defiant absolution. In the years that had turned out to be critical for David, all he had given him was a failing marriage and a bankrupt home. I should have just shot Karen and done the time, Szabo thought with a shameful laugh. The comic relief was brief. Mom in California, Dad in Montana, David in prison in Colorado: could they have foreseen this dispersion?

Razor wire guaranteed the sobriety of any visitor. The vehicles in the visitors' parking lot said plenty about the socioeconomics of the families of the imprisoned: Szabo's shiny Korean rental stuck out like a sore thumb. The prison was a tidy fortress of unambiguous shapes that argued less with the prairie surrounding them than with the chipper homes of the nearby subdivision. It had none of the lighthearted mundane details of the latter—laundry hanging out in the sun, adolescents gazing under the hood of an old car, a girl sitting on the sidewalk with a handful of colored chalk. The place for your car, the place for your feet, the door that complied at the sight of you, were all profoundly devoid of grace—at least, to anyone whose child was confined there.

David came into the visiting room with a promising, small smile and gave Szabo a hug. He had been a slight, quick-moving boy, but prison had given him muscle, thick, useless muscle that seemed to impair his agility and felt strange to the father who embraced him. They sat in plastic chairs. Szabo noticed that the room, which was painted an incongruous robin's-egg blue, had a drain in the middle of its floor, a disquieting fact.

"Are you getting along all right, David?"

"Given that I don't belong here, sure."

"I was hoping to hear from you—" Szabo caught himself, determined not to suggest any sort of grievance. David smiled.

"I got your letters."

"Good." Szabo nodded agreeably. There was nothing to look at in the room except the person you were speaking to.

"How's Grandma?" David asked.

"I think she's doing as well as can be expected. You might drop her a note."

"Oh, right. 'Dear Grandma, you're sure lucky to be growing old at home instead of in a federal prison.'"

Szabo had had enough.

"Good, David, tell her that. Old as she is, she never got locked up."

David looked at his father, surprised, and softened his own voice. "You said in your letter you'd had some health problem."

"My shoulder. I had surgery."

Szabo knew that the David before him was not the David on drugs, but, now that the drugs were gone, he still hadn't gone back to being the boy he'd been before. Maybe it would happen gradually. Or perhaps Szabo was harboring yet another fruitless hope.

"Melinda still working for you?"

"I couldn't do without her. She stayed with me even when I couldn't pay her."

"Melinda's hot."

"She's attractive."

"No, Dad, Melinda's hot."

Szabo didn't know what David meant by this, if anything, and he didn't want to know. Maybe David just wanted him to realize that he noticed such things.

"David, you've got less than a year to go. Concentrate on avoiding even the appearance of anything that could set you back. You'll be home soon."

"Home?"

"Absolutely. Where your friends are, where you grew up. Home is where your mistakes can be seen in context. You go anywhere else—David, you go anywhere else and you're an ex-con. You'll have to spend all your time overcoming that, when everyone at home already knows you're a great kid."

"When I get out of here," David said in measured tones, "I'm going to live with Mom and Cliff."

"In California?"

"Last time I checked."

Szabo was determined not to react to this. He let the moment subside, and David now seemed to want to warm up. He smiled faintly at the blue ceiling.

"And, yes, I'll write Grandma back."

"So you heard from her?"

David laughed. "About her boyfriend, Barney. I think that's so sweet. A relationship! Is Barney her age?"

"Actually, he's quite a bit younger."

As Szabo drove back to the airport, he tried to concentrate on the outlandish news of Barney's role in his mother's life, but he didn't get anywhere. He couldn't stop thinking about David, and thought of him in terms of a proverb he had once heard from a Mexican man who had worked for him: "You have only one mother. Your father could be any son of a bitch in the world." That's me! I'm any son of a bitch in the world.

He did have a mother, however, there in God's waiting room with a new companion. His late father, a hardworking trades-man, would have given Barney a wood shampoo with a rake handle. But my standing, thanks to my modest prosperity and education, means that I shall have to humor Barney, and no doubt my most earnest cautions about the forty-year age gap between Barney and my mother will be flung back in my face, Szabo thought. Suddenly tears burned in his eyes: he was back to David.

Drugs had swept through their small town one year. They'd always been around, but that year they were everywhere, and they had destroyed David's generation. The most ordinary chil-dren had become violent, larcenous, pregnant, sick, lost, or dead. And then the plague had subsided. David, an excellent stu-dent, had injected the drugs between his toes, and his parents had suspected only that he suddenly disliked them. Instead of going to college, he had apprenticed with a chef for nearly a year, before heading to prison. David didn't think that he would go back to drugs when he was released, and neither did his father. But his bitterness seemed to be here to stay, fed, likely, by his memory of the things that he had done in his days of using. Per-haps he blamed himself for the failure of his parents' marriage. The body he had acquired in the weight room seemed to suit his current burdened personality. The way he looked, he could hardly go back to what he had been.

The tractor was wet and gleaming in the bright sunlight. Barney was gathering stray bits of baler twine and rolling them up into a neat ball. He hardly seemed to notice Szabo's arrival, so Szabo carried his suitcase into the house without a word. Once inside, he glanced furtively through the hall window at Barney, then went back out.

"Good morning, Barney."

"Hi."

"This shoulder thing is behind me now. I think I'm ready to go back to work here." Barney looked more quizzical than the situation called for. "So let's square up and call it a day."

"Meaning what?" Barney asked with an extravagantly inquisitive look.

"Meaning the job is over. Thank you very much. You've been a great help when I needed it most."

"Oh?"

"Yes, I think so. I'm quite sure of it."

"It's your call, Szabo. But there's something about me you don't know."

"I'm sure that's the case. That's nearly always the case, isn't it, Barney?"

Some ghastly revelation was at hand, and Szabo knew that there would be no stopping it. "But I'd be happy to know what it is, in your instance."

Barney gazed at him a long time before he spoke. He said, "I am a respectable person."

Szabo found this unsettling. Clearly, it was time to have a word with his mother. He asked her out to lunch, but she begged off, citing the new smoking rules that, she said disdainfully, were "sweeping the nation." So he took her to the park near the river. Her size had been reduced by tobacco and her deplorable eating habits. She scurried along briskly, and any pause on Szabo's part found her well ahead, poking into garden beds and uprooting the occasional weed to set an example. They found a bench and sat. Mrs. Szabo shook out a cigarette by tapping the pack against the back of her opposing hand, then raising the whole pack, with its skillfully protruded single butt, to her lips. There the cigarette hung, unlit, while she made several comments about the weather and dropped the pack back into her purse. Finally, she lit it, and the first puff seemed to satisfy her profoundly.

"How did you find David?"

"Fine, I think. The way I get to see him down there . . . it's uncomfortable. Just a big empty room."

"Is he still angry?"

"Not that I could see."

"He was such an angry little boy."

"Well, he's not little anymore, Mom. He's got big muscles."

"Let's hope he doesn't misuse them. He got that attitude from your wife. The nicest thing I can say about her is that she kept on going."

"She married a decent, successful guy."

"What else could she do? She didn't have the guts to rob a bank."

"You forget what David was like before his problems. He didn't have an attitude. He was a nice boy."

He could see she wasn't listening.

"Barney said you told him he was no longer needed."

"He knew it was temporary from the start."

"Well, he's certainly got my place pulled together. My God, what a neatnik! And he made me insure the Russell, which I should have done a long time ago. He thinks that David's in this pickle because he got away with murder while he was growing up."

"What? He's never met David!"

"Barney's a very bright individual. He doesn't have to know every last thing firsthand."

"I think his views on how Karen and I raised David would be enhanced by actually meeting David."

"Why?"

"Jesus Christ, Mom."

"Of course you're grumpy. Barney does so much for me, and you want me all to yourself. Can't you just relax?"

Telling people to relax is not as aggressive as shooting them, but it's up there. The first time Barney had driven the tractor, he'd nearly put it in the irrigation ditch. Szabo had cautioned him, and Barney had responded, "Is the tractor in the ditch?" Szabo had allowed that it was not. "Then relax," Barney had said.

There was nothing like it: leaning on his shovel next to the racing water, the last sun falling on gentle hills crowned with bluestem and golden buffalo grass, cool air rising from the river bottom. Moon grazed and followed Szabo as he placed his dams and sent a thin sheet of alpine water across the hay crop. The first cutting had been baled and put neatly in the stack yard by Barney. The second cutting grew slowly, was denser in protein and more sought after by owners trying to make their horses run faster. All the way down through this minor economic chain, people lost money, their marvelous dreams disconnected from hopes of success.

Once winter was in the air, Szabo spent less time on his property and made an effort to do the things for his business that he was most reluctant to do. In November, he flew to Düsseldorf and stayed at the Excelsior, eating *Düsseldorfer Senfrostbraten* with Herr Schlegel while pricing robotic plasma welding on the small titanium objects that he was buying from him. The apparent murkiness of Germany was doubtless no more than a symptom of Szabo's ignorance of the language. He wondered if all the elders he saw window-shopping on the boulevards were ex-Nazis. And the skinheads at the Düsseldorf railroad station gave him a sense of historical alarm. After a long evening in the Altstadt, Szabo found himself quite drunk at the bar of the Hotel Lindenhof, where he took a room with a beautiful Afro-Czech girl, called Amai, who used him as a comic, inebriated English instructor, her usual services being unnecessary, given his incapacity. Since Szabo appeared unable to navigate his way back to the Excelsior, Amai drove him there in return for the promise of a late breakfast in the Excelsior's beautiful dining room. Afterward, she asked for his address so that they could stay in touch once he was home.

From Germany, Szabo flew directly to Denver. He slept most of the way and awoke to anxiety at the idea that this was probably the last visit he would have before David was released. In the chaotic year that preceded his son's confinement, he had never known what David was doing or to what extent he was in danger; in the last weeks of his marriage, he and Karen had admitted to feeling some relief, now that David was in jail, simply at knowing where he was. Perhaps it was that relief that had allowed them to separate. Yet Cliff's prompt appearance had aroused Szabo's suspicion: he sensed that California had beckoned while his marriage was still seemingly intact.

David was warmer toward his father this time but more fretful than he had been on the previous visit. Szabo understood that David was probably as afraid of his impending freedom as Szabo was on his behalf. He seemed, despite the muscles, small and frightened, his previous sarcasm no more than a wishful perimeter of defense. And the glow of anger was missing. Szabo wondered if jet lag was contributing to his heartache. He hardly knew what to say to his son.

"In two weeks, you'll be in California," Szabo said.

"That was the plan."

"Is it not anymore?"

"Mom and Cliff said they didn't want me. I've got to go to Plan B."

"I'm sorry, David. What's Plan B?"

"Plan B is I don't know what Plan B is."

"What made your mom and Cliff change their minds?"

David smiled slightly. He said, "I'm trying to remember how Mom put it. She said that a new relationship requires so many adjustments that introducing a new element could be destabilizing. It was sort of abstract. She left it to me to figure out that I was the destabilizing new element. Then Cliff got on the phone and said that unfortunately closure called for the patience of all parties."

"Did you say anything?"

"Yes, Dad, I did. I told Cliff to blow it out his ass."

Szabo could have taken this as evidence of David's unresolved anger. Instead, he enjoyed the feeling that they were in cahoots. "How did Cliff take that?"

"He said he was sorry I felt that way. I told him not to be. I told him I didn't feel anything at all."

They were quiet for long enough to suggest the inkling of comfort. Finally, David said, "Tell me about Barney."

"Barney! What about him?"

"Why did you send him here to see me?"

Startling as this was, Szabo did not react at first. He was quiet for a long and awkward moment. Then he asked quite levelly, "When did Barney show up?"

"While you were still in wherever. He said you sent him."

"Not exactly. Perhaps, based on our conversations, Barney thought it might be something I wanted him to do."

Szabo had no idea why he was dissembling like this, unless it was to buy time.

He suddenly recalled, from David's childhood, the purple dinosaur toy called Barney that was guaranteed to empower the child, a multimillion-dollar brainstorm for cashing in on stupid parents. "Did he explain what he was doing here? How did he get here?"

"He came in your car."

"Of course. Well, that was cheaper than flying. What was the purpose of his trip?"

"Are you asking me?"

"David, cut me some slack. I've been halfway around the world."

"Did you sleep in those clothes, Dad?"

Now Szabo was on the defensive, still in the clothes of his Düsseldorf night with Amai, whom, in this moment of bewilderment, he was certain he should have married. Escape was not so easy. If he hadn't fallen off a tractor and injured himself, this squirrel Barney wouldn't be in the middle of his life. What would he be doing? Living in Germany with Amai, siring octoroons and trying to keep her out of the bars? "I'm afraid I underpacked, David. I wore this suit at meetings and slept in it on the plane. So, Barney was here . . . for what?"

"I guess for counseling of some kind, to prepare me for the outside world."

David winced at these last two words.

"Why would Barney think he was in a position to counsel you?"

"If you don't know, Dad, I'm sure I don't, either. At least he has a Ph.D."

"Is that what he told you?"

"Dad, I'm not following this! I didn't send him here—you did!"

"I know, I know, and I'm sure it's all to the good. Was Barney helpful?"

"You tell me. He said I should go home and take over the ranch."

"It's hardly a ranch, David. It's just some property. What made him think you should do that?"

"Nothing you need to hear."

"What do you mean by that? I want to hear what some jackass with a Ph.D. had to say."

"You won't like it."

"David, I'm a big boy. Tell me."

"He said that you're incompetent and that it's only a matter of time before you break your neck doing something you have no business doing."

Furious, Szabo took this in with a false thoughtful air. Karen had said almost exactly the same thing. But her words had been motivated by a wish to replace the property with a winter home in San Luis Obispo, a town that had ranked number 1 in a *Times* survey of residential contentment.

"I trust you told Dr. Barney Q. Shitheel that you were not interested."

"I didn't tell him that, Dad."

"What did you tell him?"

David smiled at his father. "I told him I wasn't welcome there."

"You could have come there anytime you wanted."

"Right."

"What's this? Dave, why are you crying?"

David wiped his eyes with the back of his hand and spoke with odd detachment. "I knew I would never understand business, but I worked on a lot of ranches in high school. I was good at that."

Not all the fight was gone out of Szabo. Nor had he given up on the story he'd been telling himself. But even as he asked his derisive question he was reminding himself how he might have been absent for his own child. "Did you think selling drugs was a way of learning business?"

David looked weary. He didn't want to play anymore. "You're right, Dad. What was I thinking?"

"I'm not saying I'm right."

"No, Dad, you're one hundred percent right."

"Well," he said, "I'm right some of the time."

This exchange, more than anything, troubled Szabo. Here was David, broken down, imprisoned, soon to be released with his stigma. And Szabo was only adding to his insecurity, instead of trying to make the situation better.

There was plenty to do when he got home. And there was something to learn when he visited his mother: Barney had absconded with the Charlie Russell painting. The next morning, Szabo met the detective who was interviewing his mother while fanning away the smoke with his clipboard. She only glanced at Szabo, crestfallen, defeated. From the detective, a handsome fellow in a short-sleeved shirt, too young for his mustache, Szabo learned that his ranch hand's name wasn't Barney; it was Ronny—Ronny Something. Ronny's gift was for slipping into a community with one of his many small talents: the sculptural woodpile had taken him far. The painting would go to a private collector, not likely to be seen again. "This isn't Ronny's first rodeo," the detective said. "The only thread we've got is the Ph.D. There is no actual Ph.D., but it's the one thing Ronny drops every time. There's been a string of thefts, and they all lead into the same black hole. I don't know why everyone is so sure that Ronny wants to help them."

When Szabo repeated this to Melinda and saw her wide eyes, he just shrugged and shook his head. Maybe to change the subject, she asked after David, and Szabo told her that he would soon be coming home.

Stars

Only the very treetops caught the first light as Jessica started up Cascade Creek, a sparkling crevice in a vast bed of spruce needles. As she walked, the light descended the trunks and ignited balsamic forest odors, awakening the birds and making it easy to find stepping-stones to cross the narrow creek. She'd found this trail on a Forest Service map; the contour lines had suggested a climb she could manage, and by scrutinizing images on Google Earth she had seen the small watershed open into what looked like a meadow or a strip of saturated ground. Jays were foraging in the hawthorns and, as day emerged, the hurrying clouds signaled fast-changing weather. Jessica's pack held a spare down vest, a windbreaker, and an apple.

She came to a spot where the creek fell through a tangle of evergreen roots to form a plunge pool. Sitting for a moment, she followed the movement of bubbles into its crystalline depths, lost in her thoughts, free of history. Time was not the same dimension here that it was in the rest of her life, and floating like this was something to be savored. The bubbles in the plunge pool reminded her of the stars she had fallen in love with so long ago, years before she became an astronomer and began to spend her days analyzing solar data from the *Yohkoh* satellite or the

RHESSI spectroscopic imager. The stars were no longer a mystery to her; these bubbles would have to do.

After the plunge pool, the trail became steeper, and it pleased Jessica to feel her attention shift to her aching calves. She surprised a hawk on a low branch, not a soaring hawk but one that flashed through trees and seemed to take her with it. As she followed its search for an opening wide enough to ascend through, she saw a bright, grassy area ahead, a gap of light in the evergreens. She would explore there, then retrace her steps down the creek.

Once she'd reached the edge of the meadow, she stopped, unable at first to understand what she was seeing: two figures, proximate and mutually wary, one circling the other. Without moving, she grasped that a man, pistol dangling from one hand, was contemplating a wolf he had trapped; and the wolf, its foreleg secured in the jaws of a trap, was watching the man as he looked for a shot. Then the wolf turned and faced the forest in what seemed a despairing gesture. Jessica began to shout, running toward the man. She called, "You're not going to do that!"

The man turned, startled. "I sure am," he said gently. He was of an indeterminate age, tall and bareheaded in a canvas coat. His lace-up boots had undershot heels. A hat lay on the ground by his foot; his face was slick with sweat. "If this isn't something you'd like to watch, you might just want to be elsewhere."

Jessica was taken aback by his soft voice and by his peculiar tidiness. She noticed a mule tied in the trees, plywood panniers lashed to its ribs. Looking back at the terrified wolf, which was trying now to fling itself away from the trap, she heard herself say, "I'd rather shoot you than that animal."

"Oh? I don't think you know how hard it is to pull a trigger," the man said. "You have to feel pretty strongly about anything you kill. My old man used to tell me that you have to kill something every day, even if it's a fly."

He handed her the gun, and Jessica took it readily, surprised at how warm it was in her hand. She had a sense that some kind of power might shift to her, if she knew what to do with it.

"You obviously don't read the papers," she said. "People aren't having any trouble pulling the trigger these days."

"I'll take it back now, thank you," the man said patiently. "I need to go about my business, and it doesn't look to me like you feel any big need to save this animal." The wolf was on its belly now, staring at the trees, its trapped leg drawn out taut in front of it.

"I'm going to shoot you," Jessica said.

She could almost see these words go out of her mouth.

"You think you're going to shoot me."

"I know I am."

"Just wait until you try to turn him loose. That wolf isn't going to be very nice to you."

When the man seized the barrel of the gun, she felt as if she might fall, but she let him pull it away. Later, she felt that she hadn't struggled hard enough. "You need to picture this thing a little better," the man explained in his thoughtful voice. "I'm going to make a rug for my cabin out of his hide. I'm going to make jewelry out of his teeth and claws. I'm going to sell them on eBay."

Jessica started to laugh miserably, and by the time the laughter got away from her the man had joined in, as though it were funny. The wolf was watching them, up on its haunches now. The man wiped his eyes. "Honest to gosh," he said. "Where would we be without laughter?"

Maybe the laughter was an opening. Jessica tried to explain to the man that the wolf stood for everything she cared about, everything wild. But he laughed and said, "Honey, can't you hear those chain saws coming?" Her confession had gotten her nowhere.

The wolf made no attempt to escape as the man walked over and killed it.

It was the only place you could get coffee at that hour—sunrise had barely lit the front of the building—and the customers were already lined up right to the door. The young woman at the cash register, too sleepy to interact with anyone, made change mechanically, while her colleague, a young man in a woolen skullcap, seemed to hang from the levers as he waited for the coffee to pour. Jessica kept her hands in the sleeves of her sweater as she awaited her turn behind four people staring absently at their phones. Once she had the coffee, she put a second paper cup around it, went out into the morning, and felt a minor wave of optimism, ascribable to either caffeine or the sunrise.

Customers emerging from the shop were quickly absorbed by the town. As Jessica walked to Cooper Park to watch the morning dogs, the sunlight caught her, and she blew silver steam from her mouth. She had still been able to see a few stars when she left home, but they were gone now. The diehard dog people were already at the park, with others trickling in from the old houses around the neighborhood. This was the world of the cherished mongrel—rescue dogs, shelter dogs, strays that had dodged euthanasia: a part border collie that made an exuberant entrance, then spun away from any dog that wanted to play, a dignified Labrador with its nose elevated, a greyhound missing a tail, a terrier that kept getting overrun by the others only to bounce up again in furious pursuit. They all froze in tableau at the call of a crow, a distant siren, or the arrival of another dog. The owners sat at the perimeter watching, as if at the theater. It occurred to Jessica that she might have been happier as a dog. Then again, she didn't play well with others.

She had always had the stride of a country girl and felt that she had to cut through people to get anywhere. She walked at such a clip that someone asked, "Where's the fire?" On her way to the university, she bumped into an unyielding clutch of trustafarians, gathered for the day's recreation in front of Poor Richard's and one called her a douche cannon. A woman swiped at her from behind with an umbrella. She stopped only to pet dogs or to sideslip between children. In a clear stretch, she tended to run. She seemed to be clashing with everything.

Walking was how she'd met Andy Clark, on the trail along Bozeman Creek. Later, it occurred to her that it was odd for someone to hike the way he did, with his hands in his pockets. Andy was thirty years old, looked about twenty, and was in no hurry. No hurry was Andy all over. He was good-natured and full of ideas, but Jessica suspected that there was something behind that—not concealed, necessarily, but hard to know, and possibly not all that interesting. Still, Andy's boyish momentum and playfully forceful suggestions had made him good company at a time when she needed cheering up; and for a while, at least, he hadn't gotten on her nerves. It was eventually reported to Jessica that, during the production of an independent film in the city the previous summer, Andy had hung around the actresses so much that he was referred to locally as "the sex Sherpa to the stars." When Jessica brought this up, she was exasperated to see that it pleased him.

It was unclear whether Andy had a job, though he did have an office with a daybed for what he called "nooners." Jessica didn't learn this appalling term until she'd already experienced it, stumbling absently onto the daybed with him. Her previous affairs had been grueling, and she had promised herself not to do grueling ever again. She saw Andy, initially, as a kind of homeopathic remedy. But then something got under her skin. Maybe it was the karaoke machine in his bachelor apartment or his unpleasant cat or the Ping-Pong matches he pressured her into; the way he darted around in a crouch at his end of the table made it clear to her that she'd never sleep with him again.

This was something of a pattern with Jessica. Whatever interest she may have had or whatever not particularly spiritual need she felt impelled to satisfy was soon drowned by a tide of little things she would have preferred not to notice. By the time she encountered the wolf, she was sick of Andy. And that would have been that, if he hadn't continued to pursue her and if she hadn't had some creeping sadness to escape.

A few days after her hike to Cascade Creek, Andy invited Jessica to dinner at his father's house, on a ridge high above the M north of the city. She went reluctantly. On the winding road there, a white-tailed buck trotted in front of the car, wearing its horns like a death sentence. Andy led Jessica with a slight pressure on her elbow through the front door to his waiting father, who seemed to have positioned himself well back from the door he'd just answered.

"Dad, please meet Jessica Ramirez," he said. And, in a get-a-load-of-this tone, "She's an astronomer."

Mr. Clark was a tall, thin, sallow widower in an oversize cardigan, whose pockets had been stretched by his habit of plunging his fists into them. His upper lip seemed permanently drawn down, as if he were shaving under his nose. He led them to the living room in a house that appeared to be all windows. The mountains were just visible in the last of the sunset. Mr. Clark didn't look back or speak a word in their direction, confident that they were following appropriately.

In the living room, which had an adjoining bar, Mr. Clark made them drinks with a perfunctory "I hope that suits you." Jessica sniffed hers, and Andy's father aimed a hard, questioning beam at her. "Okay?"

Jessica said, "No top brands?"

My God, she thought, what is the matter with me?

Mr. Clark turned his querying look on his son, who glanced away, and by some unspoken accord the three headed over to the picture window. It was dark now, and only the lights of the city were visible. Jessica felt as if she were hovering among the constellations, and that lifted her spirits. The way that geologists are liberated in time, she thought, astronomers are freed by space. Mr. Clark touched her glass with his. He wore a piece of eight on a chain around his neck. "Well, stargazer, what's happening in the firmament today?"

"Nothing new," she said. "Some seasonal star clusters and nebulae. Are you interested?"

Mr. Clark said, "I'm afraid I miss out on all that. I'm a day guy or I'm in bed. Trout fishing is my thing. I have a collection of bamboo rods, by all the great makers. Would you like to see them?"

"No."

Mr. Clark turned abruptly and left the room. Andy gazed after him thoughtfully, before saying, "He's not coming back."

"Seriously? Because I didn't want to see his fishing poles?" Andy let a censorious silence fill the air. It worked. She briefly thought of ways to make amends, but it was too late now to pour love on the fishing poles.

Andy didn't speak as they made their way back down the winding road where they'd seen the deer. Finally, he asked, "What would you like me to do, Jessica?"

"Drop me off," she said.

Jessica's closest friend at the university was Dr. Tsieu, a fellow astronomer, barely five feet tall in generous shoes. When Dr. Tsieu's baby boy was born, Jessica was nearly the first to the maternity ward; Dr. Tsieu seemed too small to have accomplished such a thing. When Jessica got to her lab, Dr. Tsieu asked her out to lunch, but she said that she wanted to go for a walk, that she needed the exercise—which she did after a morning in front of her computer screen. But her walk up and down Olive Street and around the post office was so restless and agitated that it didn't provide relief from anything. Of course, she could not possibly have pulled the trigger. Why even go over it in her mind? Why? Why again? And what on earth had made her so sullen with Andy's father and his blasted fishing poles? She deliberated over this transgression as though it had the same importance as her failure to shoot that man. She wondered if she was just too inflexible. In time, would she become one more peevish old spinster in the hideous rest home behind the Walmart?

She drove to the mall and, without more of a plan than getting through the lunch hour, wandered into a shoe store. A lone customer stood at the display rack turning the shoes over, one after another, to look at their soles. Jessica recalled the proverb "Hell is a stylish shoe." A salesman greeted her at the door, a young man with a shaved head and a black turtleneck. Too intimate from the start, he held each selection so close to her face that she had to lean back to get a better look. She felt his breath as he pressed some studded, sparkly sneakers on her. Jessica found it fascinating that he thought she would want these, or the next pair he held up—stiletto-heeled jobs that seemed lewd, as did his smirk. The salesman didn't conceal his disappointment when she bought a pair of marked-down Vera Wang flats. She bought them because they seemed so pedestrian. Men preferred women teetering, so she chose to walk like a Neanderthal.

Traffic was thick on North Seventh, and she timed the lights wrong. Glancing at her watch, she failed to notice one turn green and heard a loud horn blast. In the mirror, she saw a cowgirl in a pickup truck giving her the finger. When she moved forward, the truck tailgated her, inches away. Jessica peered sharply into the rearview mirror, stabbed at the brakes, and the truck plowed into her. The two vehicles pulled to the side of the road.

The door of the truck burst open, and the cowgirl came wheeling toward Jessica's car. Jessica was on the phone calmly telling the secretary at her department the reason for her delay.

She rolled the window down slightly and addressed the raging cowgirl. "Let's wait for the police. Do you have insurance?"

The police arrived in a pageantry of flashing lights—a single officer, who got out and chatted familiarly with the cowgirl as she held her thick braid with both hands. Isn't it nice that they're friends? Jessica thought. There was no denying her malice, no matter how she tried to stand apart from it. Then the officer came over to Jessica's car, hardly needing to duck in order to peer into her window. "What'd you do that for?" he barked. Jessica contemplated her steering wheel. "You caused that accident by braking suddenly!"

"You know the law. She rear-ended me."

"Don't you lecture me, lady," he shouted.

Jessica gave him time to settle down before raising her eyes to his and asking, "What is this really about, Officer? Is it because you're short?"

The next day, Jessica was silent at the department meeting but asked Dr. Tsieu, the only other woman in their group, to stay afterward. Dr. Tsieu tilted her head, hands laced over her stomach, always keen to listen. Jessica said, "I'm going to take a leave."

"And?" Dr. Tsieu hardly seemed surprised.

"I'm losing my marbles."

"Anger or disgust?" Dr. Tsieu asked. "Despair, malaise, detachment, loss of purpose?"

She's trying to cheer me up, Jessica thought, complying with a grin that felt idiotic.

"It's à la carte."

There was an anger specialist right there in town, and Jessica arranged to see him, since anger was at least one component of what she was experiencing, and she was unaware of a therapist who specialized in disgust or any of the other things on Dr. Tsieu's list. A friendly giant, the therapist was dressed like an outdoorsman, in Pendleton items that were far too warm for his office. Jessica had never had counseling before and was startled to find the man so interactive. She made a summary of her concerns, and he mugged through every one of them. It seemed that he intended to cure her through his facial expressions. The prickly feeling of confinement she had in his office, the colorized photograph of his wife and children, the diplomas, the complimentary pharmaceutical notepad, and his gooberish attempts to forecast calm all convinced her that this wasn't going to work. At the end of the session, he asked her to see the receptionist, but she went sightless through the lobby.

She decided to stick to walking. If that didn't work, she would turn herself over to some program. There were now customized rehabilitation programs that combined therapy with kayaking, weight loss, and makeovers. It was part of her problem, she thought, that she could foresee a stream of self-evident lectures and desolating group sessions with people who knew why they were angry or disgusted, while her disappointment seemed to be rooted in humanity in general. In college, she had read Faulkner's Nobel Prize speech, in which he asserted that mankind would not only endure but prevail; these days, she thought that this was the most depressing thing she'd ever come across. She no longer had any idea why she had become an astronomer. Had she expected to live in space?

She walked day after day in the hills and mountains around town, in the Bridgers, the Bangtails, and the Tobacco Roots. It was autumn now, and the chokecherry thickets and hawthorn breaks were changing color. Sometimes she went with other hikers, but she rarely spoke to them. At night, she treated her blisters and planned the next day's walk. Once, she fell asleep with her shoes on, to the static of a radio station gone off the air. The phone messages piled up until her voice-mail box was full. Ho, ho, ho, she thought, this is a crisis. Before sunrise, she lay in bed staring at the window for the first signs of light. Andy's last message suggested that she go to hell. She saved that one, suspecting that she might already be there.

She ran into Dr. Tsieu at the food co-op and, feeling comradely, told her about the hikes. Dr. Tsieu smiled supportively and said, "I feel sorry for your shoes." By that time she was traveling to more-remote areas to walk, distant prairie hills and wilderness foothills. She got lost more than once and only just made it out of the hills, in flight from hypothermia. Her eyesight grew exceptionally sharp, and she could see ravens in the dark, the shadows of animals in brush, and the old footprints of her predecessors. In this state, her own hands seemed to glow, the stars fierce and the moon more than usually banal.

Jessica kept walking into winter. Twice, Andy tried to join her, jumping out of his little car at the trailhead, but the chill drove him back, shivering and waving her on in disgust. It was only a matter of time before she came to her senses, he told her the second time. He yelled something else, but he was too far away by then for her to hear.

In the gathering dark and the swirling snow, she began to

imagine voices and distantly wondered if she could still see the trail. She stopped to listen more closely, hoping to hear something new through the wind. A pure singing note rose, high and sustained, then another, in a kind of courtly diction.

Wolves.

Shaman

The Rileys lived on a small piece of land, the remains of a much-bigger property that had been diminished over the generations; but what was left was a lovely place: the two-story clapboard house, built in 1911 in an old grove of cottonwoods, was fed crystalline water by a hillside spring and graced by morning sun in the kitchen and a shelter belt of chokecherry and caragana. On the benches above the creek, the evening sun revealed old tepee rings from when the land had been Indian country. The doorstop at the front entrance was a stone hammer for cracking buffalo bones. Good hard coal from Roundup filled the shed, and on a painted iron flagpole the American flag popped in the west wind until it was in ribbons and had to be replaced. The house had a hidden fireplace vented by a center chimney, in which, during Prohibition, Pat Riley's grandfather had made whiskey, which he sold from the trunk of his Plymouth at country dances. He was thus able to reverse the contraction of the property, for the time being, which soon resumed under Pat's father, a small-time grain trader, usually described as "a fine fellow, never made a dime." The Plymouth remained, with two rusty bullet holes, the shots fired from the inside during a hijacking attempt, and was now embedded in an irrigation dam serving two neighbors, since the Rileys had lost the water rights. The property, Pat's birthright, was the Rileys' pride and joy. The point of all their work, however tedious, was to keep them on the place.

Pat was a physical therapist who made the rounds of the small hospitals and rest homes and clinics in southwest Montana. Pat loved his job, feeling that he helped people every day he worked, mostly with postoperative rehabilitation and the debilities of age. He found the residents at the rest homes especially interesting: old cowboys, state politicians, a veteran of the Women's Army Air Corps, and so on. His wife Juanita's job at the courthouse was tiresome: reconciling ledgers, posting journal entries for accruals and transfers, tracking grant revenues and expenditures, and filing, filing, filing! So it was that, on the occasion of Pat's overnight trip for a case in Lewistown, Juanita was ripe for the visit of the shaman. As a point of fact, she fancied him before even knowing he was a shaman. She just figured he was looking for a ranch job, but she never found a chance to tell him there hadn't been a cow on the place in forty years.

Juanita hardly knew what a shaman was and would have pictured someone on the Discovery Channel, feathered, painted, beaded, perhaps belled—certainly not someone dressed like this or presenting a calling card. His name was Rudy, and he seemed like an Olympian in his tracksuit and Nike shoes. He explained that he was an anthropologist and arid lands botanist, whose work had led him to discover a spiritual being living under a sandstone ledge on the Medicine Bow River, also named Rudy. It had taken seven years for the two Rudys to track each other down and become the united Rudy now standing before Juanita and touching a button of her blouse for emphasis. Juanita felt the heat rise. "I was out in the prairie. It was a hot day. All I could hear was wind and crickets or birds. Then the grass seemed to creak under my feet and I could feel the other Rudy was near and coming to me. The wind stopped as Rudy arrived. It was a lighthearted moment, Juanita. I said, 'Welcome aboard.' And that quick, I was unified. I was undivided, united as one, the one and only Rudy. But now there was . . . something else." He seemed disturbed by Juanita's hard, restless gaze. She let him follow her into the house, where she dug her phone out of her yellow, fringed purse hanging on the doorknob. She called her husband. "Pat, I've got a shaman here at the house. When are you coming home? You heard me. How on earth should I know? He says he's a shaman." She cupped the phone and said to the stranger, "What exactly is a shaman?"

"That's a long story. I—"

"He says it's a long story. Okay, sure, see you in a few."

She hung up. It would not be a few minutes, more like a day, before she saw Pat. But the ruse had an immediate effect on Rudy the shaman: panic.

"Does he mean literally 'a few minutes'?"

"Maybe five. He has to stop for cigarettes."

Rudy the shaman burst through the door at a dead run. Juanita watched him windmill down the driveway and out onto the county road, stooping to pick up some kind of pack at the corner. She grabbed the phone again.

"As soon as I told him you were about to arrive, he ran for it."

"Juanita, listen to me, you need to call the sheriff."

"And tell him what? I had a shaman at the house?"

"What does that even mean?"

"Pat! I don't know. I told you that."

"Well, call anyway and then call me back. Or I'll call them. No, better you, in case they need a description."

"Aren't you just assuming this guy is a criminal?"

"Maybe that's all a shaman is, for Chrissakes. Just call and then call me back."

At first, Juanita resisted making the call, then, realizing Pat wouldn't let it go, she picked up the phone. Sheriff Johnsrud was at a county commissioners' meeting, but she was put through to Eric Caldwell, his deputy.

"Hi, Juanita."

"Eric, some strange guy stopped by here. Said he was a—something or other. When I told him Pat was due home, he ran out the door in kind of a panic."

"That doesn't sound good."

"I don't think it's a big deal, but Pat insisted I call."

"Pat has a point. Describe this guy, would you, Juanita? What'd you say he was?"

"I can't remember, but he was wearing kind of a tracksuit, good-looking guy, maybe thirty-five, odd but with nice manners and one of those big watches tells you how far you walked, wavy brown hair, and talked educated like."

"Whoa, Juanita, you did get a pretty good look!"

"That'll do, Eric."

"Okay, we'll check it out."

"Do me a favor, call Pat on his cell or he'll fret."

Afterward, Juanita had to piece the story together. Sheriff Johnsrud came back from the commissioners' meeting and joined Eric in scouring the area between the Riley place on the county road and the edge of town, down by the Catholic church and the ball field. They confronted Rudy just past the Lewis and

Clark Memorial. When he went for something in his backpack, Sheriff Johnsrud shot him. Looking at the body, Johnsrud said, "He's done. Stick a fork in him." Eric pushed the backpack open with his foot and said there was no gun. Neither spoke until Johnsrud mused that they should go get one, and Eric nodded. "That way," said the sheriff, "it's a senseless tragedy."

Rudy, a low-risk mental patient, had just walked out of the Warm Springs hospital. The backpack contained pebbles, a dead bird, and a book on teaching yourself to dance. There hadn't been a cloud in the sky for a week in Rudy's hometown on the Wyoming border. He could have walked there in half a day.

It had been too obvious that Rudy was harmless. The doctors at the Warm Springs hospital made such a huge point of it that the whole town was embarrassed. Dan Sheare at the Ford dealership said it was like they had shot the Easter Bunny, "Town Without Pity," and so forth. So Sheriff Johnsrud conceded the terrible misfortune and took full responsibility. After all, he had fired the shot. But eventually Johnsrud changed, or everyone thought he had, though some admitted they would've changed, too, if such a thing happened to them, or else they concluded they were only imagining the sheriff was any different than he had always been. Eric, however, who had been born right there in town, moved away. Eventually people quit asking where Eric had got off to, just assuming he had landed on his feet somewhere. Probably his sister still heard from him. She lived over where the first post office burned down giving her a great view of the mountains.

When, sitting under the Dos Equis beer umbrella, Pat joked that Eric had left law enforcement, Juanita startled herself by spitting in his face. Things had started to go wrong for them, though it didn't seem so at first and not really for a while afterward, because the Cancún trip had provided needed relief, especially for Juanita, who found she could still turn a few heads on the beach. "Oh God, we're not really going back to Montana," she said on the last day. Pat said, "I hate to think how much we'll miss these warm sea breezes," but that wasn't what she meant at all, at all, at all.

During a pensive moment in the airport, while waiting to board, Pat said, "Tell me honestly, Juanita, why did you spit in my face?"

"I admit I thought about it."

"Darling, you didn't think about it, you did it. You spit in my face."

"I did?"

Juanita found this very disturbing. She knew she'd thought about it but . . . really?

Winter went on well into April, and they both were working very hard, trying to become a "unit" again, but the word itself had lost its meaning. They had been one for so long they couldn't comprehend why it had become so hard. They couldn't understand what was happening to them in other ways, either. For example, Carol Hayes, the sheriff's dispatcher, who worked at the courthouse down the hall from Juanita and was just about her best friend, right out of the blue told Juanita to her face that she was a bitch on wheels. Juanita was astonished.

"What can you possibly mean!"

"Isn't it obvious, Juanita?"

Juanita shrank into the files and deeds of her musty corner and went off to lunch with her head down. She didn't want to dignify Carol's remark by asking further what it meant, and as a result it just hung over her like a cloud. She quit going to the window and staring in the direction of their house, almost visible beyond the poplars at the fairgrounds. Oddly, she became more efficient. The small annoyance she once felt at being confined to this room was gone. There was a kind of relief in feeling she belonged here, as though the fight had gone out of her. And what good had that been anyway? Now, when asked about her job, she said simply, "It's a living."

Pat's situation had become more precarious. While rehabilitating an old priest after rotator cuff surgery, he had been a bit zealous, causing a new tear. It was quickly repaired, but the surgeon appeared at physical therapy and rebuked Pat, who would remember the vehemence, if not the words particularly, and the fact that the surgeon, still in his scrubs, wore the most beautiful pair of oxblood loafers, slippers almost, with the thinnest of soles. Pat was so friendly with the staff that he was ashamed to have been scolded in front of them like a dog or a child. They couldn't look at him, either.

The exceptionally long winters—the drifted driveway, the circles of ice in the windows, the days that abruptly ended in afternoon—might have had something to do with it, but that same hard April they decided to put the place on the market. They made no secret of thinking it a case of good riddance and didn't mind letting the neighbors and their former friends know it. They put up a FOR SALE BY OWNER out front and awaited results.

At the courthouse, Juanita held up their deed for Carol the dispatcher to see. "This will have a new name on it for the first time in ninety years. It's only a matter of time."

"Where do you think you're headed?"

"I'll let you know."

Carol went back to her desk opposite the front stairs. There wasn't any point in talking to Juanita anymore. Pat used to be so much fun, too. Now he was a regular sad sack; so maybe Juanita came by this new disposition honestly. The truth was, they didn't know where they were headed, but since they had never before known liquidity, they were sure it would come with ideas they didn't yet have, ideas resembling hopeful points on the map. This confidence came and went, and there was little to be gained by mentioning the dread that seemed to seep out of nowhere.

Someone pulled up into the driveway in a brown four-door. It was the same shade of brown as Pat's grandfather's shot-up Plymouth rip-rapping the irrigation dam upstream. They watched from the edges of the front window, careful not to seem eager. The driver's door opened, and a pair of narrow legs in old farmer pants swung out, resting on the ground. The driver gingerly slid out and shut the door: a woman perhaps just entering old age and remarkably unkempt, the wild gray hair pinned off her forehead with a red plastic comb, her barn coat done about the waist with twine. Walking unsteadily, she stared hard toward the house; she did not have the look of a prospect.

Pat and Juanita opened the door before the woman could knock. She made no attempt at introducing herself. "Yes?" said Juanita, Pat at her side attempting, "How can we help you?"

"I'm not sure you can," she said distantly, looking from one to the other, and then just stopped. She had green eyes. Later, when Pat and Juanita remarked on them to each other, it seemed to start a conversation that went nowhere.

"What brings you here?" Pat asked like some sort of radio announcer too hearty for this small stalemate.

"A glass of cold water out of that spring behind the house."

"Why, most certainly! You know, it's piped right to the faucet. So why don't you come in. I'll bet you're thirsty."

"For some of that spring water."

"You shall have it!" said Pat in that same hale voice, causing Juanita to glance quickly at him.

"How did you know about the spring?" Juanita chirped.

"I was told about it."

They sat the woman down at the kitchen table made of cottonwood planks from the old stall barn. Pat had fitted the planks together with perfect joints when they were first married. This encumbrance they also intended to leave behind, because, as Juanita said, "It weighs a ton." Pat felt they could have taken it but didn't want to argue.

Juanita went to the sink and filled her tallest glass, and as she started to turn toward the refrigerator, the woman said, "No ice," so Juanita turned back and set the glass of water before her. The woman nodded thanks. Pat sat at the far end tilting back his chair, hands behind his head in a pantomime of nonchalance.

The woman drained the glass and held it to eye level as though to look through it. Staring thus, she said, "I'm Rudy's mother, the dead boy."

Pat pulled his chair upright and set his hands close to him on the table. Juanita grinned with pain. "I'm so sorry."

Pat said, "We're both so sorry."

"Oh?"

After a long silence, Juanita asked, "Is there anything we can do?"

"Sure," she said, fishing a cigarette out of her coat and lighting it with a beat-up old Zippo. Pat and Juanita refrained from mentioning how much they hated smoking. The woman held the cigarette between her second and third fingers, as if in the middle of her hand. "You can tell me about his last day here."

"I can do that," said Juanita, getting braver. "He—Rudy— really just turned up and immediately started talking about his life like I had known him before."

"You had known him before?"

"No, I don't think so."

"Okay."

"Oh yes, and then, uh, we were just chatting in general, well, really it was quite brief, and he told me he—"

"He gave you some reason to call the law?"

"Well, ma'am, I have to be honest, he kind of frightened me the way he, the way he was talking." Juanita was startled to hear her own voice rise so quickly.

The woman took the cigarette from her mouth but kept it in her hand in front of her face. "That wasn't no lie. Rudy was a shaman."

"We don't even know what that is!" cried Pat.

The woman got up and dropped the cigarette hissing into the nearly empty water glass. "I just feel like you made a big mistake, but I guess time will tell if it hasn't already."

At the door they assured her they felt just as bad as she did. She shook her head slightly; she seemed to wonder at them. "I wouldn't have done that," she said. "I'd of had more sense."

They watched her go to her car. They expected her to say something or glance back, but no. In the house, when Juanita said she had eyes like a cat, Pat didn't seem to pick up on it, remarking instead that she must have been a great beauty in her day. He left the room, and Juanita emptied the cigarette butt into the sink before going to the window. The car was already gone.

Canyon Ferry

John's wife hadn't remarried, but she was in a stable relationship with a reliable man, while John, laid off from the newspaper a year by then, was living alone in a way to suggest he always would—all of which made visitations a study in contrasts for their son, Ethan. John could have found another newspaper job—downsizing had only marginally trumped his proficiency—but it would have meant moving away, in preference to which he stayed in town and taught welding, his former hobby, to nontraditional students at the college. And two days a week, he met with the former host of a TV "blooper" show, helping him write his memoirs, an entirely lugubrious tale of imagined suffering. The ex-host was determined for posterity to know that belying those forty years of guffawing at the pratfalls of others, he had known real anguish and been misunderstood from the day he was born in the back of a taxi, his first recollection the foldout ashtray on the back of the driver's seat.

It might have seemed that Linda and her Lucifer—actually his name was Lucius, only John called him that—would supply at least a semblance of family life, while John the bachelor, led by his tuning fork into the hungry thickets of the town, would struggle to make time for Ethan. In actuality, Linda and Lucius found their bliss as two purposeful suits, both on the way up. It made John feel that his marriage of almost ten years had served as Linda's think tank for an eventual assault on the future, an unkind and somewhat unwarranted version of facts, because she'd always said she wanted to work. She was pretty, and her life with John was meager, while Lucius was a rising star in banking, land, cattle, natural gas, and hydropower. John would learn only long after it mattered that the two had been exhausting their erotic urgency over four vigorous years of infidelity prior to the separation, which left John struggling to catch up in one sad purlieu after another, and feeling as a father nihilistic and unworthy. The three women he bedded during the proceedings were impossible to avoid, and when he ran into them, whether at the post office, the bank, or the Safeway, he just apologized. But each of these was a single unmarried woman and John was attractive, so they hardly knew how to take his contrition. If John had learned anything, it was that, once the threshold of venery was crossed, and all the furies unleashed, the aisles of the Safeway were no longer safe. A baffled if indignant former paramour in Cereals could loom with ominous incomprehension.

For the regular handoff, John appeared at Linda's new house with its wonderful view of the snowy massif of the Bridger ridge. The moment was rarely less than painful despite that it had gone on for more than a year. This time, Ethan was already dressed in a red snowsuit and an insulated hat slightly too big for him. Linda hugged herself against the cold. It was easier all around to meet her ex-husband on the front step than have him come inside. Ethan's arms hung at his sides, and he glanced at his mother several times; she responded by resting a hand on his head. Ethan peered out from beneath that shelter while John stared at Linda with hopeless longing.

"I'll have him back by supper." He didn't want to say he'd have him "home" by supper but should have known that the struggle with that terminology was long lost.

"Perfect. You guys will have fun. Right, Ethan?" Ethan nodded grimly. His mother laughed at his posturing. "He'll be fine once you get going." Reflexively she touched her lips with her forefinger, which she then touched to Ethan's, then to John's.

John led Ethan by the hand to the car. He turned to give Linda a wave, but she was already gone behind the door. It was too cold for ceremonial lingering, though Ethan, too, stared at the door before getting into John's car with a boost.

"Do you want to take off your snowsuit?"

"No."

"Do you want to unzip it?"

"No. I want to listen to the radio."

"Can we just talk a little bit?"

"Okay."

It was quiet before John, his voice thick with emotion, spoke. "Do you like doing stuff with me?"

"It's okay."

"Because today we're going fishing."

Ethan looked startled and scrutinized his father with interest. He said, "But everything is frozen." They were following a Brink's truck changing lanes without signaling.

"We're going ice fishing. You drill a hole in the ice and drop your line through."

"Are there fish under there?"

"We're going to find out."

Canyon Ferry Lake, an impoundment of the Missouri River, spread before them as a vast sheet of ice that ended at a seam of open water, perhaps the old river. John parked across the ice from Confederate Gulch at the "silos," the tall brick towers for storing grain. The Big Belt Mountains rose against a blue sky marbled with cirrus clouds streaming toward them from the Gate of the Mountains. Ethan, suddenly excited, ran around the car helping John with their gear. An iron spud for making a hole in the ice stuck out of the trunk. Ethan tried to carry it, but it was too heavy. John had spent a bewildering hour at Sportsman's Warehouse and come away with only the minimal kit but all that he could understand. He could have spent a fortune on a gas-powered ice auger, heated shelter, and underwater cameras attached to TV monitors, which, said the salesman, would set him up "good as the next guy." But John settled for a box of assorted hooks and jigs, the spud, and a skimmer to clear slush from the hole.

Ethan carried these things while John toted a coffee can of night crawlers, two plastic buckets to sit on, and the iron spud. They headed out onto the ice, and John was immediately struck by a complete lack of topographic clues as to where to spud a hole; the fish could be anywhere in such a featureless and white expanse.

One other human was visible, pulling a black plastic sled heaped with all the things that John had seen at the store. Holding Ethan's hand, John waited for him on the near shore ice. He stopped him to ask a few questions and show the man his gear.

"You got another tip-up?"

"Nope."

"You got just one?"

"Yes, that's right." He didn't want this guy giving Ethan the idea they weren't adequately equipped.

"Ooooohkay . . . ," said the fisherman, then suddenly, "Don't touch them fish, son." Ethan's hand recoiled from the man's bucket, and he looked at his father. "Why don't you go right there where I was at," the fisherman said. "I augured nine holes in a row. Counting from this side, hole number five was where most of the fish were. Put your tip-up there, but if I was you I wouldn't stay long. The wind comes up in about an hour, and it's a dad-gum typhoon. Black clouds come up past them hills right over there. When they do, you need to be long gone."

The fisherman continued on with his sled, his ice crampons allowing him a full and crunching stride, while John and Ethan slipped and skidded out onto the lake halfway to the thin black line of open water before they found the nine precise holes made by the fisherman's power auger. Together, they counted off until they reached number five, and there they set down their buckets and gear. The holes had already begun to fill in, but John had acquired that skimmer, with which he quickly scooped out the slush to reveal the surprisingly mysterious black surface of the deep water.

He put out a bucket for Ethan to sit on, round and red as an apple in his puffy snowsuit, while his father fiddled with the tip-up rig until he understood how to bend the springy wire with the tiny flag into its notch and lowered the line adorned with a sparkling green jig and baited with a twisting night crawler. It seemed he was unspooling line forever before he reached bottom. He spread the braces across the span of hole and arranged the wire and flag that would spring up when they had a bite.

Inverting his white bucket, he sat down opposite Ethan and waited with his hands stuffed up opposing sleeves.

"How long will this take?" asked Ethan.

"I wish I knew, Ethan."

"Is fishing always like this?"

"I guess you could say it's different every time."

Ethan thought for moment. "I wish fishing would hurry up."

"Are you warm enough in that thing?"

"It's boiling in here."

"How about your feet."

"They're boiling, too."

John, who could have used another layer of clothes himself, stood from time to time to bounce on the balls of his feet and clap his mittens together, at which sight Ethan nearly laughed himself off his pail. When John sat down again, he gazed around the shore, off toward the mountains; every now and then the light caught a car on the road to Helena, a quick flash, but otherwise the lake and its surroundings seemed completely desolate.

"What do you call Lucius?"

"I don't know."

You could call him Lucifer, thought John. Lucius, as John saw it, had tempted away his lively but somewhat flakey wife and turned her into a career woman fit to stand beside him at the Consumer Electronics Association. They hadn't come out as a couple for a whole week before she was talking about the glass ceiling. Lucius was fifteen years older than Linda, who, though contented with the relationship, had shown no interest in becoming his fourth wife, something Lucius expected to happen sooner or later, as indeed it did. Lucius would tell his friends that the wedding was to be small and intimate; he wouldn't be inviting them this time. They'd slap him on the back and offer to come to the next one. This, with Linda on his arm. She seemed to take it in stride. Her eyes had by now opened to a much-larger world, if weekly trips through airport security were a gateway to such a thing. She must have thought so, because in an unguarded moment after she'd remarried, she called John a bump on a log. He felt betrayed. He'd always thought he'd been doing fine right up until his paper was restructured. But greater than his hurt was his worry about what place there would be for Ethan in Linda's new life.

The small red flag popped up, and Ethan was so startled he tumbled from his pail. John was able to lift him to his feet by a handful of snowsuit at his back. He set the tip-up to one side and felt the tautness on the line slowly traveling from the spool. He gave the line to Ethan who grasped it in both hands and smiled in amazement to feel the life in it. At John's direction he pulled fist over fist, the loose line falling behind him until with a heave the fish flew out of the hole into the air then bounced around on the ice. John held the fish, a yellow perch, close to Ethan who stared at its keen eye. "Throw him back?"

"Yes, please, back in the hole," said Ethan. John unhooked the perch and slipped it back in. Ethan leaned close and peered into the blackness. "He's gone."

John reset the tip-up and noticed that Ethan was more concentrated on its operation now that he had seen it work. He asked a few questions after he thought about the fish and its friends and what there was to eat down there. Then he said his feet were cold.

"Mine, too. Let's jump up and down." The two hopped around the fishing hole, and then Ethan fell on his back laughing until

John picked him up by the front of his red one-piece like a suitcase. "Put your mittens on."

"Okay."

"And tell me if you get too cold."

"Uh-oh-kay."

"Are you cold now?"

"Okay."

"Ethan, be serious, are you cold?"

"No-kay. What is that?"

"What is what?"

"That black thing."

To the northwest, a storm cloud was climbing fast, dark and full of turbulence. John glanced at their fishing rig hoping the flag would pop up soon; he could see Ethan was eager for another fish. But then the wind was upon them, picking up with startling speed, sweeping shards of ice toward the seam of open water with an unremitting tinkle.

"Ethan, I think we should reel this thing up. This weather is—I don't know what this weather is doing."

John bent over the hole in the ice and was carefully spooling in the line, when he saw the little flag flutter in the corner of his eye. Just then a fish grabbed the bait and began pulling the line again. "Uh-oh, Ethan, we've got another one," he said as the wind rose to a screech. "I'm going to have to break it off. I hope that's okay—" No answer. "Okay, Ethan? Ethan, okay if we just let it go?"

John looked up and saw the boy forty feet away, tumbling like a leaf in the wind. He dropped the fishing line and stood, barely able to keep his own balance. Ice particles chimed in the air accompanying Ethan's jubilant laughter. John made for him, the wind pushing him forward, and each time Ethan got to his feet, crouching arms held apart for balance, he tumbled forward and skidded some more. John hurried but Ethan kept sliding faster. The black cloud roared like an engine overhead bringing a whirl of heavier snow that made Ethan harder to see as he slid yelling joyfully toward the open water. Trying to overtake him, John fell again and again, now with only the sound of laughter to guide him. He no longer knew where the water was, whether it was even in the general direction in which he was stumbling. He fell and crawled until he became aware of the stickiness of blood on his hands. Certain he had lost his way he stopped to listen, straining to distinguish any sound in the din of the storm. He had no idea which way he should go. Every impulse to move was canceled as soon as it arose.

The cloud passed overhead to the south and the Missouri River valley. The wind died, as the remaining snow was sifted onto the ice slowly unveiling a blue sky. Some forty feet away Ethan was clear as day in his red snowsuit. He was sitting crossed-legged next to the open water. "Daddy! Let's fish here!" As they crossed the ice toward the car, John saw his son look back toward the black line of water, and he knew he was troubled.

Linda met them at the door. Lucius was out. Ethan jumped into her arms, and John handed her the bundled snowsuit. "Mom, we had so much fun! We caught a fish and went sliding, with Daddy trying to catch me!" But looking back at his father in confusion, he seemed about to cry.

Linda asked, "Where was this?"

"Over toward Helena."

"A pond?"

"Not really."

"Oh, well, never mind. It sounds like a great place."

"I'll take you sometime."

Linda smiled, looked into his eyes, and gently rapped his chest with her knuckles. "Time to move on, Johnny, you know?"

John glanced away, pretending to look for Ethan. "Where'd he go?"

Hoagy Brown, the TV host, had lost interest in his memoirs. He let John see the sex and fart bloopers that could not be broadcast; but after the sufferings of his deprived childhood had been recounted in full, he found he hardly cared about revisiting his later life, his several wives or his son, a La Jolla Realtor. To John he seemed tired of living, having used up all the Schadenfreude that had propelled an illustrious career. He still had a dirty mind, though that too was fading, or perhaps he noticed John's lack of enthusiasm for his tales of conquest among women, most of whom were, even by Hoagy's account, dead anyway.

John didn't expect to be paid now that he was leaving the project, and Hoagy never offered it. Instead, he followed John to his car and said, "You're brushing me off, aren't you?"

"Not in the least, Hoagy, but I don't think at this late stage I have much to offer you."

"What late stage? I'm just getting started."

By then it was his time to have Ethan with him again, and he was excited about his plan for a hot-air-balloon ride, arranged and paid for at a popular "balloon ranch" in the foothills south of town. He paused before knocking on the door, a great oaken thing with a letter slot. On last year's Christmas card it had been adorned with a splendid wreath, in front of which Linda and Lucius beamed, with Ethan in the foreground between them in a little blazer and bow tie. John had felt some incomprehension at the assertive formality of this scene and wondered what it was about the heavy front door that even now made him feel affronted.

He knocked, and Lucius answered. "Oh, John, what a pleasure. Let me get Ethan. Ethan! It's Dad, get your things!"

Lucius ducked out of the doorway with a small, self-effacing bob that nevertheless left John waiting on the step looking into the hall. There he remained for a long time, his impulse to shut the door against the draft suppressed at the thought of again facing the letter slot and the expanse of varnished wood.

At length Lucius reappeared, wearing a frown of concern. He faced John silently in his cardigan, one arm clasped across his waist, the other holding his chin in deep thought. "I gather, John, that last week's experience at Canyon Ferry was pretty darn frightening for Ethan. Is that how you understand it, Linda?"

Linda answered from someplace inside. "It is."

"Linda's trying to watch *Mary Tyler Moore*," Lucius explained. "Some classic episode."

"And, what, Linda?" John called to her.

"And he doesn't want to go with you," came Linda's voice in reply. "Do you mind? Why prolong this?"

"May I speak to Ethan?"

"If that's what you require. Ethan, come speak to your father!"

Lucius seemed to be twisting with discomfort. He looked straight overhead and called out, "Please, Ethan, right now."

Linda said, "Sorry about not coming to the door, John, but I'm not decent."

Ethan appeared in flannel pajamas, a bathrobe, and rabbit slippers, head hung and glancing offstage in the direction of his mother. Lucius rested a hand on his head. John said in a voice of ghastly jocularity "What d'you say, Ethan? Aren't we going to have our day together? I've planned something you'll really like."

Ethan said, "I don't want to go with you."

John was amazed at his directness.

John got interviews at several papers. His record was good, and the owners all apologized for the pay. Three of the seven made the same remark: "It's a living." And so without great conviction, John found himself in charge of the news in Palmyra, North Dakota, which served an area identical in size to the principality of Liechtenstein, or so the *Herald*'s owner liked to say. Over the course of many years, John learned all there was to know about Palmyra, and almost nothing of the place he'd left, except that Linda had died, that Ethan had finished college and lived in Fresno, at least according to the last update he'd received quite some time ago. John assumed he was still around there somewhere—Ethan, that is. Lucifer could be anywhere.

River Camp

"Anytime you're on the Aleguketuk, you might as well be in heaven. I may never get to heaven, so the Aleguketuk will have to do—that, and plenty of beer! Beer and the river, fellows: that's just me.

"Practical matters: chow at first light. If you ain't in the chow line by o-dark-thirty, your next shot is a cold sandwich on the riverbank. And don't worry about what we're going to do; you'll be at your best if you leave your ideas at home.

"Now, a word or two about innovation and technique. You can look at these tomorrow in better light, but they started out life as common, ordinary craft-shop dolls' eyes. I've tumbled them in a color solution, along with a few scent promulgators distilled from several sources. You will be issued six of these impregnated dolls' eyes, and any you don't lose in the course of action will be returned to me upon your departure. I don't want these in circulation, plain and simple.

"The pup tent upwind of the toilet pit is for anyone who snores. That you will have to work out for yourselves. I remove my hearing aid at exactly nine o'clock, so snoring means no more to me than special requests. From nine until daybreak, a greenhorn can be seen but not heard.

"Lastly, the beautiful nudes featured on the out-of-date welding-supplies calendar in the cook tent are photographs of my bride at twenty-two. Therefore that is a 1986 calendar and will not serve for trip planning."

Marvin "Eldorado" Hewlitt backed his huge bulk out of the tent flap, making a sight gag of withdrawing his long gray beard from the slit as he closed it. Sitting on top of their sleeping bags, the surgeon Tony Capoletto and his brother-in-law Jack Spear turned to look at each other. Tony said, "My God. How many days do we have this guy? And why the six-shooter?"

Tony, the more dapper of the two, wore a kind of angler's ensemble: a multipocketed shirt with tiny brass rings from which to suspend fishing implements, quick-dry khaki pants that he'd turned into shorts by unzipping them at the knee, and wraparound shades that dangled from a Croakie at his chest. His pale, sharp-featured face and neatly combed hair were somewhat at odds with this costume.

"I have no idea," Jack said. His own flannel shirt hung loose over his baggy jeans. "He seemed so reasonable on the Internet."

Some sharp, if not violent, sounds could be heard from outside. Tony crawled forward in his shorts, carefully parting the entry to the tent to look out. Jack considered his friend's taut physique and tried to remember how long he'd had his own potbelly. Tony was always in shape—part handball, part just being a surgeon.

"What's he doing, Ton'?"

"Looks like he's chopping firewood. I can barely see him in the dark. Not much of the fire left, now."

"What was that stuff he made for dinner?"

"God only knows."

The tent smelled like camphor, mothballs; the scent was pretty strong. When Jack let his hand rest outside his sleeping bag, the grass still felt wet. It made him want to take a leak, but he didn't care to leave the tent as long as Hewlitt was out there.

Tony went back to his sleeping bag. It was quiet. A moment later his face lit up with blue light.

"You get a signal?"

"Are you kidding?" said Tony. "That would only inspire hope."

Tony's wife—Jack's sister—was divorcing him. There were no kids, and Tony said the whole thing was a relief, said that he was not bitter. Jack was quite sure Tony was bitter; it was Jack's sister who was not bitter. Jack had seen Gerri at the IGA, and she'd been decidedly unbitter—cheerful if not manic. She'd hoped they would have an "outtasight" trip. This was part of Gerri's routine, hip and lively for a tank town. Tony might have been a bit serious for her, in the end. Maybe he needed to lighten up. Jack certainly thought so.

Jack's wife, Jan, was one of the sad stories: having starred, in her small world, as a staggeringly hot eighteen-year-old when Jack, half cowboy and half high-school wide receiver, had swept her out of circulation, she had since gone into a rapid glide toward what could be identified at a thousand yards as a frump, and at close range as an angry frump. Gerri and Jan had driven "the boys" to the airport for their adventure together, each dreading the ride home, when in the absence of their men they would discover how little they had to talk about. In any case, they could hardly have suspected that they would never see their husbands again.

But the divorce wasn't the reason that Tony was so bent on a trip. He'd made some sort of mistake in surgery, professionally not a big deal—no one had even noticed—but Tony couldn't get it out of his mind. He'd talked about it in vague terms to Jack, the loss of concentration, and had reached this strange conclusion. "Why should I think I'll get it back?"

"You will, Ton'. It's who you are."

"Oh, really? I have never before lost concentration with the knife in my hand. Fucking never."

"Tony, if you can't do your work in the face of self-doubt, you may as well just quit now."

"Jack, you think you've ever experienced the kind of pressure that's my daily diet?"

Jack felt this but let it go.

Marvin Eldorado Hewlitt was now their problem. Jack had tried plenty of other guides, but they were all either booked or at a sportsmen's show in Oakland. He'd talked to some dandies after that, including a safari outfitter booking giraffe hunts. At the bottom of the barrel was Hewlitt, and now it was getting clearer why. So many of the things they would have thought to be either essential or irrelevant were subject to extra charges: fuel for the motor, a few vegetables, bear spray, trip insurance, lures, the gluten-free sandwich bread.

"But Marvin, we brought lures."

"You brought the wrong lures."

"I'll fish with my own lures."

"Not in my boat."

Lures: $52.50. Those would be the dolls' eyes.

"Marvin, I don't think we want trip insurance. I'm just glancing at these papers—well, are you really also an insurance agent?"

"Who else is gonna do it? I require trip insurance. I'm not God, but acts of God produce client whining I can't deal with."

Trip insurance: $384.75.

"Tony, give it up. There's no signal."

Tony looked up. "Was that a wolf?"

"I don't think it was a wolf. I think it was that crazy bastard."

The howl came again, followed by Marvin's chuckle.

"You see?"

Tony got out of his sleeping bag and peered through the tent flap.

"He's still up. Sitting by the fire. He's boiling something in some kind of a big cauldron. And he's talking to himself, it looks like. Or it's more like he's talking to someone else, but there's no one there that I can see. We're in the hands of a lunatic, Jack."

"Nowhere to go but up."

"You could say that. You could pitch that as reasonable commentary."

Jack felt heat come to his face. "Tony?"

"What?"

"Kiss my ass."

"Ah, consistency. How many times have I prayed for you to smarten up?"

Jack thought, I've got him by forty pounds. That's got to count.

The two fell silent. They were reviewing their relationship. So far, Tony had come up only with "loser," based on Jack's modest income; Jack had settled for "prick," which he based on the entitlement he thought all doctors felt in their interactions with others. This standoff was a long time coming, a childhood friendship that had hardened. Probably neither of them wanted it like this; the trip was supposed to be an attempt to recapture an earlier stage, when they were just friends, just boys. But the harm had been done. Maybe they had absorbed the town's view of success and let it spoil something. Or maybe it was the other thing again.

Outside, by the fire, Marvin was singing in a pleasant tenor. There was some accompaniment. Jack said, "See if he's got an instrument." Tony sighed and climbed out from his sleeping bag again. At the tent flap, he said, "It's a mandolin." And in fact at that moment a lyrical solo filled the air. Tony returned to his bag, and the two lay quietly, absorbing first some embellishment of the song Marvin had been singing and then a long venture into musical space.

Shortly after the music stopped, Marvin's voice came through the tent flap.

"Boys, that's all I can do for you. Now let's be nice to one another. We've got our whole lives ahead of us."

In a matter of minutes, the camp was silent. Stars rose high over the tents and their sleepers.

Morning arrived as a stab of light through the tent flap and the abrupt smell of trampled grass and mothballs. A round, pink face poked through at them, eyes twinkling unpleasantly, and shouted, "Rise and shine!"

"Is that you, Marvin?" Tony asked, groggily.

"Last time I looked."

"What happened to the beard?"

"Shaved it off and threw it in the fire. When you go through the pearly gates, you want to be clean-shaven. Everybody else up there has a beard."

The flap closed, and Jack said, "I smelled it. Burning." Then he pulled himself up.

Jack fished his clothes out of the pile he'd made in the middle of the tent. Tony glanced at this activity and shook his head; his own clothes were hung carefully on a tent peg. He wore his unlaced hiking shoes as he dressed. Jack was briefly missing a shoe, but it turned up under his sleeping bag, explaining some of the previous night's discomfort.

Tony said, "It's time for us to face this lunatic if we want breakfast."

The sunrise made a circle of light in the camp, piled high with pine needles next to the whispering river. Hewlitt had hoisted the perishable supplies up a tree to keep them away from bears; a folding table covered by a red-and-white-checkered tablecloth was set up by the small, sparkling fire. Stones on either side of the fire supported a blackened grill, from which Hewlitt brought forth a steady stream of ham, eggs, and flapjacks.

Jack rubbed his hands together eagerly and said, "My God, it's like Chef Boyardee!" Tony rolled his eyes at this and smiled at Hewlitt, whose surprisingly mild and beardless face had begun to fascinate him. The beard, it was explained, was something Hewlitt cultivated for sportsmen's shows: he hated beards.

"I'm not ashamed of my face," he said. "Why would I hide it?"

Hewlitt had already eaten, and so Jack and Tony sat down at

the table while he headed off toward the trees. Halfway through the meal, Jack noticed the man making slow, strange movements. Tony, thoroughly enjoying this breakfast, which was miles off his diet, hadn't looked up yet.

Finally Jack said, "I think the guide is having some kind of a fit."

Tony glanced up, mouth full of unsaturated fats.

"No, Jack, that's not a fit. That's Tai Chi."

"Like in the Kung Fu movies, I suppose."

"No."

They continued to eat in a less-pleasant silence until Hewlitt bounced over and joined them. Tony smiled as though they were old friends and asked, "Chen?"

"Uh-uh," said Hewlitt.

"Yang?"

"Nyewp."

"I'm out of ideas," Tony admitted modestly.

"Wu," said Hewlitt, in subdued triumph.

"Of course," said Tony. "What was that last pose?"

"Grasp-the-Bird's-Tail."

Jack listened and chewed slowly. He let his eyes drift to the other side of the river: an undifferentiated wall of trees. The water seemed so smooth you'd hardly know it was moving at all if it wasn't for the long stripe of foam behind every boulder. Invisible behind the branches, a raven seemed to address the camp.

Fried eggs on a metal plate. Jack ate more cautiously than usual: Tony was always on him about his weight. But then Tony was a doctor, and Jack felt he had his well-being in mind despite the often-annoying delivery. It was pleasing to notice these signs of old friendship, such as they were. Jack knew he should take better care of himself, and he had complied when Tony had wanted him to give up the cigarettes. It had been hard, and they were never completely out of his mind. In an odd way, that had been his own gesture of friendship, despite Tony's main argument having been that financially Jack really couldn't afford to smoke.

Tony was telling a story to Marvin that Jack already knew. He'd heard it a hundred times.

"We went on vacation to Mexico one year, and I brought back these little tiny superhot peppers to cook with. We had Jack and his wife, Jan, over for dinner one night, and I told Jack what I just told you, that these were the hottest little peppers in the world. Well, Jack, he's had about five longnecks in a row, and he says, 'Nothing's too hot for me!' right before he puts a spoonful of them in his mouth. Buddy, that was all she wrote. Tears shoot out of his eyes. His face turns . . . maroon. His head drops to the table, and what do you think he says?"

"I don't know," said Hewlitt.

"He says, 'Why is it always me?'"

Hewlitt stared at him for a moment. Then he said, "What's the punch line?"

Tony's face fell with a thud. Hewlitt got up to feed the fire.

"Our host doesn't seem to have much of a sense of humor," Tony said, when the man was gone. Jack just smiled at him.

There were a lot of Italians around the meatpacking plant, and that's where Tony's people had settled. He had come a long way. Jack's family was cattle, land, and railroad: they'd virtually founded the town but hadn't had a pot to piss in for generations.

Gerri liked to point out that half of her and Jack's relatives were absolute bums, which generally made Jack's wife respond that Tony's family was right off the boat. Nobody crossed Jan: she wasn't witty; she was angry. He may be a doctor to you, but he's a wop to me. Jack was fundamentally too fragile for this kind of badinage, unfortunately, because he had to admit that Tony and Gerri were far less snippy when Jan was around. She'd say to Jack, "You want respect, you better be prepared to snap their heads back." Or she'd put it the way Mike Tyson did: "Everybody's got an attitude until you hit them in the face."

Jack's roots in town were so deep that he thought that Jan's bellicosity was just a result of having grown up somewhere else. She was from Idaho, for crying out loud. This was before he found out Jan had had a slipup with Tony back in the day, while Jack was off doing his time with the National Guard.

When Tony and Gerri took them to New York to see *Cats*, that's when it really hit the fan. Tony had made a big thing about *Cats* winning a Tony Award, which Jan thought was such a hoot because Jack had no idea what a Tony Award was. He'd thought Tony was flirting with Jan again, with his so-called humor. Jack and Jan moved to their own hotel, leaving the room Tony had paid for empty. In their new room, Jan went on the defensive and blamed alcohol for the flirtation. She seemed to think that with this citation, the issue was settled. Jack didn't buy it, but he'd never been willing to pay the price for taking it further. Instead, he absorbed the blow. Having Tony know he just took it was the hardest part.

But somehow the problem between the two of them evaporated when they were back in town. "New York just wasn't for us," Tony said, amiably, and Jack accepted this gratefully. Jan, however, twisted it around; she took it to mean that she and Jack just weren't good enough for New York.

"Who wants to go there anyway?" she'd say. "All those muggers, and that smelly air!"

Meanwhile her slipup was consigned, once again, to history. Full stop. Jack couldn't stand any of it.

They all pitched in to tidy up the camp, and then they headed for the boat. It was tied to a tree, swinging in the current; a cool breeze, fresh and balsamic, was sweeping up the river. Hewlitt carried a Styrofoam chest—their lunch—to the shore and put it aboard. Fishing tackle had been loaded in already.

A moment later the three men climbed in, and Hewlitt started the engine. Once he was sure it was running properly, he stepped ashore and freed the painter from the tree, sprang aboard again, and turned into the current. Tony said, "This is what it's all about."

Jack nodded eagerly and then felt a wave of hopelessness unattached to anything in particular. Maybe catching a fish, maybe just the day itself. Hewlitt gazed over the tops of their heads, straight up the river. He seemed to know what he was doing.

He had looked more competent when he'd still had the beard. Now he looked like a lot of other people. God was always portrayed with a beard—for Jack it was impossible to picture him without one, even if he strained to imagine what he assumed would be a handsome and mature face. The only time you ever saw Jesus without a beard, he was still a baby. Tony had grown his own beard right after med school. Sometime later Jan had told Tony that he needed to get rid of it; that was one of the worst arguments Jack and Jan had ever had. Jack had said it was for Gerri to say whether or not she liked the beard, since it was her husband. Jan said that a person was entitled to her own opinions.

"Who taught you to cast?" Tony said. They had started fishing.

"You did," Jack replied.

"Obviously you needed to practice."

Jack just shrugged it off. He was still getting it out there, wasn't he? Maybe not as elegantly as Tony, but it shouldn't have made any difference to the fish. The casting was just showing off. It seemed to have impressed Hewlitt, though, because he took Tony upriver to another spot, leaving Jack to fish where he was, even though nobody had gotten a bite. Jack thought it was probably a better spot, this new one, and of course it was perfectly natural that Hewlitt would take Tony there, since it was Tony who was paying for the trip. Nevertheless, after another hour had passed, he felt a bit crushed and no longer expected to catch a fish at all. He thought, None of this would be happening if I had more money.

The sun rose high overhead and warmed the gravel bar. Jack's arm was getting tired, and eventually he stretched out on the ground with his hands behind his head. The heat felt so good, and the river sounded so sweet this close to his ear. Let Tony catch all the fish, he thought; I am at peace.

"How are you going to catch a fish that way, Jack?"

Tony was standing over him. He hadn't even heard the motor.

"I'm not. Did you catch anything?"

"No."

"See? You could have had a nice nap."

Tony sat down next to Jack on the gravel and glanced over at

Hewlitt, who was carrying their lunch box from the boat to the shore. "You know what old Eldorado did before he was a wilderness outfitter? Guess."

"Lumberjack?"

"Way off. He was a pharmacist."

"I'm surprised they even had them up here."

"This was in Phoenix."

Jack thought for a moment, and then asked, "Do you think he knows what he's doing?"

"No."

"Are we going to catch fish?"

"It seems unlikely."

They were interrupted by a cry from Hewlitt, whose rod had bent into a deep bow.

"Jesus. I didn't even see him cast," Jack said.

The two men hurried over. Hewlitt glanced at them and said, "First cast! He just mauled it."

The fish exploded into the air and tail-danced across the river.

"Looks like a real beauty," said Tony grimly, his hands plunged deep in his pockets.

After several more jumps and runs, Hewlitt had the fish at the beach and, laying down his rod, knelt beside it, holding it under its tail and belly. It was big, thick, and flashed silver with every movement as Hewlitt removed the hook. Tony and Jack craned over him to better see the creature, and Hewlitt bent to kiss it. "Oh, baby," he murmured. Then he let it go.

"What'd you do that for?" Tony wailed. The fish was swimming off, deeper and deeper, until its glimmer was lost in the dark. "We could have had fresh fish for lunch!"

Their guide, in response, got right in Tony's face. "Don't go there, mister," he said with an odd intensity. "You don't want that on your karma." Then he walked back to the boat and dragged the anchor farther up the shore.

"My God," Tony said. "What have we got ourselves into?" But Jack was simply pleased with everything.

A few minutes later, he even made a possibly insincere fuss over the bologna sandwiches. "Is there any lettuce or anything?"

"Doesn't keep without refrigeration. Where do you think you are?"

"The Aleguketuk. You already told me."

"Nice river, isn't it?"

"I wish it had more fish," said Tony. "Although it's obviously not a problem for you."

"Nyewp, not a problem."

As Hewlitt went to the boat to look for something, Tony said, "Ex–pill salesman."

"But fun to be with."

Jack had gone through times like this with Tony in the past: just be patient, he knew, and his friend would soon be chasing his own tail. It had already started. Tony had come unglued once when both couples had gone to a beginners' tennis camp in Boca Raton—thrown his racket, the whole nine yards. Jack had just let it sink in with Jan, what she had done with this nut. He knew he shouldn't feel this way: Jan had made it clear she regretted the whole thing, but he felt doomed to rub it in for the rest of their lives, or at least until she quit marveling over how fit Tony and Gerri were. He always suspected she included Gerri only as camouflage when she mentioned it. He'd seen this fitness language before: buns of steel, washboard abs, power pecs—all just code for Tony hovering over Jan like a vulture. And now, because Tony and Gerri were divorcing, Jack feared that further indiscretions might be on tap.

Tony threw his bologna sandwich into the river. "I can't eat it."

Hewlitt had his mouth full. "Plan on foraging?"

Tony sat down on the ground, elbows on his knees, and held his head in despair.

No other fish were caught that day, and neither man slept well that night. The next day a hard rain confined them to their tent; Tony read Harvey Penick's *Little Red Book: Lessons and Teachings from a Lifetime in Golf,* and Jack did sudoku until he was sick of it. The weather finally lifted in time for the third night's evening fire, and Hewlitt emerged wearing only his long underwear to prepare the meal, which was a huge shish kebab with only meat the entire length of the stick. When it was cooked, Hewlitt flicked the flesh onto their tin plates, which were so thin you could feel the heat through their bottoms. Afterward Hewlitt recited a Robert Service poem—"There are strange things done in the midnight sun"—so slowly that Tony and Jack were frantic at its conclusion.

"Where exactly was that drugstore you worked in?" Tony asked.

Hewlitt stared at him for a long time before speaking. "A pox on you, sir."

Back in the tent, Jack asked, "Aren't you concerned that he'll confiscate the impregnated craft-shop dolls' eyes?"

"What difference does it make? They haven't worked so far."

"Tony, it was a joke. Jesus, for a fancy doctor with a five-thousand-square-foot home on the golf course, you sure haven't lost your sense of humor."

"Fifty-two hundred. Get some sleep, Jack. You're getting crabby."

Jack had worked for the county all those years since the National Guard. In '96 he had denied Tony a well permit for his lawn-sprinkling system, and Tony had never gotten over it. It was payback for the little nothing with Jan, he was convinced, even though in reality it was no more than a conventional ruling on the law, which Tony, as was often the case, thought should be bent ever so slightly. Jack had explained the legal basis for his decision without denying that it was pleasant seeing Tony choke on this one. Tony had put his hand in Jack's face and said, "This is for surgery, not for holding a garden hose."

"You might want to tone down the square footage, if your time is limited," Jack had replied. "That's an awful lot of lawn."

"What the fuck are you talking about!" Tony had shouted back. "You don't even have a lawn, you have fucking pea rock!"

Hewlitt must have been throwing more wood on the fire. You could see the flare of the flames through the walls of the tent. From time to time, he laughed aloud.

"Do you suppose he's laughing at us?" Tony asked.

"Things can still turn out. We have time."

"At least we got away together," Tony said. "We used to do more of this. It's important. It makes everything come back. We're kids again. We're who we used to be."

"Not really," said Jack. "You used to be nicer to me."

"You're joking, aren't you?"

Jack didn't answer. He wished he hadn't said such a thing, and his throat ached.

"What about Cancún in 2003? It didn't cost you a nickel."

Jack didn't know how to reply. He was in such pain. The tent fell silent once more. When Tony finally spoke, his voice had changed.

"Jack. I don't have another friend."

Jack wanted to make Tony feel better then, but it wasn't coming to him yet. Tony was right about one thing: they were who they used to be. Jack was still doing okay in his little house, and Tony was still just as lonely by the golf course as he'd been by the meatpacking plant. He had to take it out on somebody.

In the morning, there was frost on everything. Jack and Tony, arms stiff at their sides, watched as Hewlitt made breakfast and merrily reminisced about previous trips.

"Had an English astronaut here for a week, just a regular bloke. Loved his pub, loved his shepherd's pie, loved his wee cottage in Blighty."

Tony and Jack glanced at each other.

"Took a large framed picture of the Queen Mother into space. Ate nothing but fish-and-chips his whole month in orbit, quoting Churchill the entire time."

Tony whispered to Jack, "There were no English astronauts."

"I heard that," Hewlitt said, standing up and waving his spatula slowly in Tony's face.

"Did you? Good."

Hewlitt resumed cooking in silence. The silence was worse.

He served their meal without a word, then went to his boat with his new bare face, and in his hand he grasped a handful of willow switches he had cut from the bank. With these, he scourged himself. It was hard not to see this as a tableau, with the boat and the river behind him and Hewlitt, in effect, centered in the frame. His audience, Jack and Tony, turned away to gear up for a day of fishing and standing with their rods at their sides like a sarcastic knockoff of *American Gothic.*

Right out of the blue, Hewlitt stopped his thrashing and turned to fix them with a reproving gaze. "I've spent my entire life as a liar and an incompetent," he said.

"Don't be so hard on yourself, Eldorado," Tony said, with poorly concealed alarm.

"Bogus vitamins on the Internet? How about swingin' doors and painted women?"

"That's all behind you, now."

"If only I could believe you!" Hewlitt cried.

Tony was paralyzed by the strangeness of this, but Jack stepped forward and snatched the willow switches away. He got right in Hewlitt's face.

"How much of this do you think we can stand?"

"Well, I—"

"We're not on this trip to hear about your problems. We don't even know you. I came here to be with my friend because we need to talk. This is a freak show, and we shouldn't have to pay for it. We thought we'd catch some fish!"

This seemed to sober Hewlitt, who replaced his look of extravagant self-pity with one of caution and shrewdness.

"I'm the only one who can get you out of here, son. No brag, just fact. You make me feel respected or you're SOL. I'd like to be a fly on the wall when you try backing this tank down a class-five rapid. That's the only way home, punk, and I'm unstable."

"Jesus," said Tony. "This is insane! This trip was my reward as a vassal of Medicare!"

Hewlitt responded by pretending to play a violin and whis-tling "Moon River." Jack raised a menacing finger in his face, and he stopped. Then Hewlitt was talking again.

"How about you try going broke on eating-disorder clinics to wake up to find your wife still gobbling her food? Forty K in the hole and she's facedown on a ham!"

Jack turned back to Tony. "I don't know what to do."

Hewlitt's lament rushed onward. He had dug deep in his pharmacist days to throw a big wedding for his daughter, appar-ently; she had married way above their station thanks to her big blue eyes and thrilling figure. It was, in Hewlitt's words, a hoity-toity affair with the top Arizona landowners, the copper royalty, and the developers, and Hewlitt's caterer food-poisoned them all. Several sued, his wife and daughter blamed him, and in this way Hewlitt found himself at the end of his old life and the beginning of the new. He took a crash course in wilderness adventures at an old CCC camp in Oregon, graduating at the top of his class and getting a book on the ethics of forestry in recog-nition. Hewlitt seemed to think that this was all an illusion, that no one really cared about him at all.

Tony and Jack maintained compassionate, respectful smiles throughout this tirade. By the end Hewlitt was so upset his cheeks trembled. When he finished, Jack raised an imploring hand in his direction, but to no avail: Eldorado Hewlitt walked past them and into his tent.

"Doesn't look like a fishing day," Jack said.

Once they were back in the tent, Jack stretched out on his sleeping bag, and Tony turned to grab a thick paperback from his pack, a book about zombies with the face of someone with white eyeholes on the cover. He slumped back on his bedroll, drew his reading glasses from his shirt, and was on the verge of total absorption when Hewlitt flung open the tent flap. Tony slowly lowered the zombie book.

"Sorry to disturb you," the man said, though there was no evidence of that. "I have to ask: What is your problem? 'Old friends'? Is that what you are, 'old friends'? Grew up together in the same little town? I know I have problems; I'm famous for my problems. I'm told by qualified professionals that I have ruined my life with my problems, but these few days with two 'old friends' have completely unnerved me. What did you two do to each other? Where is this bad feeling coming from? I'm terrifically upset, and I don't know what it is. But it's coming from you two, I've figured out that much. Can't you work this out? You're killing me!"

Hewlitt hurled down the flap and left. Jack and Tony looked at each other, then quickly glanced away.

"What was that all about?" Tony asked, unpersuasively.

Jack said nothing. He had found his box of lures and was lifting one up as though to examine it. A blue frog with hooks.

After a minute he got to his feet. He went out of the tent, looked around, and came back in with their rods. He made a show of breaking them down and putting them back in their travel tubes. Tony, staring determinedly now at a single page of his zombie book, barely lifted his eyes to this activity, which caused Jack to raise the intensity of it. He held up a roll of toilet paper in his hand. Tony couldn't look at him.

"Might as well take a shit. Nothing else to do around here."

Tony kept his eyes on the book and gave him a little wave.

A short time later, the toilet paper flew back into the tent, followed by Jack. He slumped on his bedroll with a sigh.

"I've got another book," said Tony.

"I hate books."

"No, you don't. You loved *The Black Stallion*."

"I was twelve."

"So don't read. Who cares?"

"What's the other book?"

"*Silent Spring.*"

Jack snorted. "Thanks a bunch."

Tony dropped the book to his chest. "Jack, what do you want?"

"In the whole world?"

"Sure."

"I'd like you to tell me in plain English what my wife saw in you."

Tony exhaled through pursed lips and looked at the ground. "We did this a long time ago. Either you shoot me or throw her out, but otherwise there's nothing more to say. The whole thing is both painful and negligible to me, and kind of an accident and kind of ancient history. We have managed to stay friends despite my very serious personal crime against you. It is a permanent stain on my soul."

"What do you mean by that?" Jack said. "You don't even believe you have one."

"Well, you do, and you're innocent. I have a soul that is blemished by shame. All right? I'm not proud of myself."

Jack lay facedown on his bedroll, chin on laced fingers, and looked miserably toward the tent flap. He fell asleep thus, after a while, and so did Tony, glasses hanging from one ear. Hours later, they were awakened by the cooling tent and diminished light.

Jack got to his feet abruptly, seeming frightened, and rifled through a pile of clothing until he found his coat.

"You going to find us something to eat?" Tony asked.

"I am like hell. I'm going to have a word with our guide."

Tony raised a cautioning hand. "Jack, we're dealing with a very unstable—"

"Well put, Tony. That's exactly what I am, but I plan to do something about it. I'm upset. And it's his fault."

"Jack, please—"

But Jack had already gone. Tony slumped back with his hands over his face. It went through his mind that patiently putting up with Jack was an old habit. That's what had started their mess. Jack had done something dumb—gotten drunk and driven his car on the railroad tracks, in fact, nearly ruining it—that had caused Jan and Tony, in an accidental encounter at the post office, to commiserate with each other, and the next thing they knew they were in bed, bright sunlight coming through the thin curtains of the Super 8. It wasn't anything, really, but Jan threw it into an argument with Jack the next year during the Super Bowl, and the half-life was promptly extended to forever.

Jack came back in through the tent flap, slapping it open abruptly. He crouched down, staring at Tony. Then he said, "He's dead."

Tony sat up. The zombie paperback splattered on the dirt floor. He stood and walked straight past Jack, out through the flap, then came back in, kicking the book out of his way, and lay down again.

"He sure is," he said.

"So what happened?"

"He took something."

"Jesus. Did you see this coming?"

"No. I thought it was an act."

"Is the food in there with him?"

"He hauled it back up the tree. Where the bears couldn't get it."

"Bears. Jesus, I forgot about bears." Jack dashed out of the tent once more. When he returned, dangling Hewlitt's gun by its barrel, he had a wild look in his eyes. Tony knew what it was and said nothing.

"I'll get a fire going," Jack said. "We've got to eat something. Why don't you get the food down and see what we've got."

Outside they felt the strangeness of being alone in the camp, the cold fire, Hewlitt's silent tent. The boat meant everything, and separately they checked to see that it was still there. Tony ended up crouched by the fire pit, shaving off kindling with his hatchet, while Jack puzzled over the knots on the ground stake: the rope led upward over a branch, suspending the food supplies out of reach. Once the rope was free, he was able to lower the supplies to the ground and open the canvas enclosing them: steaks, potatoes, onions, canned tomatoes, girlie magazines, schnapps, eggs, a ham. He dragged the whole load to the fire and stood over it with Tony, not quite knowing what to do next.

"If I'm right about what's ahead, we go for the protein," Tony said.

It was getting darker and colder; the flames danced over the splinters of firewood. Jack was quite still.

"What's ahead, Tony?"

"The boat trip."

"Oh, is that what you think?"

"That's what I think."

Jack looked up at the sky for a moment but didn't reply. Instead, he lifted two of the steaks out of the cache and dropped them onto the grill.

The bedrolls became cocoons without refuge. They were in a dead camp with a dead fire and a corpse in a tent. They thought about their wives—even Jan's misery and Gerri's demand for freedom seemed so consoling now, so day-to-day. Tony's small slip with the scalpel was now nothing more than a reminder of the need for vigilance—a renewal, in a sense. Jack had a home and all his forebears buried on the edge of town. He could wait for the same. No big deal, just wink out. Nothing about this bothered him anymore. He had sometimes pictured himself in his coffin, big belly and all, friends filing by with sad faces. He belonged.

They couldn't sleep, or they barely slept; if one detected the other awake, they talked.

"I don't know what the environmentalists see in all these trees," Jack said.

"Nature hates us. We'll be damn lucky to get out of this hole and back to civilization."

"Well, you want a little of both. A few trees, anyway. Some wildflowers."

"You try walking out of here. You'll see how much nature loves you."

There was no point worrying about it, Tony said; they would have the whole day tomorrow to work on their problems.

"So what do we do with the body?" Jack asked.

"The body is not our problem."

It couldn't have been many hours before sunrise by the time the bears came into the camp. There were at least three; they could be heard making pig noises as they dragged and swatted at the food that had been left out. Tony tried to get a firm count through a narrow opening in the tent flap while Jack cowered at the rear with Hewlitt's gun in his hands.

"It's nature, Tony! It's nature out there!"

Tony was too terrified to say anything. The bears had grown interested in their tent.

After a moment of quiet they could hear them smelling around its base with sonorous gusts of breath. At every sound, Jack redirected the gun. Tony tried to calm him, despite his own terror.

"They've got all they can eat out there, Jack."

"They never have enough to eat! Bears never have enough!"

Tony went to the flap and tied all its laces carefully, as though that made any difference. But then, as before, the sound of the bears stopped. After a time he opened a lace and looked out.

"I think they're gone," he said. He hated pretending to be calm. He'd done that in the operating room when it was nothing but a fucking mess.

"Let's give them plenty of time, until we're a hundred percent sure," Jack said. "We've got this"—Jack held the gun aloft—"but half the time shooting a bear just pisses him off."

Tony felt he could open the flap enough to get a better look.

First light had begun to reveal the camp, everything scattered like a rural dump, even the pages of the girlie magazines, pink fragments among the canned goods, cold air from the river coming into the tent like an anesthetic.

Tony said, "Oh, God, Jack. Oh, God."

"What?"

"The bears are in Hewlitt's tent."

Jack squealed and hunkered down onto the dirt floor. "Too good, Tony! Too good!"

Tony waited until he stopped and then said, "Jack, you need to take hold. We've got a long day ahead of us."

Jack sat up abruptly, eyes blazing. "Is that how you see it? You're going to tell me to behave? You're a successful guy. My wife thought you were a big successful guy before she was fat. So tell me what to do, Tony."

"Listen, start by shutting up, okay? We're gonna need all the energy in those big muscles of yours to get us out of this."

"That's straight from the shoulder, Tony. You sound like the old guinea from down by the meat processor again."

"I'm all right with that," said Tony. "Up with the founding families, piss poor though you all are, it must have been hard for you and Jan to know how happy we were."

"Somebody's got to make sausage."

"Yes, they do."

"Linguini, pepperoni, Abruzzo. Pasta fazool."

"I can't believe you know what pasta fazool is, Jack."

Jack imitated Dean Martin. "'When the stars make you drool, just like pasta fazool.' Asshole. Your mother made it for me."

He was gesturing with the rifle now. When the barrel swung past Tony's nose, the reality of their situation came crashing down on them as though they had awakened from a dream. Jack, abashed, went to the front of the tent and peered out. After a moment, he said, "All quiet on the western front."

Tony came to look over his shoulder, saw nothing.

"They're gone."

The two men emerged into the cold, low light, the gray river racing at the edge of the camp. There was nothing left of the food except a few canned goods scattered among the pictures of female body parts. The vestibule of Hewlitt's tent was torn asunder, to the point that the interior could almost be inspected from a distance. Jack clearly had no interest in doing so, but Tony went over gingerly, entered, then came out abruptly with one hand over his eyes. "Oh," he said, "Jesus Christ."

They picked through the havoc the bears had left until they'd found enough undamaged food for a day or so in the boat. They put their bedrolls in there, too, but the tents they left where they were. Any thought of staying in camp was dropped on the likelihood of the bears returning at dark.

"We'll start the motor when we need it," Tony said. "All we're doing is going downstream until we get out."

Jack nodded, lifted the anchor, and walked down to the boat, coiling the line as he went.

The river seemed to speed past. As they floated away, Tony thought that this was nature at its most benign, shepherding them away from the dreaded camp; but Jack, looking at the dark walls of trees enclosing the current, the ravens in the high branches, felt a malevolence in his bones. He glanced back at their abandoned tents: already, they looked like they'd been there for hundreds of years, like the empty smallpox tepees his grandpa had told him about. This might be good country if someone removed the trees and made it prairie like at home, he thought. With the steady motion of the boat, he daydreamed about the kinds of buildings he'd most like to see: a store, a church, a firehouse.

Tony said, "My dad was a butcher, and I'm a surgeon. I'm sure you've heard a lot of jokes about that around town."

"Uh-huh."

"The funny thing is, I didn't want to be a surgeon—I wanted to be a butcher. The old second-generation climb into some stratosphere where you'll never be comfortable again. Where you never know where you live."

"I don't think you'd like it back there at the packing plant."

"Not now—I've been spoiled. But if I'd stayed . . . I don't know. Dad was always happy."

"And you're not?" Jack asked.

"Not particularly. Maybe after Gerri goes. Now that I'm used to the idea, the divorce, I can't wait. I think I'm overspreading my discomfort around."

"Jan and I don't have the option," Jack said. "There's not enough for either one of us to start over on. We're stuck together whether we like it or not." He was thinking of how life and nature were just alike, but he couldn't figure out how to put it into words.

Boulders, submerged beneath the water, could be felt as the boat rose and fell, and the river began to narrow toward a low canyon. In a tightening voice, Tony said, "Most of humanity lives beside rivers. By letting this one take us where it will, we'll be delivered to some form of civilization. A settlement, at least."

He reached inside his coat and pulled out a wallet. "I thought we better bring this."

"Is that Hewlitt's wallet?"

"That's not his name. There are several forms of identification, but none of them are for a Hewlitt." He riffled it open to show Jack the driver's licenses and ID cards, all with the same picture and all with different names.

"He had a lot of musical talent," Jack said, and let out a crazy, mirthless laugh.

"See up there? I bet those are the rapids he was talking about."

"Oh, goody. Nature."

Indeed, where the canyon began, and even from this distance, the sheen of the river was surmounted by something sparkling, some effervescence, a vitality that had nothing to do with them. Shapes appeared under the boat, then vanished as the river's depth changed, the banks and walls of trees narrowing toward them and the approaching canyon walls. You couldn't look up without wanting to get out through the sky.

At the mouth of the canyon was a standing wave. Somehow the river ran under it, but the wave itself remained erect. A kind of light could be seen around it. Tony thought it had the quality of authority, like the checkpoint of a restricted area; Jack took it for yet another part of the blizzard of things that could never be explained and that pointlessly exhausted all human inquiry. Carrying these distinct views, their boat was swept into the wave, and under; and Jack and Tony were never seen again.

Lake Story

Glendive was unbearably hot in August, and for half of it I rented a cottage on the western shore of Flathead Lake, a little getaway in sight of Wild Horse Island and built a long time ago between two rocky points barely thirty yards apart, the lawn between them leading down to a pebbly shore and the deep green water in a kind of pool. The place was only available because the neighbor whose starter castle towered over the next small bay had died in the spring. A Kansas City resident who had made a fortune trading carbon credits and ringtones, he owned the kind of craft normally at the service of drug runners, a vastly powerful cigarette boat whose daily thunder made the nearby rental cottages uninhabitable. Pleas went unacknowledged, the petition thrown out as the smell of fuel continued to drift up from his dock. So after the boat owner died, concluding a prolonged battle with pancreatic cancer, Memorial Day in the small surrounding neighborhood was given over to celebration. The jubilant air persisted as FOR SALE signs appeared on his property, then through its deterioration, especially as islands of quack grass started pushing up through the clay tennis court. Suddenly the small cottages, each with its tiny green bay and an evergreen-crowned rocky ridge running to the lake, were all back in business. I felt very lucky to have scored one of them on short notice, a one-bedroom clapboard house with a mossy shingled roof and overstuffed chairs fished out of winter homes elsewhere, before the age of dedicated cottage furniture. The fireplace was made of round stones from the lakeside, and a huge incongruous print of Niagara Falls was the main room's only decoration. "Were these people all short?" Adele asked, noticing that every lamp lit us at waist level unless we slumped into one of the low-slung chairs to thumb the swollen copy of *Redbook*. At night, above these lamps, all was darkness.

I was having an affair with Adele, a married woman whose availability was also made known to me at the last moment. We'd been doing this for nine years, nine short-term rentals, each begun just as her husband finalized his schedule, which included an annual visit to his mother in rural South Africa, where communications were conveniently, if uncertainly, faulty. Adele and I otherwise avoided deceit of any kind, operating on a don't-ask-don't-tell basis, each suspecting that ours was the kind of flourishing relationship that would wither in the full light of day. Sunlight may be the best disinfectant, but it fades passion like everything else. I'm a widower with grown children, but Adele's were of an impressionable age, and God forbid they ever found out about us. They couldn't possibly have understood. We relished this covert life and didn't mind in the least that we could be deceiving ourselves, lost as we were in its pleasures and logistics.

Usually, we arrived in separate cars, but this time Adele came on the train from Seattle, where she'd gone for a design show. I picked her up at the station in Whitefish, observing our customary artifice—"You never know who you'll run into in

Montana"—before we took a look around from inside my car and began kissing. By now, there was no need for any foreshadowing in these early parts: we knew what was coming. As I drove out and turned onto the highway for the lake, Adele said, "Seattle was wonderful, but then it's summer. You smell salt water, and there are cranes and freighters and container ships like a real seaport. You don't get that in San Francisco. And I met the coolest cowboy, a professional rodeo cowboy, and he could talk about anything. He was reading a book!" Adele looked great in a cotton summer dress, this one blue with tiny silver zigzags.

"And?" I asked.

"He was too big for a Pullman berth."

I didn't know if she was serious. I don't think she was. It's possible she had a wild side, but you wouldn't know it by our relationship, which had almost nothing wild about it. Perhaps monogamous cheaters were commoner than I thought.

I loved Adele, and Adele loved me, but we were not in love, and she couldn't make me jealous, though that principle was untested. I once pretended to be in love with her, and my saying so was greeted by silence arising from contempt. It was instructive. I barely made up for it by deferring ejaculation for about ninety minutes, which left me stooped for two days with lower back pain. I took some ibuprofen, and Adele read to me from *Tartarin of Tarascon* in recognition of my sacrifice. When we got to the part where Tartarin is unable to decide whether to cover himself with glory or with flannel, we closed the book and fell asleep with plenty of room between us on the bed, where we always left whatever we'd been reading and, lately, our reading glasses.

That evening at the lake, we sat out on the weathered deck and watched the blue twilight dwindle until the broad silver of its surface was lit with stars. Perhaps, Adele glanced at me, or I at her, but some wordless signal passed between us, and we entered by the screen door, just a crack, so as to exclude the moths, and made for the bed, which proved a squeaking seismograph that registered the tiniest movement. Even reaching to turn off the lamp produced a cacophony. This bed was good for nothing, and so we dragged the mattress to the floor, where there were only our own sounds to contend with. I touched her with my fingertips.

"You're tracing. You can't remember me from one year to the next?"

"I like being reminded."

"You're looking for change."

"Nope."

In the morning, I caught several very small cutthroat trout from the dock, using a child's rod found in the garage and worms from beneath the paving tiles that ran from the house to a tiny garden shed. Adele woke up to fried eggs, fresh trout fillets, and sourdough toast served in bed. This was all a bit easier for me, as I lived alone, while Adele was married, happily married, to a very nice guy about whom I should have felt some guilt except that he was known for straying himself and had caused Adele a bit of pain over this. I mean, you looked at these things and you could see possible retribution in every direction, if that's what you wanted, but I didn't. Besides, some of my pleasure consisted in just having company.

We read on the shore until late morning, when it was warm enough for a swim. That is, the air was warm enough: the lake is never warm, but we dove in naked, paddled for a very short time, floating on our backs and gazing up at the cheerful little clouds over the Mission Range, then clambered out into the warm air, and had dried off by the time we fell into sex on one of the Adirondack chairs at the bottom of our sunny ravine, the glare on the cottage windows suggesting a steady stare. When we stood up, we laughed at the sight of each other before Adele, glancing back at the chair, said, "Eww, I'll get it." That's when I had the idea that ruined everything.

The cottage came with a battered aluminum boat, an old Evinrude motor on its transom and a litter of things strewn in its bottom, life jackets, a mushroom anchor and line, a net with a broken handle, a Maxwell House bailing can, one oar, and a sponge. I looked into the red gas can; it was full, and the fuel smelled fairly recent. "I say we make a run across the lake and have lunch in Big Fork." In my defense, it was a perfect day for it, windless and sunny, the mountains to our east wonderfully green and regular. Summer traffic glinted from the highway for miles across the water and along the ripening cherry orchards.

The motor started on the first pull. Adele in her summer dress and white-framed sunglasses sat facing forward atop a life jacket, while I, with an arm behind me on the motor's handle, maneuvered us out of our little bay into the open water. I tried to memorize the position of the cottage in the landscape so we could find our way home, knowing as I did it wouldn't be long after lunch that we'd be longing to drag the sagging mattress onto the floor again. We tended to overdo these exertions in what time we had, even though, as Adele reminded me, it's not something you could store for later. I supposed that was true, as there was nothing routine about each renewal of ardor, though we did get better at it every year. If we were not as attractive as we once had been, we had the advantage of knowing what we liked with greater certainty, even as it had grown more unmentionable in polite company.

The surface of the lake sparkled green, and its placidity belied the occasional squall that popped unexpected out of the mountains, drowning kokanee fishermen, whose bodies sank like stones in the cold water. Now it was as delightful as a rain forest on a sunny day. I gave the pressure bulb on the gas line an extra squeeze, and Adele, sensing my movement, turned to smile, then rolled her eyes heavenward in bliss over our surroundings. Leaving a bubble trail and a straight wake, the little Evinrude pushed us slowly to the other side.

"We're a long way from shore. Want to fuck in the boat?"

"No, I want lunch."

I resumed cruising speed, and in a short time we were at the dock south of the golf course. I tied up without interference from the marina staff, who may have been eating. We climbed from the boat, Adele straightened her dress as she looked around, and with my hand on the small of her back, I led her to a pathway along the Swan River, where youngsters were swimming off docks in front of well-kept cottages nearly lost in greenery. By now we were uncomfortably hungry and followed a boardwalk to the nearest restaurant, which looked popular, at least with locals. The obvious tourists were pouring into a bigger place across the street with water views and outside dining. Once seated, we were encouraged by the originality of what was on the blackboard menu. They seemed especially proud of something called MISSION RANGE BASIL TOMATO GREEN CHILE MEAT LOAF. That item ran the length of the board, unlike FRIED

CHICKEN or SOUP OF THE DAY. We ordered it and received startlingly sincere congratulations from the waitress, a rawboned brunette with a cigarette behind her ear and a shamrock tattoo on her forearm. I was glad to get our orders in, because the restaurant was filling up, and already other couples were standing in front waiting for a table. Adele remarked that we became an ordinary couple once a year, the South African part of the year; when we relied on ordinary opportunity, we were just garden-variety adulterers. "There was a good bit of that at the design show, I think. Trade shows seem mostly for that. Couples just getting acquainted, regret in their faces. Getting out of town. Departing from duty for desire."

"Sounds like a bus route," I said.

"For some, it is a bus route."

"We're solitary travelers. Smartphones, a boat, meat loaf."

With the dining room full, the noise picked up, and Adele and I drew closer. Our food arrived. My state was such that I could feel the least adjustment of her chair in my direction. Someone waiting outside for a table was smoking a cigarette, and our waitress closed the door in his face. Adele held a forkful of meat loaf in front of her and said, "Eat up, get the bill, and take me back to the cottage." My heart raced at how effortlessly she could reduce all else to preliminaries.

A heavyset woman dining alone walked toward the cash register holding her bill like a specimen. She glanced our way, then glanced again, and then headed toward us. Adele didn't see her coming until she was nearly at our table, by which time Adele went white and jumped to her feet, clutching her napkin in grotesque exuberance. "Esther!" It came out as little more than a croak at which she clutched her throat, as if to blame an unchewed bit of food for the strange sound. By the time I was on my feet, wiping my mouth, causing a shower of crumbs from my napkin, I knew I was hosed. Esther, Adele's sister-in-law, a woman in late middle age, was possessed of a kind of authoritarian face, an effect unrelieved by her close-cropped yellowish hair and a red summer blazer. I was a "colleague" from Glendive.

"You didn't go to South Africa with Marty?" Esther said.

"I was at a design show in Seattle. With Marty away, I thought I'd take a leisurely train ride here, grab something to eat, and rent a car to drive home. Walked in and here he was. Old Home Week." I guessed that was me, though Adele was pointing in case there was doubt.

"Matching meat loaf!" I cried stupidly. Esther, evidently no fan of wordplay, gave me a bit of a look.

"What brings you here?" Adele asked with a grimace.

"Damage control: one of our legislators got drunk and T-boned a travel trailer with his speedboat. Ran it right off the lake into the middle of an RV park."

"Esther does PR for . . . who exactly?"

"Anyone with American money. Looks like you're nearly finished. Ride home with me and save on that rental. I can wait for you in the car. No hurry."

"Are you sure you won't join us?" I asked, but Esther laughed grimly, perhaps tellingly, and went out the door without another word.

"I hate her," said Adele. "Three hundred fifty miles in a white Honda Civic is not what I had in mind. And she's got breath like kerosene." The waitress brought the check.

Adele stared into my eyes. "I'm sure you could see, as I could see, that she's onto us."

"I'm not particularly intuitive but, yes, I thought there was something there."

"Something unpleasant as if . . ."

"We'd been nabbed."

"Well, maybe not so clear as that but suspected, perhaps. Can I ask you a favor?" she said.

"Of course."

"Don't ever do this to me again."

"And all this time, I thought it was mutual." I didn't know what else to say, or why I more or less sang these words. I'd never seen Adele angry before, and I was startled at the transformation.

"This strikes you as a good time for irony?!"

"Adele, people are staring."

"Staring! I'd love to be able to worry about stares."

Esther appeared in the doorway and came toward us in big strides, like a forest ranger. "Everything okay?" She glanced back and forth between us with transparently insincere concern. Adele's mottled face made an implausible attempt at reply.

"Just winding up here, Esther. I'll be right along. Sorry to hold you up."

Esther backed away giving us a good long look at her quizzical expression, then strode out the door again. I perhaps felt less vulnerable than Adele and believed that while Esther was happy to exhibit her intuitions, hers was still a theory masquerading as a fact. She had nothing to go on.

"I'd better leave."

I didn't dare try an affectionate farewell given Esther's circling. I said, "Well, kiss, kiss."

Adele said, "Same." She got up, gave me a small waist-level wave, and went out. I wasn't proud of the speculating I began. I barely knew Adele's husband, Marty, a petroleum geologist originally from South Africa and something of a lady's man, as I said. There might be a tiny contretemps just on principle, with some awkwardness on those rare occasions when we met again; or the shit might really hit the fan, with Adele winding up out on the street and Marty drawing me into fisticuffs, for which I have no particular talent. I was cringing at how quickly my erotic stream of consciousness had evaporated into a haze of measliness and fear. Adele came back and sat down.

"Screwed. She left. She's going to turn me in."

"Adele, honestly I doubt it."

"I'm toast, and you know it."

Part of me wanted to exploit this heightened state erotically, but that seemed a dangerous idea, and so in the end we made a gloomy pair heading across the lake to the cottage, Adele facing the bow while I steered. The lake was still quiet except for cat's-paws and the wakes of birds. Just past midway, I could smell the piney breeze from shore as I dwelled on Adele's shape through her blue dress, and as she braced herself on the seat. Her hair was loose, stirred around her shoulders by the air moving across the boat. I thought that at some point she might look back at me, but she never did. In our nine years of meeting I had given her very little to go on, and now I could see that it wasn't enough.

I tied the boat up and tilted the engine on the transom. Adele was already walking up the dock but stopped halfway, her forefinger crooked and pressed it to her lips in thought. "Maybe I'm overreacting." I followed her partway, encouraged that she was taking a more hopeful view of things; but what I had to say put an end to that.

"Deny everything. Esther wasn't here. Marty wasn't here. Tell them their data is corrupt."

Adele's arms fell to her sides in disgust as she walked the rest of the way to the cottage. I could only follow and then watch her throw her belongings into her suitcase. I may have breached the bedroom door too enthusiastically; it banged against the wall behind it, causing Adele to look up sharply from her packing. "Is this your James Cagney moment?"

"No, no, it isn't," I said mildly.

"I'm so sorry," she said tearfully. "This has always been inevitable. I should have taken it better. I love Marty. What the fuck have I been doing?"

I had a flippant answer for that, too, but it would have only revealed my bitterness. I hardly needed to be reminded of her love for Marty, who had always seemed pretty and bland and devious to me, although I probably made that up. All I really knew of Marty was that women found him presentable. I thought his expensive clothes were odd on a petroleum geologist, and that to me suggested a real slyboots in his finery. But I also knew my inferences were utter crap.

Either Adele didn't want to be seen with me on arrival in Glendive, or the long ride together would have been too fraught; either way, we ended up at the nearer Kalispell airport to rent her a car, a Kia that made her seem bigger than she was as she gave me a forlorn wave and departed. Kaput.

I moped around the cottage for another day and headed out. The day I got home, Esther and I met for coffee at her request. She hadn't abandoned Adele at the restaurant after all; she'd gone for gas. When she returned and discovered us gone, she searched frantically for Adele and finally gave up and drove to Glendive. I suppose she was aware of what we were up to together; but taking Adele away must have seemed the perfect chance to break it to her that Marty wasn't coming back anytime soon. He'd met someone in South Africa, an English girl working at a branch office of Deutsche Bank.

I had dinner with Adele that winter at Walkers American Grill in Billings, always crowded with local suits, but now it didn't matter who saw us together. She was working hard and living alone, her marital situation still unresolved. She blamed herself for everything but placed her hopes on Marty's irresolute arrangement with his girl in Johannesburg. "He honestly doesn't know where it's all going," she said, smiling uncertainly. "He told me he just wants to live it out."

I guess I'll have to wait. Esther thinks I'm being a dope, but she's so instinctively protective I can't take her seriously. She's a specialist in damage control, adequate company, and may see more in me than is actually there. We're kind of in the same boat.

Crow Fair

Kurt was closer to Mother than I. I faced that a long time ago, and Mother pretty well devoured all his achievements and self-aggrandizements. But there came a day when the tide shifted, and while this may have marked Mother's decline, it was a five-alarm fire for Kurt. He had given Mother yet another of his theories, a general theory of life, which was the usual Darwinian dog-eat-dog stuff with power trickling down a human pyramid whose summit was exclusively occupied by discount orthodontists like himself. Kurt had successfully prosecuted this sort of braggadocio with Mother nearly all his life; but this time she described his philosophy as "a crock of shit." This comment had the same effect on Kurt as a roadside bomb. His rapidly whitening face only emphasized his moist red lips.

Kurt and I put Mother in a rest home a few months back. I don't think you can add a single thing to putting your mother in the rest home. If ever there was an overcooked topic, popping Ma in the old folks' home has to be a leading candidate. Ours has been a wonderful mother and, in many ways, all the things Kurt and I aren't. We are two tough, practical men of the world: Kurt is a cut-rate tooth straightener; I'm a loan officer who looks at his clients with the view that it's either them or me. The minute they show up at my desk, it's stand-by-for-the-ram. Banks love guys like me. We get to vice president maybe, but no further. Besides, my bank is family owned, and it's not my family. Kurt goes on building his estate for Beverly, his wife, and two boys, Jasper and Ferdinand. Jasper and Ferdinand spent years in their high chairs. Beverly thought it was adorable until Ferdinand did a face plant on the linoleum and broke his retainer. What a relief it was not to have them towering over me while I ate Beverly's wretched cuisine. Her Texas accent absolutely drove me up the wall. Kurt has lots of girlfriends in safe houses who love his successful face. His favorite thing in the world is to make you feel like you've asked a stupid question. Beverly has some haute cuisine Mexican recipes no one has ever heard of. She has to send away for some of the ingredients. She says she'd been in Oaxaca before she met Kurt. Some guy with his own plane. It was surprising that Kurt and I turned out like we did. Our dad was a mouse, worked his whole life at the post office. In every transaction, whether with tradespeople or bankers like me, Dad got screwed. To make it even more perfect, his surgeon fucked up his back. Last three, four years of his life, he looked like a corkscrew and was still paying off the orthopod that did it to him.

But Mother—we never called her Mom—was a queen. Kurt said that Dad must have had a ten-inch dick. When we were Cub Scouts, she was our den mother. She volunteered at the school. She read good books and understood classical music. She was beautiful, et cetera. Like I said. This is the sort of shit that happens when kids fall in love in the seventh grade, brutal mismatches that last a lifetime. Dad's lifetime anyway, and now Mother's in God's waiting room and going downhill fast.

Kurt and I always said we hoped Mother cheated on Dad, but we knew that could never possibly have happened. She was above it, she was a queen, and despite our modest home and lowly standing, she was the queen of our town. She gave us status, even at school, where Kurt and I had to work at the cafeteria. People used to say, "How could she have had such a couple a thugs?" meaning me and Kurt. Some words are born to be eaten.

Kurt and I have lunch on the days we visit her in assisted living. These are the times we just give in to reminiscence, memories that are often funny, at least to us. In the seventh grade, Mother took all of our friends to the opera, *La Bohème*, in her disgraceful old Pontiac, five of us in the backseat chanting, *"Puccini, Puccini, Puccini."* She was worried as she herded us into our seats under the eyes of frowning opera fans. We stuck our fingers in our ears during the arias. One little girl, Polly Rademacher, was trying to enjoy the show, but Joey Bizeau kept feeling her up in the dark. Mother would've liked to have enjoyed herself, but she had her hands full keeping order and succeeded almost to the end. When Mimi dies and Rodolfo runs to her side, we shrieked with laughter. The lights came up, and Mother herded us out under the angry eyes of the opera patrons, tears streaming down her face. It was a riot.

The Parkway was a nice but short-lived restaurant that didn't make it through the second winter. Before that we just had the so-called rathskeller and its recurrent bratwurst, but it had turned back into a basement tanning parlor with palm-tree and flamingo decals on its small windows. While we still had the Parkway, Kurt was picking at his soufflé as the waiter hovered nearby. Kurt shook his head slightly and sent him away. Kurt has natural authority, and he looks the part with his broad hands and military haircut. He rarely smiles, even when he's joking: he makes people feel terrible for laughing. I'm more of a weasel. I don't think I was always a weasel, but I've spent my life at a bank; so I may be forgiven. "Remember when she got us paints and easels?" We laughed so hard.

Several diners turned our way in surprise. Kurt didn't care. He has a big reputation around town as the guy who can get your kid to quit looking like Bugs Bunny; no one is going to cross him. It was a tough call selling our crappy childhood home, but it helped pay for assisted living. Mother would've liked to have had in-home care—that is, when she was making sense—but the day was fast arriving when she wouldn't know where the hell she was, unless it was the chair she was in. Anyway, we've got her down there at Cloisters. We just hauled her over there. It's okay. Kurt calls it Cloaca.

Mother's days are up and down. Sometimes she recognizes us, sometimes not, but less and less all the time. Or that's what Kurt thinks. I think she recognizes us but isn't always glad about what she sees. When she is a little lucid, I sometimes feel she is disgusted at the sight of us. I mean, that's the look on her face. Or that we're hopeless. Or that I am: she never could find much wrong with Kurt. This used to come up from time to time, a kind of despair. She once screamed that we were "awful" but only once, and she seemed guilty and apologetic for days, kept making us pies, cookies, whatever. She felt bad. If she'd had any courage, she'd have stuck to it. We were, and are, awful. We will always be awful.

We were in Mother's room at the center. I won't describe it:

they all have little to do with the occupant. Me and Kurt in chairs facing Mother in hers. Her face is pretty much blank. Someone has done her hair and makeup. She still looks like a queen, keeps her chin raised in that way of hers. But she just stares ahead. Kurt bangs on about a board of supervisors meeting; then I do a little number about small-business loans, naming some places she might recognize. Mother raises her hand to say something.

She says, "I gotta take a leak."

Kurt and I turn to each other. His eyebrows are halfway to his scalp. We don't know what to do. Kurt says to Mother, "I'll get the nurse." I stole around in front of Mother to get the call button without alerting her. I couldn't find it at first and found myself crawling down the cord to locate it. I gave the button a quick press and shortly heard the squeak of the approaching nurse's shoes. Kurt and I were surprised at how hot she was, young with eye-popping bazongas. Kurt explained that Mother needed the little girls' room. Ms. Lowler winced at the phrase. Kurt saw it, too. He's quicker to take offense than anyone I know, which is surprising in someone who so enjoys making others feel lousy. When Mother came back from the bathroom, she was refreshed and a little communicative. She knew us, I think, and talked a bit about Dad, but in a way we hadn't heard before. She talked of him in the present tense, as though Dad were still with us. "I knew right away he wasn't going anywhere," she said. We were thunderstruck. Mother yawned and said, "Doozy's tired now. Doozy needs to rest."

Outside, Kurt splayed both hands and leaned against the roof of his car. "Doozy? Who the fuck is Doozy?"

"She is. She's Doozy."

"Did you ever hear that before?"

The door was open to Ms. Lowler's office, which was small and efficient and clean, and refreshingly free of filing cabinets. Little uplifting thoughts had been attached to the printer and computer. Have-a-nice-day level. I took the initiative and asked if we could come in. "Of course you can!" she said with a smile and hurried around to find us chairs. Kurt introduced himself, booming out "Doctor" and I made a small show of modesty by just saying, "I'm Earl."

"Your mom has good and bad days in terms of her cognition generally, but she never seems anxious or unhappy."

"She got any friends?" said Kurt.

"I think that's a bit beyond her Her friends are in the past, and she mostly lives there."

Kurt was on it. "Who's this Doozy? That name mean anything to you?"

"Why, yes. Doozy is your mother. That's her nickname."

"Really?" I said. "We've never heard it."

"Doozy is the nickname Wowser gave her."

"Wowser? Who's Wowser?"

"I thought it might be your dad."

I just held my head in my hands. Kurt asked if this had gotten out. Ms. Lowler didn't know, or didn't want to know, what he was talking about.

Kurt and I love to talk about Mother because we have different memories of her before she lost her marbles, and we enjoy filling out our impressions. For example, Kurt had completely forgotten what a balls-to-the-wall backyard birder Mother was. We went through a lot of birdseed we really couldn't afford. Dad shot the squirrels when Mother was out of the house. By holding them by the end of the tail, he could throw them like a bolo all the way to the vacant lot on the corner. Naturally, Mother thought the squirrels had decided the birds needed the food more and had moved on.

Kurt remembered her gathering the cotton from milkweed pods to make stuffing for cushions. He was ambivalent about this because we both loved those soft cushions, but it seemed to be a habit of the poor. Dad was the one who made us feel poor, but through her special magic Mother made us understand that we had to bow our heads to no one. By being the queen she transformed Kurt and me into princes. It stuck in Kurt's case. Wowser and Doozy put all this at risk.

Two weeks later we were summoned back to the home by Ms. Lowler, who this time wore an all-concealing cardigan. She'd had enough. It seems Mother had been loudly free-associating about her amorous adventures in such a way that it wasn't always best that she occupy the common room during visiting hours. She had a nice room of her own with a view of some trees from her window and a Bible-themed Kinkade on the opposite wall and where she couldn't ask other old ladies about whisker burn or whatever. That's where we sat as before, except this time I located the call button. Kurt and I were in coats and ties, having come from work, Kurt shuffling the teeth of the living, me weaseling goobers across my desk. She smiled faintly at each of us, and we helped her into her chair. Kurt started right in. I kind of heard him while I marveled over the passage of time that separated us from when Mother ruled taste and behavior with a light but firm hand and left us, Kurt especially, with a legacy of rectitude that we hated to lose. Kurt was summarizing the best of those days, leaning forward in his chair so that his tie hung like a plumb bob, his crew cut so short that it glowed at its center from the overhead light. Mother's eyes were wide. Perhaps she was experiencing amazement. As Kurt moved toward what we believed to be Mother's secret life, her eyes suddenly dropped, and I first thought that this was some acknowledgment that such a thing existed. Kurt asked her if she'd had a special friend she'd like to tell us about. She was silent for a long time before she spoke. She said, "Are those your new shoes?"

I followed Kurt into Ms. Lowler's office. "I would like to speak to you, Ms. Lowler, about our Mother's quality of life."

"What's wrong with it?"

"She's no longer here at all, Ms. Lowler."

"Really? I think she's quite happy."

"Ms. Lowler, I'm going to be candid with you: there comes a time."

"Does there? A time for what?"

"Ms. Lowler, have you had the opportunity to familiarize yourself with the principles of the Hemlock Society?"

"I think it's quite marvelous for pets, don't you?"

Later, when Mother started thinking Kurt was Wowser, he really got onto the quality-of-life stuff. I waited before asking him the question that was burning inside of me. "Have you ever done it?"

"I've never done it but I've seen it done."

There were times when Mother seemed so rational apart from the fact that what she told us fitted poorly with the Mother we used to know. She said, for example, that Wowser always wore Mr. B collars with his zoot suit.

Kurt told me that he never knew what would happen when he

visited Mother. Lately she's shown an occasionally peevish side. Today she suggested that he "get a life." This was about a week after Mother had started confusing Kurt with Wowser, and a few days after Kurt had started addressing Mother as Doozy in the hopes of finding Wowser before he could add his own stain to our family reputation. "You're in a different world when your own mother doesn't recognize you, or thinks you're the stranger who gave her a hickey."

This brought up the Hemlock Society all over again. I told Kurt to forget about it. "Why?" said Kurt. "That's the only way we get our real mother back. The human spirit is imperishable, and Mother would live on through eternity in her original form and not, frankly, as 'Doozy.' They really should weigh the spirit just to convince skeptics like you. I see the expression on your face. You could weigh the person just before and just after they die. Then you'd see that the spirit is something real. Scientists have learned how to weigh gravity, haven't they? It's time to weigh the spirit."

I'd give a million dollars to know why Kurt is in such a lather about our "standing" in town. Does anyone actually have "standing" in a shithole? Well, Kurt thinks so. He thinks we have standing because of Mother's regal presence over the decades, which, I will admit, was widely admired but which seems to be under attack via these revelations about Wowser and Doozy. I shudder to think what would happen if Kurt found out who Wowser is. Sadly, we know who Doozy is. Doozy is our mother.

I said to the shining young couple across my desk, "If you take this loan, at this bank's rates, at this point in your lives, you could find yourselves in a hole you'd never dig out of." Was this me speaking? This was an out-of-body experience. I didn't tell them that if I went down this road I'd be in the same mess I was recommending they avoid. Feeling my heart swell at the prospects of this couple was more than a little disquieting. From their point of view—and it wasn't hard to see it in their eyes—I was just turning them down. They would have liked me better if I'd hung this albatross around their necks and let them slide until we glommed the house. After they were gone, I slumped in my chair—a butterfly turning back into a caterpillar. I hadn't felt quite like this since I repeated ninth grade with Mrs. Novacek busting my balls up at the blackboard doing long division.

Kurt has this habit of picking up his napkin between thumb and forefinger as though letting cooties out. It's his way of showing the restaurant staff that nobody is above suspicion. He was on his third highball when I said, "There were times when Mother could be pretty hard."

"Where do you come up with this shit?"

I felt heat in my face. "Like when she was den mother."

"Of course she was hard on you. You were still a Bobcat after two years. What merit badges did you earn?"

"I don't remember . . ."

"I do. You earned one. Handyman. You earned a handyman merit badge. I never ever knew anyone who even wanted one. I had athlete, fitness, engineer, forester, and outdoorsman in year one. And Webelos. I didn't find Mother hard, ever. Unless you mean she had standards. Where are you going? You haven't even ordered!"

After the lunch I missed, Edwin, our bank president, came to my desk for the first time since spring before last and asked when I would start moving product like I used to. The young couple must have complained,

Visiting Mother with Kurt was getting to be too hard. The last time we tried, Mother got a mellow, dewy look on her face, and at first Kurt thought it was her pleasure at seeing us. Then he seemed to panic: "She calls me Wowser, I jump out the window."

Mother said, "Wowser."

Kurt was blinking, his nose making a tiny figure eight, but he didn't jump out the window. So I started seeing Mother on my own. I didn't try to make anything happen when I was with her, and we mostly just sat in silence. She would look at me for a long time with a watery unregistering look, and then, once in a while, I'd see her eyes darken and focus on me with a kind of intensity that lasted for a good long time. I think I knew what was going on, but I was darned if I would start yammering at her like Kurt did to get her to put into words what couldn't be put into words and only produced some crazy non sequitur from her deepest past. Of course if it featured Wowser, Kurt was on the warpath. If she just chattered about this, that, and the other without naming names, then Kurt would announce she was talking about Dad. But mostly he couldn't handle her obvious mental absence.

"Mother, I just heard the sprinklers go off. Now that's summertime to me. Mother! Are you listening to the sprinklers? It's summertime!"

"Kurt," I said. "It's not registering."

"Mom! The sprinklers! Summertime!"

Kurt had a brainstorm, and it turned out very badly. I say this not knowing how it went down, but I know it wasn't good.

He decided that since Mother was mistaking him for Wowser, he would just go ahead and be Wowser—"Wowser for a day." He came home shattered. I really don't know what happened, unless it was Mother's golden boy turning into some vanished adulterer, a role in some ways similar to the one he'd been playing around town and in his safe houses for years. Finally, and without telling me anything, he calmed down. He said, "I think I have a headache. Do I? Do you think I have a headache?" It was getting to him.

When we were young, I was always a little stand-offish. That is, I was a social coward. But not Kurt. By the time he was twelve, he'd be sticking out his big paw and telling grown-ups, "Put 'er there." They liked it, and it kind of made me sick. Now he revealed an uncertainty I hadn't seen before; but it didn't last. He was soon on the muscle again. Kurt: "I see literally—literally—not one thing wrong with my taking on the identity of Wowser in pursuit of truth."

Mother's love of excellence was not something I always embraced. It certainly raised Kurt to the pedestal to which he had become accustomed, but it unfairly cast my father in a negative light. Truth be told, I was far more comfortable with Dad than with our exalted mother. What you saw was what you got. He was a sweet man, and a sweet old man later, who was not at war with time. He noticed many things about life, about dogs and cats and birds and weather, which were just so many impediments to Mother. Kurt was right: left to Dad we would have probably not gone very far, nor been nearly so discontented.

I'm on the hot seat looking into the piercing eyes of my boss: "Earl, how long have you been with the bank?"

"Twenty-two years."

"Like to see twenty-three? Not much coming over your desk except your paycheck. Desks like yours are financial portals. You know that."

"My, what big teeth you have." I was fired that day.

Where had I been all my life? I had grown up under so many shadows they were spread over me like the leaves of a book. Only Dad and I were equals, just looking at life without being at war with it. There was no earthly reason I should have been a banker beyond serving the shadows. By all that's reasonable, I should have been at the post office like Dad, taking packages, affixing stamps. Reciting harmless rules, greeting people. I loved greeting people! In my occupation, you had to screw someone every day, even if it was your own family.

I went to see Mother on my own on a beautiful day with a breeze coming up through the old cottonwoods along the river and cooling the side street where the rest home sat in front of its broad lawn and well-marked parking spaces. The American and Montana flags lifted and fell lazily. It was hard to go indoors. A few patients rested in wheelchairs on the lawn, the morning sun on their faces. I recognized old District Court Judge Russell Collins. He had no idea where he was, but his still-full head of hair danced in the breeze, the only part of Judge Collins moving. The others, two women who seemed to have plenty to talk about, barely glanced at me.

I sat with Mother in her room. It seemed stuffy, and I got up to let in the air. A glance at the spruces crowding the side lawn made me want to run out into the sun as though these were my last days on earth. I was unable to discern if Mother knew I was in the room. She rested her teeth on her lower lip, and each breath caused her cheeks to inflate. It was very hard to look at, which doesn't say great things about me.

I'd had enough of these visits to feel quite relaxed as I studied her and tried to remember her animation of other days. Why had she married Dad? Well, Dad was handsome and for thirty-one years held the Montana state record for the 440-yard dash. He looked like a sprinter until he died. His luck and happiness as a successful boy lasted all his life. Even Mother's provocations bounced off his good humor when she attempted to elevate his general cultivation with highbrow events at the Alberta Bair Theater in Billings. Dad liked Spike Jones, "the way he murders the classics." I remember when he played "Cocktails for Two" on the phonograph when Mother was at a school board meeting. I loved the hiccups, sneezes, gunshots, whistles, and cowbells, but Kurt walked out of the house. I thought Dad held his own with Mother. Kurt thought she made him look like a bum.

Kurt asked me to come over and help him get some things out of his garden, a jungle of organic vegetables that he plundered throughout the season as part of his health paranoia. He said that he intended to share some of this provender, as though to suggest that I would be suitably compensated. He was pouring with sweat when I got there, shirtless, his ample belly spilling over the top of his baggy shorts. He had on some kind of Japanese rocker shoes that had him teetering down the rows and doing something or other, strengthening his calves or his arches, I don't know. He took me to a cucumber trellis that was sagging with green cylinders of all sizes and told me to take my pick. I had a big brown shopping bag, and I started tossing cukes in there until he insisted on picking them himself, giving me the worst ones, ones with bug holes and brown blemishes.

"Doozy has completely confused me with Wowser."

"I think you're encouraging that, aren't you?"

"I'm learning way too much about Wowser, Earl. All their adventures. Roadhouses, et cetera. God-awful barn dances in the boonies. I imagine Dad is spinning in his grave."

Maybe Dad strayed, too. I didn't think so, and it wouldn't really fit for him. Dad was as plain as a pine board; but Mother, with her art and opera and shiny pumps—well, I could see it. Ambition is never simple. "Kurt, she has dementia. She could be making this all up."

Then he was right in my face. I could feel his breath as he rapped my elbow with a trowel. "How little you know. Dementia means she *can't* make it up."

Kurt wanted me there to knock down his potato pyramid: he'd start his plants in an old car tire, and as they grew he began stacking tires and adding dirt until the whole assemblage reached eye level. Now was the payoff, and he wanted me there. "Ready?" I said I was, and he pushed over the stack of tires, spilling dirt and hundreds of potatoes at our feet. He put his hands on his hips, panting, and smiled at the results. "Take all you want." I took a few. He'd be hiking up and down the street giving the damn things away.

I had a sudden insight. "Kurt," I said, "you seem to be competing with Wowser."

He slugged me. The cucumbers and potatoes fell from my hand. He must have fetched me a good one because I could hardly find my way out to the street.

I let it go. I can't believe it, but I did. I just wanted to keep these things at a distance. Kurt continued to press the staff at "Cloaca" about whatever Mother might be saying that others would hear. He was obsessed by the unfamiliar nature of her coarse remarks, which he said reflected the lowlife thrills she had experienced with Wowser. I had dinner with Kurt and his wife at the point that things seemed to be deteriorating. Their two boys were displeased to have me, their uncle, even in the house. These are two weird, pale boys. I don't think they've ever been outdoors. I always ask if they've been hiking in the mountains. They hate me. Beverly was quite the little conversationalist, too. She asked why I didn't have any girlfriends.

"They just haven't been coming along."

"They may find you drab. I know I do."

Beverly had made some desultory attempt at meal preparation. She'd been drinking—nothing new—and there was not much left of her former high Texas sleekness besides her aggressive twang. Kurt always looked a bit sheepish around her and was anxious when, over the sorry little meal, she brought up Mother, a subject Beverly found hilarious. Years ago when Mother was at her best, she had made no secret of her disapproval of Beverly, whom she called a tart. Local wags said that she and Beverly were competing for Kurt, and there may have been something to it, as I could bring around a rough customer with a gold tooth or neck tattoo and Mother would greet her like a queen. Of course I resented it, and of course I was pleased when Beverly, having gotten wind of Mother's new interest in Junior, said, "Old Doctor Kurt got his tail in a damn crack, ain't he?" I haven't really liked Beverly since the day of their marriage, when she called me a disgrace. There'd been a bunch of drugs at the bachelor party, and I had an accident in my pants; the word got out, thanks to Kurt.

"It's just all part of the aging process, hon," Kurt said pandering to Beverly. "The sad aging process."

"That right, Doc? Just don't drag your mother over here and give her a shot."

Like I said, she'd been drinking.

Mother had nearly hit bottom. She was still following things with her eyes, like a passing car or a cat, but not much. No, not much. I continued to see her, but I didn't know why. No, it's hard to say why I went. I'd say now that she was damn near a heathen idol, propped here or there, in a window or facing something, a picture, a doorway; it didn't seem to make much difference. It wasn't pretty at all. But Kurt kept at it until something went wrong. Evidently he broke some furniture, kicked down a door, shouted, cried. Police were involved on the assumption he was drunk. Fought the cops, got Tased, booked, released, and then a day later fucked up his rotator cuff yanking on a venetian blind. It was a week before I felt I could go near him. I thought it might be best to quietly approach Ms. Lowler.

"It has been a nightmare," she said. "And not just for me. The other residents were terrified. We've had the doctor here for them. It's a full moon, and they don't sleep well anyway. Ever since your brother started pretending to be your mother's boyfriend, she has become more and more agitated. I personally think it has been quite cruel. Then he wanted to move her to his own house, which seemed I hardly know what."

He wanted to put Mother to sleep like an old cocker spaniel. I don't know why this agitated me so; she was all but asleep anyway—I suppose it was the unexpected memories that rushed back at the thought of her no longer existing—Mother hurtling along in our old Econoline with a carload of kids, bound for a dinosaur exhibit, an opera, a ball game, or off to Crow Fair to watch the Indian dancers and eat fry bread. Crow Fair was right in the middle of when Dad and I liked to fish the Shields, which I would have preferred, while Kurt was happy to drink in all the culture with the possible exception of Crow Fair, which he considered just a bunch of crazy Indians. Maybe not fishing with Dad was why my memory was so sharp.

Or why it came to me: Mother was herding a little mob of us like a border collie through the tepees and concessions, thousands of Indians and spectators, smoke drifting from campfires, Crow elders in lawn chairs talking in sign language, young dancers running past us to the competitions in a rush of feathers. Our guide was Mr. White Clay, who helped Mother lead us to the rodeo grounds, the powwow, the fry-bread stands, and the drumming of the Nighthawk Singers. Mr. White Clay looked more like a cowboy than an Indian in his jeans, snap-button shirt, and straw hat. He was tall and dark like many Crows, and it was surprising how Mother deferred to him and how well they seemed to know each other. He had quickly familiarized himself with our group and was vigilant in rounding up anyone who strayed. It was wonderful to see Mother so relaxed, so willing to let Mr. White Clay handle things. We kids had to call him Mr. White Clay. Mother called him Roland.

My face was burning. I cut my conversation with Ms. Lowler so suddenly she was startled. I went home, burst through my front door, and picked up the phone. I called information for Crow Agency and requested a number for Roland White Clay. He answered. He answered! I told him who I was, who my mother was, who my brother was, how old we were then. Mr. White Clay was silent. I asked if we could come to see him, and he said with odd formality, "As you wish."

I had found Wowser.

I will never know why I told Kurt, but that's what I did. It took him a while to absorb this and determine for himself if I was imagining it. But he remembered, too. He remembered. He said that when he was "Wowser," "Doozy" had given him the impression that after the war Wowser no longer belonged in a tepee. Kurt said, "In case you hadn't noticed, I have forensic skills." I told him I hadn't noticed; but he went on rather plausibly. Evidently Wowser's stationing in Southern California had briefly transformed him from Plains Indian to Zoot Suiter; and more troublingly, Mother had gone from den mother to tart. Maybe they had fun. But Kurt wasn't happy. He said it looked like he would have to move. My brother move away? After all these years? I couldn't possibly face that. Kurt was there at the Grass Dance with Mother on that faraway and now sadly beautiful day. He said, "We're gonna drag that Indian back up here and let him and Mother have a grand reunion. That's when this Wowser retires."

We drove to the Rez in his little MG, which he stores most of the year. I couldn't think of a worse car to drive on a hot day on the interstate, our hair blowing in the heat, our faces getting redder. Kurt thought it would cheer him up, but by the time we got near Laurel, where fumes from the refinery filled the little two-seater, tears were pouring from his eyes. At first I thought it was the appalling conditions of driving this flivver among the sixteen-wheelers, pickup trucks, and work-bound sedans. But that wasn't it. He was remembering throwing a fit at assisted living. Surely I knew that. I waited until we slowed for the Hardin exit to ask him what happened. He unexpectedly swerved onto the shoulder. Our dust cloud swept over our heads and dissipated downwind. Kurt stared at me.

"She came on to me."

"It's your own fault!" I shouted.

"Searching for the truth about our mother? You're actually calling that my fault? To my face? You never cared about Mother!"

"Mother never cared about me!"

Kurt lowered his voice, "Earl, there was a problem of course. The problem was that you were uneducable."

"Ah. I thought Dad was uneducable. That's what she said. What luck she had you."

"I think she felt that way," he said with a slight toss of his head.

"Was this when she was fucking the Indian?"

"You need to be careful, Earl." I could see violence rising in Kurt's face. "You need to be very, very careful."

"Just asking, Kurt. It shouldn't be controversial. I'm only trying to establish a time frame."

"'Fucking the Indian' is not a time frame. It's ignorant. Remember John Wayne in *Hondo* where he plays a half-breed army scout? My point is he has a hard time being accepted by Indians and whites, per se."

"Are you saying we might be half-breeds?"

"Not per se. We just don't want any questions like that hanging over us."

"Can we stop for water? What happens if we have mechanical problems on the Rez? You can't even buy tires for this thing." I was trying to change the subject, and I guess I was successful because Kurt started the motor and pulled back onto the highway, the tiny four-banger sneezing under the hood. I knew perfectly well that I didn't pass inspection around our house except with Dad. Kurt was trying to see himself in the mirror, his hair windmilling around in the heat. Then he'd look at me like a dermatologist. It didn't take me long to figure out that he was wondering if we were half-breeds.

Roland White Clay was some kind of emeritus tribal chairman. His office was at the end of a corridor past the drinking fountain, and sparsely furnished, a military portrait behind the desk. He wore a sport coat over his jeans and a sky-blue western shirt, his Stetson resting upside down on his desk. He met us with cordial suspicion and occasionally glanced out of his window as we met, seemingly anxious to be outdoors again. Kurt and I sat in front of his desk, as though interviewing for a job.

"Chief—do you mind if I call you Chief?"

"Suit yourself," said White Clay with a wintry smile.

"Chief, I read all the Montana and Wyoming papers pretty much every day, and I see an issue that affects Indian people very negatively." Here White Clay perked up. "And that is: rolling cars. My research indicates that with each six inches of wheelbase, the likelihood of rollovers is reduced by eighteen percent." I spotted this as bullshit from the get-go. "My thought is to appeal to the automobile industry as an altruistic salute to Native American culture to manufacture special editions of their standard vehicles with wider wheelbases to help prevent rollovers." The acid look in White Clay's face was a wonder to behold. White Clay spoke after long silence.

"If you think I should," said White Clay, "I can have tribal council sit in."

"No," said Kurt. "We're just trying to learn more about our mother. She has dementia and she's slipping away."

He gazed at us. "Well, we were close."

"How close?" said Kurt. You could hear the demand in his voice. White Clay mused comfortably as he looked back at him. Finally, he smiled. Just then three little boys ran in: White Clay's grandchildren. He introduced them. All had short, crisp names, Chip, Skip, and Mick. He reproached them affectionately for their muddy jeans and T-shirts. They tagged White Clay and shot out as quickly as they'd come.

"I never married," he said.

"That's all you're going to say?"

"That's all I'm going to say."

The photograph behind the desk, grainy from being blown up, showed a smiling GI on a riverbank, propped against his M1. I couldn't tell if it was White Clay or just another Indian kid. We had deferments, which Kurt said was the only way to go if there was nothing more to fight than gooks. My asthma exempted me, but Kurt could easily have been drafted if Mother hadn't gone to the board. She had something on the woman who was running it.

"Is Caroline suffering?"

Caroline. When had someone last called Mother that? "No," I said. "Except during her so-called good spells when she is confused." I didn't say a word about what she might have been going through while Kurt was impersonating him, not when we were sitting across the desk from the genuine Wowser.

"Whose idea was it to come and see me?"

Kurt barked an artificial laugh. "We just thought you might want to see her. Might do her a lot of good."

A truculent cloud crossed Kurt's face. "Our mother enjoys an unparalleled and dignified standing in our community that will never change." All I could think was that if he took a stand at this moment he could plan on being Wowser for the rest of Mother's life. White Clay picked the Stetson up off his desk and thrust it onto his head. He stood, still tall if bowlegged, but broad shouldered and erect. "Caroline and I were . . . there wasn't room for it. I'll come to see her, if you think it would help. Might help me!"

One look at Kurt's MG and he said he'd take his pickup. Going back in that hot headwind was awful. It nearly stopped that silly little car, and our faces roasted as we headed into the afternoon sun. "How about the three papooses that showed up in the chief's office? What'd he call 'em? Snap, Crackle, and Pop? Something like that."

"Caroline," said White Clay. "It's me." Her eyes moved slightly in White Clay's direction, and Kurt threw his head back and mouthed some words to the ceiling. For him, it was all over. White Clay just moved his head very slightly from side to side, as if saying no. In a while he got up, bent over, and kissed Mother on the cheek. You couldn't tell if she noticed. White Clay turned to speak to us. He said, "You were a couple of cute little boys. I understood why your mother wouldn't go off with me. Now I see you again, and you are grown men. I must tell the truth.

There doesn't seem to be much to either one of you." He nodded to me and went out. Then Kurt left, leaving me alone. I sat and watched Mother. There was nothing in her face, nothing like life, nothing except the rise and fall of her breathing. It felt safe, after so long, to ask her if she loved me. It was just the two of us. No reply. I didn't expect one.

I met with Kurt at his clinic in the old ice-cream plant that had been stylishly renovated to house fashionable new businesses, but fashionable new businesses failed to arrive except for a doomed florist and a malodorous brisket palace. I couldn't wait to speak to him, and sitting in one of his examination chairs, I felt I was confessing after a long interrogation. Kurt, who is never off duty, wandered around in his white tunic inspecting his weird tools while I told him the story.

"I spent almost three hours with Mother, and don't ask me why, she was pretty lucid."

"Lucid about what?"

"I'm going to tell you. Maybe the visit from White Clay, I don't know, but she was kind of excited, kind of agitated, you could say, and I just sat there, and finally I said, 'What's on your mind?'"

"You think she has one?"

"Kurt, honestly."

"All right, so go on."

"Remember when Dad had his gallbladder surgery?"

"And the septicemia?"

"Exactly, and do you remember when it was?"

"No."

"Well, I'll tell you when it was. It was the same week as Crow Fair, one year later."

"Earl, that's not something I would ever remember. And in some ways it speaks to some of your issues, always looking back, always regretful."

I ignored this. I felt it was important that Kurt hear the story and that it would maybe change his views of Mother and help him realize she was only human. "Well, when Dad was in the hospital you remember his sister Audrey came out from Spokane to help care for him. And Mom felt it was kind of insulting, and she went off by herself."

"I vaguely remember. As I recall, Esther was a hell of a cook. But repetitious."

"Oh, you thought it was a big improvement. That's another thing that may have gotten Mom, this big fuss over Audrey. Anyway, she left."

"Where did she go?"

"Crow Fair," I hissed.

"You heard this today? What did they do?"

"I'll tell you what they did. They took two horses and went on a day's ride up the Bighorn River and camped under the stars."

"They camped under the stars."

"They camped under the stars. They ate antelope. Mom said it tasted just like chicken."

"It's like you're reading a fucking poem. Antelope doesn't taste like chicken."

"They swam in the Bighorn and gathered wild berries. He took her to the secret graves of the warriors. They dried their clothes on the willows." Kurt winced, clutching a dental tool. "In two days, she was back at Dad's bedside."

Kurt said with feeling, "Our mother was a cheating housewife."

I hoped my story provided a gentler interpretation of our mother and the choices she made. Of course I made the whole thing up. My only regret was some bucktoothed kid coming in and finding himself in the hands of an agitated orthodontist. But. It may have been a mistake. Kurt didn't take it at all as I had intended. It made him see our dad as a victim. "He's there recuperating from surgery eating that awful stuff Audrey kept making over and over." Now Audrey was a bad cook. I thought it would be strategic to egg him on. Dishes we called shit-on-a-shingle and buffalo balls.

"Dad definitely was getting the short end of the stick. Mom out there in the tepee." What tepee? I could see he was moving his allegiance to Dad. Soon I'd be an orphan.

Kurt had a big job and had all the time in the world to work through our family history. I was broke and out of work. Also, my phone had been turned off. I thought I knew why, but at first I was unwilling to borrow someone's phone to find out. In the end I put on my game face, borrowed an office at my old bank for a morning, and, braving a gauntlet of smirks, arranged an interview at a bank in Miles City and put several hundred miles of prairie between Kurt and me.

It was my luck that the president of the bank in Miles City, who wore a cowboy hat at all times, regarded the president of the bank that fired me as a "pilgrim and a honyocker." I didn't entirely follow this but sensed it was in my favor; and indeed it was. I was offered the job on my word alone. In middle age, I had the chance to move away from home for the first time. I was terrified because it meant leaving Mother in Kurt's hands. Soon I was at a very similar desk doing very similar things with the same clients but with more cowboy boots. I was clawing for volition and tried to develop a personal algorithm that would predict the date I would be fired all over again. I developed a garish fantasy life for what my last stop would be and came up with cleaning port-a-pottion at Ozzfest.

Then Kurt called to tell me that he had instigated a forensic inquest into the finances of Ms. Lowler that revealed minor malfeasance, easily challenged. But Ms. Lowler wouldn't stand for it and quit. I knew what was next: he was taking Mother to his home. "She gave so much, it's time to give back."

"She'll be lucky to make it a month," I said. I was paralyzed.

Kurt said, "Never be ruled by hatred."

"And forfeit the merit badge?"

In the last five weeks of Mother's life, I really should have been fired, but the staff at the Miles City bank was just fascinated by my torpor, wishing to see how far I might go toward complete ossification. In some way I was kind of fun for them. They were like happy children watching a frog.

I had the oddest feeling going to the funeral and at the funeral itself a kind of helium levitation. Kurt and his loudmouth wife, Beverly, were there gaping with fascination at the sight of me. I never spoke to them. There were lots of people there, lots of elderly people mostly, and some others, too. It was a crowd. It seemed like they were underwater, and I alone had a boat, such a nice little boat. I was pretty much sunning myself and the waves were gentle. Occasionally, I looked over the side. I was sailing away.

I rose rapidly at the bank, if you call five years rapid. I grew fond of Miles City and bought an old Queen Anne house on

Pleasant Street. I loved banking so much—funneling the universal lubricant—and led our expansions to five midsize cities. Lately, I've been riding a carriage at the annual Bucking Horse Sale, waving to everyone like an old-timer, which I guess is what I'm getting to be.

CLOUDBURSTS
Collected and New Stories

For more than four decades, Thomas McGuane has been heralded as an unrivaled master of the short story. Now the arc of that achievement appears in one definitive volume—forty-five stories, including two new and six previously uncollected pieces. Set in the seedy corners of Key West, the remote shore towns of the Bahamas, and McGuane's hallmark Big Sky country with its vast and unforgiving landscape, these are stories of people on the fringes of society, whose twisted pasts meddle with their chances for companionship. Moving from the hilarious to the tragic and back again, McGuane writes about familial dysfunction, emotional failure, and American loneliness, celebrating the human ability to persist through life's absurdities.

Fiction

GALLATIN CANYON

The stories of *Gallatin Canyon* are rich in the wit, compassion, and matchless language for which Thomas McGuane is celebrated. Place exerts the power of destiny in these tales: a boy makes a surprising discovery skating at night on Lake Michigan; an Irish clan in Massachusetts gathers around its dying matriarch; a battered survivor of the glory days of Key West washes up on other shores. Several of the stories unfold in Big Sky country: a father tries to buy his adult son's way out of virginity; a convict turns cowhand on a ranch; a couple makes a fateful drive through a perilous gorge. McGuane's people are seekers, beguiled by the land's beauty and myth, compelled by the fantasy of what a locale can offer, forced to reconcile dream and truth.

Fiction

THE LONGEST SILENCE

From the highly acclaimed author of *Ninety-two in the Shade* and *Cloudbursts* comes a collection of alternately playful and exquisite essays borne of a lifetime spent fishing. The forty pieces in *The Longest Silence*—including seven collected here for the first time—take the reader from the tarpon of Florida to the salmon of Iceland, from the bonefish of Mexico to the trout of Montana. They introduce characters as varied as a highly literate Canadian frontiersman and a devoutly Mormon river guide and address issues ranging from the esoteric art of tying flies to the enduring philosophy of a seventeenth-century angler to the trials of the aging fisherman. Both reverent and hilarious by turns, and infused with a deep experience of wildlife and the outdoors, *The Longest Silence* sets the heart pounding for a glimpse of moving water and demonstrates what dedication to sport reveals about life.

Essays

ALSO AVAILABLE

The Bushwhacked Piano
The Cadence of Grass
Driving on the Rim
Keep the Change
Ninety-two in the Shade
Nobody's Angel
Nothing but Blue Skies
Panama
Some Horses
Something to Be Desired
The Sporting Club
To Skin a Cat

Printed in the United States
by Baker & Taylor Publisher Services